A JOY TO BE HIDDEN

A JOY TO BE HIDDEN

a novel

ARIELA FREEDMAN

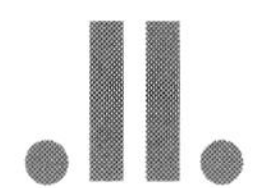

The following is a work of fiction. Many of the locations are real, although not necessarily as portrayed, but all characters and events are fictional and any resemblance to actual events or people, living or dead, is purely coincidental.

Cover photograph © 2013, Charlotte Colbert. "Staircase," "A Day at Home," 2013, by Charlotte Colbert is published with permission of the artist.
Cover design by Debbie Geltner
Book design by Tika eBooks
Printed and bound in Canada.

Library and Archives Canada Cataloguing in Publication

Freedman, Ariela, 1974-, author
A joy to be hidden : a novel / Ariela Freedman.

Issued in print and electronic formats.
ISBN 978-1-77390-008-7 (softcover).--ISBN 978-1-77390-009-4 (HTML).--
ISBN 978-1-77390-010-0 (Kindle).--ISBN 978-1-77390-011-7 (PDF)

I. Title.
PS8611.R4227J69 2019 C813'.6 C2018-905128-0
C2018-905129-9

The publisher gratefully acknowledges the support of the Government of Canada through the Canada Council for the Arts, the Canada Book Fund, and Livres Canada Books, and of the Government of Quebec through the Société de développement des entreprises culturelles (SODEC).

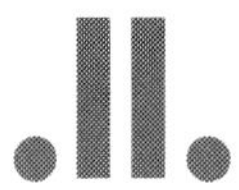

Linda Leith Publishing
Montreal
www.lindaleith.com

"It is a joy to be hidden, and a disaster not to be found."

D. W. Winnicott

PROLOGUE

November 1998

When my grandmother died, I was the first to go through her things. Well, not the first. The woman we hired to look after her was there before me, and she had taken my grandmother's two fur coats, the otter and the mink. I mourned the loss of the coats more deeply than the loss of my grandmother, a difficult and distant woman who wielded her reading glasses and books to keep others at a distance, like a sword and shield. In the last month of her illness, I had grown to know her a little better, but her hospital self, bedridden, drug-addled, loopy and confessional, confusingly affectionate, was unrecognizably different from the termagant of my childhood. When she suddenly and expectedly died—suddenly because every death is a shock, expectedly because the doctor had been cruelly clear about the one to four months she had left to live—I was not sure whom or what I had lost.

Those coats were like pets to me when I was a child. They were the singular attraction of our rare visits to my grandmother's house. My grandmother did not like noise, was not particularly comfortable with children, and her apartment was full of tiny Swarovski sculptures and porcelain shepherdesses that we were not allowed to touch. But my sister and I were allowed to take the coats out of the closet, to model them and stroke them. We both always wanted the mink, which was silver white, and not the otter, black and sleek. I was the eldest, so I claimed the mink as right of primogeniture.

When we first played with the coats we would drape them over ourselves and crawl on the floor and pretend we were animals. When we were older we stood upright and pretended that we were ladies, even though being a lady was much less interesting than being an animal. Being a lady was a static game. After we had arranged our hair over the collars of the coats, had done up the fascinating Chinese frog and ball fasteners, twirled two or three times like dancers to see the coats balloon out, and declared our intention to go to tea or lunch, we were usually at a stalemate, hypnotized in front of the full-length mirrors on the closet doors, unwilling to take off the coats but hot and burdened by their dead weight.

Or sometimes we hung the furs up at the far end of the long closet. I was Lucy and she was Edmund (younger sisters have to take the boy parts). We walked in the darkness to the back to the closet, feeling our way through the rows of polyester and crushed velvet and the smells of baby powder and tobacco—*l'eau de grand-mère* and, as the ad would have it, priceless. When we came to the sleek heavy furs, I parted them with my hands and said, "Edmund, it's getting lighter," and each time I was disappointed not to see the lamppost in the forest, not to feel the sharp cold spikes of snowflakes on my hand.

My grandmother did, coincidentally, have Turkish Delight on a high shelf in the kitchen. When we played that game, we always asked for it, seduced every time by the queen's description, and every time disappointed by the gelatinous perfumed powdered cubes which were nothing like what we thought of as candy.

As we grew older, we no longer played at dogs or ladies, but instead imagined a feral thing in the closet that wanted to eat us, that lived in the dark. We did not come out until one of us was crying, though our grandmother, who was so seldom left in charge of us, never really seemed to notice, or mind.

Though the loss of the furs was most potent for me, my grandmother's helper also ran up a phone bill of about eight hundred dollars to an astrology call line.

"You were right about her," my mother said on the phone. "I feel terrible about that, and how she must have treated grandma."

I had sounded the alarm about the caregiver a couple of months earlier, after the second time I visited my grandmother in the hospital. The helper left as soon as I reached the room, and said she'd be back in ten minutes. It was over an hour before I tracked her down, smoking outside the hospital.

"I don't trust her," I told my mother on the phone later that day. "She seems completely uninterested in grandma. She's supposed to help her. I don't like the way she talks to her."

My mother was still reeling from her own recent widowhood. She lived a seven-hour drive away, and was tethered by a midlife net of multiple responsibilities: my twin eight-year old brothers, her own ailing parents, the transformation and abdication of my sister. After my father died, my sister declared that she had found God, became ultra-orthodox, and moved to a yeshiva in the hills of the Galillee. My mother was in no way prepared to manage the care of a mother-in-law who had always despised her. Nonetheless, she called her brother-in-law in New York, my grandmother's last living son, to pass on my concerns. He told her she had no right to be critical, living as she did at a distance. Then he got angry. How dare she say anything at all? My mother hung up the phone and they did not speak again until the day of my grandmother's funeral. Even then, it was no tearful reconciliation, just a phone call, mutual expressions of hurt and rebuke, and a receiver hung up as violently as the slamming of a door.

Everyone should have to clear out an apartment after the death of the owner. It is a stoic exercise. Nothing else will convince you as quickly of the futility of stuff, the absurdity of the accumulation of objects, and the vanity of ownership.

Because almost everything in that house was trash. The romance novels, hundreds of them, their covers each a variation on the other: women with luxurious auburn hair, or blonde, or brunette, men with or without moustaches, wearing top hats and cowboy hats, posed against the sunset, in the desert or the city, swooning and flirting. Among the romance novels was a small, shabby paperback titled *Every Woman's Standard Medical Guide*. I took it off the shelf, curious. The publication date was 1948, the year my father was born. I slipped the book into my bag even as I discarded the novels.

No antique dealer wanted to take the furniture, the heavy unfashionable bureaus, the glass octagonal display case, the long hard sofa encased in Mandarin silk. In the end, the Salvation Army took some of it away, but we had to pay for the truck. I expected that I would regret that sofa, since enough time had passed to transform it from relic to kitsch to timeless. But it was just a problem, too big to get into the elevator, too heavy to carry down the stairs. Like the signs said on the storefronts that are perpetually going out of business, everything had to go.

Her drawers I emptied directly into garbage bags, and I carried the housedresses out of the closet by the armful. They were every extravagant print and colour, paisley to daisy. In her old age my grandmother had become voluminous, she billowed, and the last few times I visited her at home, housedresses were all she wore.

All her jewelry was in the safe, which was lucky, so at least the help didn't help herself to that. Most of it was paste, anyway, but I took one piece of value, an enormous amber pendant in a web of gold wire. It looked like something that should have magical properties like the power to tell the future or summon the dead.

I wondered what the helper had done with the furs. She was a large woman, and the furs belonged to a svelte and younger version of my grandmother. I suppose she must have sold them, though it is hard to imagine her getting a fraction of their value. I imagined her trying them on, pinched by the narrow shoulders, leaving the coats unbuttoned. The mink had bracelet arms, cut wide and short in order to display the adornment of elegant and ornamented wrists.

The helper had also left the bottle of Chanel No. 5 on the dresser, where it always sat. I poached that perfume many times as a child. It was a large and heavy bottle, and there was only an inch or two of the amber liquid at the bottom. I sat on the bench at the foot of the bed and sprayed it. It smelled warm and soft and crumpled, like an old woman's skin, like a room where the windows were never opened, like a pile of coats on a bed. Alfred Beaux designed the scent to smell like cold water at midnight, frozen rivers and icicles like diamond drop earrings hanging off the branches of fir trees, but this was a fussy indoor odour, the smell of old age. The perfume had no magic for me anymore.

At the back of the closet were her purses. When my grandmother was young, women had a wardrobe of purses, different sizes and colours for day and for night. I pulled them out and lay them on the bed. The helper must not have thought they were worth anything, or perhaps the back of the closet was too deep for her to invade, or maybe, like the door to Narnia we used to imagine we had found, these had only appeared for me. There was a Chanel purse, real or fake, gold chain and patent leather. I could not imagine carrying such a thing, but I put it aside in case my aunt might want it. A large red leather purse I wanted to be bold enough to carry, a beige purse full of pockets, and in those pockets crumpled tissues and a broken compact that had dumped flesh-coloured powder into the crevices at the bottom. When I was a child, I thought my grandmother had a false nose because she used to miss the line between her nose and her cheek. There was a difference in both colour and in texture as if, like my beloved potato-head toy, you could attach and detach her appendages. Face powder, purses—how much of this armature of femininity had my generation abandoned! It all deserved its own wing in a museum, beside the slippers of women whose feet had been bound, and the Lysol once used as brutal contraception. The last purse was barely worth the name, a shapeless sack of burlap with a braided shoulder strap, neither beautiful nor useful, but as I flung it on the bed it felt oddly heavy and there was the slither and clink of something inside it.

I wasn't thinking at that point, I felt like I was in a dream, when one action follows another like a leaf follows a current in the river. I sat down on the bed again to see what I had found.

I opened the bag and there was a smaller purse, black and covered in sequins, with a long satin shoulder strap and a heavy clasp. I snapped the purse open and emptied it on the bed, and a pile of coins fell out. They were different than any coins I had seen before, a buttery gold, thick and heavy. I picked one up and weighed it in my palm, but I needn't have bothered, because on its face was the marking of the weight: one ounce. I spread them out on the bed and counted them, ten gold coins, and then I piled them up in pairs to count them again. I reached into the purse to check if I had missed any, and found a ring at the bottom, a fire opal in a platinum band set with small chips of what looked like diamonds. I slipped it on and the ring fit perfectly. When I held it up to the light the milky stone threw back flames of scarlet and the blue glitter of ice. To say that it felt as though it was meant for me is not to excuse the fact that I took it. I took the ring off, balanced the cool weight in my palm, and slipped it back in the purse, and then I felt something else, a crinkle of paper. I reached in once again. There was an inner pocket in the purse, made of fabric, and inside was an envelope. Inside the envelope a photograph, and a thin piece of paper, mimeographed and so creased and handled it felt soft as skin.

The photograph was a portrait in black and white of a man in a pale suit and hat standing in front of a painting. The painting took up most of the wall behind him and was abstract, strips of variegated shades which in the photograph all came out as different intensities of grey though they might have been any colour. His face was half in shadow. but you could see that he was handsome, he held that even in his carriage, the ontrapasso of his slim hips, his loose arms. He had a strong chin and looked fair-haired. I turned it over and there was a date, scribbled in pencil in the lower right-hand corner. A name, Oliver. And an inscription:

> For when I see thee a little I have no utterance left, my tongue is broken down and straightaway a subtle fire has run under my skin, I have no sight, my ears ring, sweat pours down, and a trembling seizes all my body, I am paler than grass, and seem in my madness a little better than one dead. But I must dare all, since one so poor…

Sappho. I had studied the fragment as an undergraduate, imagining each poem unwrapped and deciphered from the cartonnage of mummies and the trash heaps of antiquity. What did my grandmother have to do with Sappho, or with a strange man in a pale suit, what did she have to do with secrets? The return address on the envelope was in New Mexico. I'd never heard my mother talk about New Mexico. From her world, ten square Brooklyn blocks, that seemed as far away as Atlantis.

I carefully unfolded the piece of paper, so small I might have missed it, worried that it would come apart in my hands. The paper was deeply creased, something that had been folded and unfolded many times. It was a release form from a hospital, a place with a familiar, even notorious name. The year was the same one marked on the photograph.

My grandmother had a will, but it said nothing of a secret purse. Everything was to be divided between her children, but two of her three sons were dead, so my uncle swept in to sell the apartment and dissolve the estate. My uncle's family was wealthy, they didn't need the money, but like so many rich people they were rich precisely because they held onto money beyond need—I remembered how irritated my father would be when they went out to dinner, ordered the cheapest thing on the menu, would not drink, and at the end after dividing the bill left a tight ten percent on the pre-tax cost of their own meal. I had no idea if any of the money from the estate would find its way to my mother, and I didn't know anything about her financial situation, which must have been strained—two children still at home, widowed before fifty, and her own career a patchwork of childcare and part-time labour. If I told her about the coins, the ring, she would certainly tell my uncle, and then perhaps she would see none of this unexpected windfall.

I put the trash bags in the alleyway, swept the apartment broom-clean, left the donations by the door—my uncle would be by later to pick them up. Then I left with a new weight in my backpack but a lifting in my heart. Not just about the ring, but about the mystery.

My grandmother liked riddles, it was her one gift with children.

Most of the time she sat silent in a corner, reading her book, but occasionally, oracular, she would make a pronouncement from her seat, after you'd forgotten she was even in the room. White horses on a red hill, first champ, then stamp, then stand still. That phrase still set up a semantic confusion in my brain, white horses stuck in a swollen mouth, or teeth sown in a red bog. A rapid lightning gallop in a field of flesh. And these coins, this picture, this scrap of a poem, were like a prophetic mouth opening and then closing fast shut.

She had never written me a letter, but this felt like a letter from beyond the grave.

Since this is her story too, I should call her by her own name.

Helen.

PART ONE

1.

September 1998

I only began to really know my grandmother—and that word suggests too much, since as I learned more about her she only became more enigmatic—during the last month of her life. I first went to the hospital in September. She had already been there for two months, and I had no plans to go, only guilty, endlessly deferred intentions. I was very busy, and we never were close. When my mother asked me to visit, I was full of excuses. The hospital was in Brooklyn, two trains away and a walk. It would take me at least an hour to travel each way. I had my classes and I was also teaching, I needed that time to make some money to support my studies.

There was a long silence, so long I thought we might have lost the connection. Then I heard my mother's voice again. "I'm sending you a cheque for a thousand dollars so you don't have to work so much," she said tersely. "Go once a week."

It is embarrassing to admit that you visited your dying grandmother because you were paid to do so. We never discussed how long the visits would last, exactly how that thousand dollars broke down into hours of my time and the last hours of her life. It is ignoble, but I do not want to cover the last weeks of her life with any false claim of altruism or nobility. I went because I was paid, although after the first time, I would have kept coming anyway.

I lived on St. Mark's Place, in the heart of the East Village. The street was legendary, but it was an accident that I landed there. I followed a roommate notice on a bulletin board at the university, and this is what I found. If I had lived in a different era I would have called it fate. The East Village was emerging past the notoriety of the eighties, though I still found people nodding out on my doorstep in the early morning who had been sitting there all night. On one side of the building was a nightclub, and we were lucky to live on the other side; our neighbours heard the bass *thrum thrum thrum* until the early hours, and in the late nineties, there was nothing but bass. We lived a few blocks from CBGB and around the corner from St. Mark's Church. Those years held explosive performances and historic readings and epic literary apprenticeships and life-risking, live-saving encounters. I missed all of it, I was too dutiful. I was insufficiently seduced by the chance to squander my youth.

Allen Ginsberg died that year, and even I was aware of that. He lived only a few blocks away from me. His last poem was a scribbled list titled "Things I'll Never Do Again." The list included exotic places where he would never travel or to which he would never return: Potala, Bali, Adelaide, the Sphinx at sunrise. But more moving were the mundane losses: the stairs of his 12th Street apartment, the graves of his family at Bnai Israel cemetery. He subtitled the poem "Nostalgias."

Though it made no sense at all, I lived that period with a pre-emptive sense of nostalgia. Soon, after all, it would become the past. It seemed perverse to be nostalgic for the present, not only because I inhabited it, but also because everyone else was busy being nostalgic for the storied years of the seventies and eighties, for the city on fire. When I first arrived in New York it was already beginning to lose its edge, to become safer, more comfortable. The East Village was changing because of people like me, writers and artists and students living east of Third, and taking their first baby steps into Alphabet City. The week I moved in, I was welcomed by an anti-gentrification march down the street. It was not aimed at me directly but it might as well have been.

But it turns out I was right to feel like there was something precious and vanishing about that time. For all that New York had already changed, it was about to change much more. We thought that history was over and that liberal democracy would last forever. Giuliani was mayor and the Twin Towers still stood. In retrospect, it was a golden period, albeit a late-decadent, fin-de-siècle fool's gold, a false sense of freedom. The internet existed—I had a dial-up connection, an AOL account, and there were rumours that the library was digitizing its catalogue—but we were not yet all tangled in the net that would grow so fast and so big that it would ensnare us all before we had a chance to think about it, nor in the web of surveillance that would follow the fall of the towers. Our fall.

In graduate school in the nineties, it was fashionable to believe not in reality but only in "the real," the scare marks enclosing what could not be truly named. Still, that was the last time in my life that truly felt real, and I don't think anything else has been entirely real since. I felt so much back then, in the first years of my twenties, before the false apocalypse of Y2K and the true disaster of 9/11, before the billionaire mayor and the Disneyfication of Times Square, before the East Village was little Japan and back when Hell's Kitchen still deserved the name for its combination of butchery and vice. In the last years of the century, in the last years of the millennium, at the end of the empire, in the first years of my twenties. In the last months of her life.

2.

On Sunday morning, the subway was dour and empty, with a few tired early-shift employees making their way to work, and bedraggled and exhausted partiers making their way back home. I took out Blanchot, which I was reading for my Derrida class. Our class started that week, and I was excited because Derrida himself was flying in to teach for a month, which seemed as improbable and thrilling as David Bowie stopping by to teach strumming or Meryl Streep dropping in on a class in elocution. Those were celebrity-addled days in theory, and academic stars wafted down the hallways surrounded by young and eager disciples.

"But good for Derrida," my teacher said. "I knew him back when he had nothing. I remember when he didn't have a penny to his name, I'd buy him a sandwich at conferences or else he'd end up skipping lunch to save money. Let him have his embroidered vests, his silk ascots, he deserves it. He paid his dues."

He said it magnanimously, as if he was himself the distributor of all elegant waistcoats, of all brightly coloured and elaborately folded flags of silk in shades of rust and amber.

The Blanchot story was short, only a few pages, and I checked the assignment sheet twice to see that I was not mistaken about the reading. "*L'instant de ma mort*," it was called. The moment of my death. Of the author, I had only the vaguest associations. I imagined him an old man with a white beard, which was incorrect, and probably the fault of the "blanche" in the name Blanchot. In fact, Blanchot was aggressively, militarily clean-shaven.

This would be our primary text for the next month, and I could not imagine how Derrida would spin eight hours of content out of the spare and enigmatic story. The first sentence sounded like a fable and posed the paradox of a young man prevented from dying by death itself. What all this had to do with deconstruction—which I imagined as itself a garment, the seams inside out, with odd cuts and appendages, for instance, a missing shoulder, and an arm extending tentacular from the torso, a garment neither practical nor attractive but with its own hypnotic fascination—I could not tell.

Later on, the encounter between Derrida and Blanchot would prove a famous one, would mark an ethical turn in deconstruction towards ideas of death and welcome and hospitality. Even as it happened, it was passing into history. Everyone in that auditorium came to be a witness, felt the moment freezing into the monumental past. Blanchot, who in the story described his own near-brush with death as a young man, was still alive as we sat in the classroom. He would not die until 2003, at the age of 95, an impossible age for a man who lived through two World Wars to reach. Derrida would die a year later. My grandmother, who was in a hospital bed waiting for the instant of her own death, had two more months to live, though she was told that she had six. As for me, I had checked two different online auguries and they gave me dates ten years apart and halfway through the next century, the century that in 1998 had not yet been breached. I was glad to know that I would die in the spring. I would be older than my grandmother and Derrida, but younger than Blanchot. The websites offered me a helpful clock with which to count down the days, the hours, the minutes, a *memento mori* that could live in the corner of my screen. I was oddly soothed by the stoic reminder.

Reading the story, I nearly missed my stop. I then had trouble finding the hospital in an unfamiliar corner of Brooklyn. September was as hot as August, the city a humid marinade of trash and urine and traffic fumes, and by the time I stepped into the building I was drenched and exhausted. Once inside the hospital, I couldn't find the room, as if it had been constructed by some Daedalian architect, not as clinic but as maze.

Even when I found the room, I had trouble recognizing her.

She was like a fish, her stomach bloated, the blue veins legible on her arms, her legs lost in the blankets. But she had also lost weight so you could see her bone structure, the heart-shaped face, age spots dark on her pale skin. She had been heavy all my life, her features lost in flesh and hidden behind her cat's-eye glasses. Without them on, she looked much younger. She looked like me. I hadn't meant to say it out loud, but then she said, "I always thought so," and I was surprised. It was the most intimate exchange we'd ever had, from a likeness that had long been hidden.

When my grandmother was young she was beautiful. She fully channeled the glamour of the forties and the fifties in America, a combination of genetics, zeitgeist, and a now unimaginable effort. In the small black and white photographs held in her albums by faded cardboard corners, her lips are dark, her hair luxurious in smooth back-swept rolls. She is dressed to type, in Esther Williams swimsuits and dresses cinched tightly at the waist, stockings clinging to her shapely calves, her feet in pumps. She was zaftig, as Leo Rosten defined it in the 1968 *The Joys of Yiddish* (my grandparents had the paperback in their bathroom)—a word which "describes in one word what takes two hands, outlining an hourglass figure, to do."

Zaftig. You didn't need to know what it meant to know that it was juicy. The word was onomatopoeiac, a sound that held a shape, which sometimes worked even for words that had no ostensive meaning, like the famous example of bouba and kiki: one benign and round and the other spiky and abrasive. All my life, my grandmother appeared to be bouba, which sounded very close to bubby, Yiddish for grandmother. Her zaftigness expanded into the shelf of her bosom, the pillow of her stomach. But inside she was always a little Kiki. Somehow, I could tell, even when I was very young, that there was a sharp kernel inside of her and that none of us was allowed to get too close.

Still, in her early life she was vibrant, bursting with life, and when I puzzled over the old pictures, I was in part investigating that mystery, the discovery that she was once as young as me. How incredible it was, that our grandparents were full of life and lust and beauty, as much as I ever was myself, more, indeed, since her looks chimed with her era, and mine clashed with an age enamoured of hollow-eyed girls too thin for breasts, or sporty amazons who looked like they had just stepped off a polo field, swinging long manes of hair and smelling like cut grass and money.

And what was even more incredible, from the vantage point of my youth: that I would also grow old. Once, before my grandmother had moved to the hospital, I visited her in her nursing home. An old man seated at her table made obscene noises at me as I leaned over to help her with her fork and spoon. When I would not respond he abruptly grew silent and then gestured at my grandmother. "Well, look at her," he said. "You can see she was a beautiful woman once, though you wouldn't think it now." He swallowed, unstuck his dentures from his gum and stuck them back on again with his tongue, ruminating. "You'll be like that someday," he said, punishing me.

I laughed at him. When you are young you don't care. Then you grow up and your old indifference is a daily rebuke.

For the first time in my life, Helen greeted me warmly. Perhaps it was the drugs they gave her that loosened her tongue, because in that hospital bed she seemed, for the first time I had ever known her, *relaxed*. She had always been still and silent, but she was never serene, she was just hidden.

At least, from her family. Later on, at the funeral, friends would describe her as the life of the party. They would talk about her vibrancy and wit and wicked mahjong skills. This slightly loopy hospital version of my grandmother was the only way I could make sense of the woman they described. She laughed, she seemed happy, she had even taken out her mirrored compact and put on lipstick, though she didn't have the steadiness to put it on straight, and I fought the urge to hold out a tissue and wipe the red smear on the side of her mouth as a mother wipes strawberry jam off the face of her child.

"Did I ever tell you how I caught your grandfather?" she said.

"No," I said. "Never." She'd never told me anything. My ear snagged on that strange word "caught."

"I was fourteen years old. He was eighteen." She saw my raised eyebrows and laughed. "I know, he thought I was too young also, but I knew what I wanted. I was friends with his sister. You know, when we came to America, I was eight years old, my mother had to work for a living. My father was good for nothing by then. *Gut-far-gornisht!* My mother was in a garment factory. She came home later than I got out of school, so I used to go to my friend Rachel's house every day, then she'd pick me up on her way home. That started when I was ten, eleven years old, so really, we were like sisters. He wasn't interested in us, I was his little sister's friend. As far as he was concerned, we were both of us pains in the *tuchus*."

Her lipstick lolled on the hospital tray and I could read the sticker on the bottom of the golden tube: poppy.

"He didn't even want to know from us. But I'd been watching him and really, he hadn't grown up badly. He was going to be a handsome man, this I knew. And ambitious! He'd applied to Harvard. He could have gone to Columbia, but he wanted to leave New York. I didn't blame him, his mother was obsessive about her children, I mean, obsessive. He couldn't take a piss without her asking if he was alright. He was valedictorian that year, and everyone thought he would get in, he was going to be the first in the school to go to the Ivy League, not just the Ivy League, but the best of the Ivys. Harvard! That day he got the letter, and he took it to his room, and by some miracle his mother wasn't home."

She swallowed hard, and smoothed the blanket with her trembling hands.

"So, we know now about the quotas. That's how all that *narishkeit* started, you know-the interviews, the personal statements. It was a way of weeding out the Jews, because after they started to let them in, pretty soon they were taking over the university, and that scared them, the goyim, they were being pushed out of their own places. The first affirmative action was for those, the goyim. It's still true. That's how we ended up with Bush for president. Not the first, I mean the second one, the idiot."

She started coughing hard, and her body shook under the sheet. I brought her a plastic cone of water from the sink—how stupid to give a patient a cup you can't even set down—but she impatiently waved it off. She took a tissue in her shaking hand. Her veins were dark and prominent, like worms snaking under the skin, and when she set the tissue down, it was stained red. Not blood, lipstick, and I was in front of the closet in her bedroom in my mind's eye, I had just doused myself in the powdery effluence of the large bottle of Chanel No. 5 on her dresser, following the advice I'd read in a woman's magazine (spray the bottle in front of your face and then, eyes closed, stride through the mist—spray, stay, walk away) and I looked down, and there was an open trash can filled with crumpled tissues stained in red, each kissed and then discarded until they almost overflowed the pail.

"I knocked on the door," she resumed. "I knew. He said, go away, but I came in anyway. He was sitting on the edge of his bed, it was narrow, he was too big for it. He was too big for that room. He was always very tidy for a man, later on that was one of the things we used to fight about, he wanted me for to keep the house more nice, and I couldn't see the point of it, doing it all over again every single day. And his bed was tightly made. Military. But in front of him there was a pile of paper. At first, I didn't understand what it was, he'd ripped up that letter into such tiny pieces you couldn't have made out a single word, not the logo of the university, not a signature, and not a refusal, he had destroyed it. It was like—like what they have at parades—right, confetti. And I kneeled down and started to pick up the pieces slowly. I was sitting almost between his legs, and he was leaning back. He put his hand on my head, very lightly, it was a strange thing to do. I was embarrassed, but I liked it. I didn't want to move. I stayed down there as long as I could, hunting for pieces of paper in the carpet, and then I stood up and he was looking at me, not at his little sister's friend, at me. Thank you, he said, and I didn't trust my voice to say anything, just turned around and went to the toilet not the kitchen to throw it out—I knew he wouldn't want his mother to see the letter—and when I went into Rachel's room, she was stiff and angry and she said, aren't you a little old to need babysitting every afternoon, and after that we were never friends again. She would not forgive me for falling in love with him. She didn't even want to come to our wedding."

She coughed again, and her head sank further into the pillow. Dying was a process of subtraction; flesh, colour, consciousness. I once saw an exhibition by an artist who had painted his dying wife through all the stages of her illness until she was just a pale disturbance in the bedsheets, like the imaginary landscapes in the sky, distant shimmering hills and valleys that form before the light of day gives way to darkness.

"Your grandfather was a very good man," she said. "I'm tired now. Come back another day. Where is Andrea?"

The helper comes without helping. Kafka wrote that at the end of his life, when he had lost his voice to tuberculosis and was dying, like his own hunger artist, of slow starvation. His final words were fragmentary notes written on slips of paper, because he could not speak. He envied the lilacs in his window because they could drink water. How thirsty he was.

3.

The very best thing about my roommate was that she was rarely home. We found each other on a noticeboard in the university, found the apartment through a phone number on a lamppost just a day later, before we had a chance to get to know each other or had any idea how different we were in our basic sense of how to be a person in the world. I think she was sorry she hadn't opted for a sterile dorm room, a cube in a building of cubes closer to Washington Square. I am being unfairly dramatic, there was nothing objectionable about her, which was precisely why I took objection, she was such a normal girl. She collected stuffed animals, she loved chocolate pudding, she wore primary colours, she was certainly a virgin. She mounted stuffed animals on the wall like trophies, it was a massacre.

Our differences were intellectual and aesthetic in that she had no interest in either category. We never fought, but I tried to colonize the apartment with my gloom and existential doubt, and that must have felt like poison for her, just like her wall of stuffed animals and cheery affirmations felt like being gassed with cotton candy to me. Soon she was out all the time, studying in the library or at choir practice or in the gym, daily, which puzzled me since her ebullient figure seemed entirely resistant to being pared or tamed, like her very curly hair, which all of the storage space in our bathroom was dedicated to smoothing. I thought that everything in her life was designed to constrict and discipline, from her control top underpants to the graduate degree in accounting that she seemed determined to master but did not seem to like, except all of this was accompanied with sticker charts and smiley-face stickers and posters of rainbows and unicorns as if to affirm that this jolly joyless grind was the best of all fates in the best of all possible worlds.

Her sneakers were bright pink, and always waiting by the door—she took off her shoes in the house and my negligence in remembering to do the same brought her nearly to tears.

Our first week living together, I sat in our narrow kitchen drinking a cup of coffee by the thin diffused light of the air shaft. Brenda burst past me. "I'm going jogging!" she said cheerfully. "And then I'm going to meet Jess at Starbucks!" She always announced her plans before leaving the house, and had an endless list of friends I'd never met to whom she referred as if I'd recognize them.

"Byyyye," she said, and I heard the soft click of the door closing.

As soon as she closed the door, I started smoking out the kitchen window, something Brenda did not allow. "I just have two rules," she said when we decided to move in together. "Absolutely no smoking in the apartment. And shoes off in the house." "Of course," I said airily. "Anyway, I don't smoke." Three days in I was smoking, my shoes up on the kitchen table. When she came home, I'd blame the smell on the air shaft and the neighbours below us. "God," she'd say, wrinkling her pert nose. "The air circulation is so bad, it's like they were smoking inside the house. I'm going to say something to them." "You absolutely should," I said, thinking of our downstairs neighbours, who were either lovers or Nabokovian siblings, tiny and black-haired and with actual violet eyes. They flinched when I passed them on the stairs, and I thought Brenda's exuberance would terrify them entirely, so much that they wouldn't have the nerve to tell her that neither of them were smokers.

When I heard a knock at the door, I thought Brenda was home unexpectedly, that perhaps she'd forgotten her keys. I quickly put the cigarette out in my cup of coffee and then threw the butt out the window, I swung my feet off the table and slipped my shoes off at the entrance, opened the door to find no one. Then I looked down.

"Hello," the girl said. She stood about as high as my chest.

What capricious Giants we must be to the world of children, what Brobdingnagians! She wore a summer dress that looked too small for her, smocked at the top, covered in tiny blue flowers. Her legs were bare, and she wore a woman's red pumps, her feet precariously perched in them like a bird's claws on a twig. I couldn't imagine where she'd come from. The residents of the building were students and artists, as far as I could tell. There was a crackhouse across the street, a club next door, an S&M shop nearby, all corsets and masks and whips in the window. It was no place for children. Was she eight, nine, ten years old? I couldn't tell.

"May I come in?" she said and I stepped out of the doorway to let her stride through, apparitional.

"My name is Persephone," she said, and then she paused and looked at me. "Oh," I said. It took me a minute. "I'm Alice." "Charmed to meet you," she said, and then she put one foot behind the other and bent her knees in a quick curtsy.

"Where in the world did you come from?" I said in wonder.

"Downstairs," the girl with the name of a goddess said. "May I come in for a cup of tea?"

Brenda had a collection of mugs emblazoned with affirmative

messages: "Goal Digger" and "Don't Quit Your Day Dream" and "World's Best Daughter" and "Better Late Than Never". Persephone stood reading them on the shelf, her hands clasped behind her back, while I boiled the water. "I like this one," she said, pulling out the chipped, gold-limned small teacup that was mine, bought in a Salvation Army on the Lower East Side. A pattern of rose buds and twined green stems. I filled a glass pot with a tea-flower I had bought in Chinatown. With a serious expression, she watched the flower unfurl into a spiky creature, more sea urchin than flower, and fill the pot, spiraling out in tendrils as it infused the hot water. "You buy them in Chinatown," I said. "Not a flower at all, but tea leaves and flowers bound together—a trick. They bloom into the water. This one is green tea and jasmine."

"I like that," she said. "But usually I drink Earl Grey."

She sat very straight at my narrow kitchen table, and her feet rested on the ledge of the chair because they could not reach the floor. I looked for the sugar before I remembered I had discarded it, the white crystals swarmed with black ants, but there was honey in the refrigerator so I took it out, opened the cold lid sealed tighter with stickiness, and watched her.

She took a tablespoon, then a second one. She stirred the tea delicately, for longer than she needed. She resembled a Tenniel illustration, long straight hair and solemn eyes, and she seemed at once perfectly at home and curious about everything.

My mother had named me for Tenniel's Alice—her image of a little girl—but I looked nothing like her. In Tenniel's illustrations, which had pride of place on my childhood shelf, Alice had long fair hair brushed back from a high forehead, symmetrical features, and rosebud lips. I would recognize her face a decade later in the marble bust of a young girl at the Met who could easily have been his model, and whose immobile perfection seemed to explain Alice's statuesque integrity and charm, her harmonious and cool imperturbability. If anything, I looked more like Alice Liddell—petite, with black eyes and short bangs I had kept from when I was a child, and a face that had often been described, perhaps uncharitably, as old-fashioned. I couldn't imagine the Alice of the books looking like Alice Liddell herself, who was too slight, too sly. But I could imagine this girl in her too-small dress and too-large shoes tumbling down a deep well and remaining entirely composed. She looked around the room as if she was taking notes.

"Where is your mother?" I said.

I had finally remembered that I was the adult. I had little experience with children. There was my sister, true, eleven months my junior, but I didn't think of her as a child since we were so close in age we shared our childhood. And then there were the twins, but they were only two years old when I left home.

"My mother is asleep," Persephone said. "She doesn't mind if I leave the apartment as long as I don't leave the building by myself. Would you like to take me to the park? After we have our tea. And do you have any cereal, please? I haven't had breakfast. We can leave her a note."

My morning stretched in front of me, three books to finish for class and my computer screen. Autumn still thought it was summer, and St. Marks hadn't yet woken up. The street was quiet but filled with the lemon of early morning light.

"I don't have cereal but I have oatmeal," I said, taking a package out from Brenda's neatly arranged boxes. "We can go to the park. Do you know where your name comes from?"

"My mother likes mythology," Persephone said. "Ovid is her favourite writer. I like the story of Arachne better. Spiders are natural artists."

Thinking back on our meeting now, it is hard to believe that she spoke that way, like a tiny Liberal Arts student rather than like a child. But sometimes, when children are raised by books and not by grownups, they end up precociously composed, made up of gleaned stories, poorly-understood morals, and words whose meaning they know but whose sounds they consistently mispronounce. Raised by libraries, rather than raised by wolves, though books had their own dangers. I had been a little like that myself. When I was a little girl, we went to meet a famous politician, who circulated in the crowd as politicians do, robustly shaking hands. When he came to me, I seized his hand and kissed it, like a knight might kiss the hand of a lady in an Arthurian romance. He looked down in surprise at the six-year old girl kissing his hand, and swept me up in his arms, to the fond adoration of the masses. The photograph of the politician and child made the newspapers the next day. Some years later, he ran for president, and lost, though if he had won it would have made a better story—the moment a little girl saw him in a crowd and recognized him for what he was, a king.

Persephone ate one package of oatmeal, then another. Through the window, I could see my downstairs neighbour ascending the fire escape along the airshaft, first his head, then his slim shoulders, then his pale and narrow chest, followed by his altogether, he liked to sunbathe nude on the roof in the mornings. She sat calmly, her back to him, her entire focus on the spoon. I was so tired of reading Heidegger, and maybe this was the answer to it, watching the sun pick out the freckles on a little girl's nose on a Sunday morning.

"You can't wear those shoes," I said, and I thought, I sound like my mother. I picked up her bowl and washed it out. It was calming to do something for someone else. On my own I would have left the bowl on the table.

"No," she said. "I guess not." She sighed, as if that was a regrettable necessity. "I'm ready now," she said, standing up.

She walked over to the living room, her ankles wobbling with every step, a baby giraffe. She looked at the wall of stuffed animals and I said, "They aren't mine, but you can have one." How likely was it, that Brenda kept track? She shook her head. "I don't like dolls," she said. She then walked over to the tall French windows with their deep ledges, the windows that had sold me on the place before I realized Brenda would block them with her bed and screens and cheerful clutter. "Our view is just like this," she said, "only not so high up." Across the street there was an exotic dancer who practised with the curtains open in the red light of a draped lamp, there was a stumbling after-midnight line of visitors to the crackhouse, there was a social worker's checklist of things she should not have seen. Even so, for the moment it seemed like a glorious thing to be a city child, like Eloise at the Plaza. She turned away from the window. "Shall we?" she said, and she offered me her narrow bare arm.

I slipped a twenty in my pocket, slid on my Birkenstocks and grabbed my keys, I stuck Heidegger's *Basic Writings* in a tote bag from the Strand. I had no idea what you did at a kid's park, maybe there were spare moments for reading Heidegger. We went down two flights, and then she put her fingers to her lips, hush, and slid a key out of her pocket and into the door.

The place was just like mine, but less tidy, heaps of clothes on the floor. I could see dishes piled in the sink as we passed the kitchen. Persephone pointed to the closed door of the bedroom and mimed sleep, I nodded, and we made our way to the front room where a corner marked off her living space from the rest of the apartment, a narrow bed, neatly made, a milk crate bookcase, and true to her word, no stuffed animals or dolls. She took off the red shoes and lined them up beside her bed, pulled out a pair of sandals, pink jellies. They were everywhere that year. She took a crayon and left a note on a piece of construction paper—at the park with a friend—and then she pinned it to the bedroom door with a thumbtack like a small Martin Luther.

I wasn't used to being outside so early on a Sunday in New York. It was a different city, washed clean in the morning light, uncrowded, the shops still dark and shuttered, the clubbers finally asleep. We went east, to Tompkins Square. Brenda had warned me about Tompkins Square when we first moved in. Our apartment was as far East as she ever went. I'd been further, but I hadn't yet been to the park. I'd forgotten it was even there.

Persephone slipped her small hand into mine as soon as we crossed the first street, and I felt touched and alarmed at once—who was this girl, so free to give away her trust in the big city? I looked around for predators, but there was just an old woman, bent almost double under the curve of her own spine, and a man crossing the street in the other direction, holding the hand of a boy who seemed around Persephone's age. He smiled broadly at me and I flushed until I realized what he was smiling at was our fellowship, two parents driven out early on a Sunday morning on the whim of our children. He had mistaken me for a mother. For her mother.

"Can you let go of my hand please?" Persephone said. I must have tightened my grip, and I hadn't even realized it, but we had reached the park. She ran straight for a boy sitting in a pile of woodchips and, spotting her with delight, he stood up and threw the handful he'd been playing with in the air as if it was light as paper. His hair was the colour of ketchup, and he had a pale, pointed face. He must have been younger than her by three or four years. Later on, I would learn she had no friends her own age—only children and adults, whom she was poised between like a coin spinning on its side.

They settled in the hollow of a bush at the edge of the children's park, and I tried not to worry about what other activities the bush might have sheltered. I sat down on a bench in the sun. This wasn't so bad.

"Would you like a ticket?" I must have dozed off in the sun because the boy was at my side and Persephone beside him. He held out a woodchip, solemn.

"Yes," I said. "Of course."

I pulled invisible bills out of an imaginary pocket with a flourish.

"Where am I going?"

"That's a magic ticket," he said. "That will take you anywhere you want to go. Take good care of it."

I slipped it into my bag and he did not look away until it was safely secured.

"Good," he said.

"Good," I said. I had a magic ticket that would take me anywhere I wanted to go. What more did I need?

4.

I knew that my grandmother had gone through periods of what her era rarely dared to call depression. My father had said that after he and his brothers grew up and left the house, there were days she would never get dressed. She wore housedresses and slippers and spent the days indoors with a novel and the television remote, cups of tea and cigarettes smoked out the window, long games of solitaire played at the kitchen table. "Not good," my grandfather said, and after that he came directly home after work and demanded they go out. They went to dinner every night, or to a friend's house to play mahjong or bridge. She would still spend the day in her housedress, but by 5:15 she was showered and dressed, she had plucked her eyebrows and coloured her lips her favourite shades of peony and poppy. She was ready.

Years they lived like that, until he died first, as men do. At the age of sixty he collapsed in the bathroom while shaving. That is the way to die: instantaneously, while looking in the mirror, at a version of yourself not yet too blurred by age. My father feared his mother would slip back into what they called "her moods," but actually the opposite happened, and she had ten lively and useful years, you could say she was a different person, until her son died and she declined. Complications from her diabetes put her in the hospital and she was told she had six months.

I went to the hospital a second time, and this time I felt less lost, though the journey took just as long. In the week of my absence, my grandmother had grown thinner and paler. This time she had not bothered to put on lipstick or brush her hair, which was a thin, permed tangle on her scalp, the tips red and the roots white. She tried to lift herself up when she saw me, and then collapsed.

Her helper was there, hovering by the bed, but she didn't assist her. "She lazy," she said. "Good for nothing. She got to learn to do it for herself, right Helen?"

I could not believe my ears. I said, "Don't talk to her like that," but my grandmother flushed and giggled and seemed pleased and embarrassed, as if the abuse was a kind of flirtation.

"I'm going for my break," the helper announced, and my grandmother began to cry. It was awful, and made it seem as though in the last week she had regressed to infancy. Like an infant, her face was red and wrinkled I barely recognized her without the familiar mask of makeup. Her eyebrows were sparse and uneven, and her pale lips had fallen in to the wet cave of her mouth. I saw that her dentures were in a glass on the table beside her. "Andrea, Andrea," my grandmother said, and I felt embarrassed that I had not thought to ask her name.

"Don't be a baby," Andrea said. "You know I be back. She always cry like that when I go," she said to me. "She forget in a minute. Her mind is gone." She drew a spiral by her ear with a finger. She leaned over and squeezed my grandmother's hand with swift and surprising warmth, and left the room.

I did not know whether to sit or stand. The blankets were disturbed and my grandmother's leg, withered and naked, was exposed almost to the hip. I straightened the blanket, not certain whose modesty I was protecting, hers or my own. She was a woman who once would not leave the house without stockings, without what she called "putting on her face." Finally, I settled on the chair beside the bed and perched on the very end of it, as if I were prepared to leave at any moment.

Andrea was right. My grandmother settled in a minute, sank back into her bed, and then opened her eyes again. She groped for the tissue box secreted in the folds of her bed, and wiped her face. Then she jerked her hand—the knuckles too swollen to put on her wedding ring—towards the bedside table. I wasn't sure what she wanted, and she jerked her hand again, impatient. "My teef," she said. "My teef." I passed her the glass but her grasp was palsied and the water spilled on her sheets. "Just a minute," I said, and reached in to give her the dentures. She fumbled, her hands clumsy, but once she had settled them in her month she seemed herself again. I helped her raise herself on her pillows and sat down again.

"Do you have any cookies?" she said. I was surprised. But I did have a cookie, I bought it in the subway, and it sat wrapped in plastic in my purse. I gave it to her, and she tore off the plastic wrap, already seeming more dexterous. She took a piece of cookie—crumbs in the sheets—and stuffed it in her mouth quickly, as if she was afraid it would be taken away from her, as if she knew that life had a limited amount of sweetness left on offer and she needed to consume it as quickly as possible.

"Thank you," she said decorously, although her mouth was still full and crumbs tumbled onto the front of her hospital gown. She smiled at me as if we had never met. She blinked like a doll and her eyes shifted back and forth, as if looking for something, and then I realized it was me, she was trying to identify me.

"Grandma," I said. "Grandma. It's me, Alice."

She lifted the corners of her mouth and folded her hands over the blanket.

"Very nice," she said. "Nice to meet you."

"No, Grandma, Alice. Moshe's daughter. Moshe, your son Moshe. I'm your first granddaughter, remember?"

She drew back in surprise. "Moshe?" she said. "Where is Moshe? Is Moshe here?"

"No," I said. I was alarmed. At his funeral, she had keened with sorrow. I had never seen a grief so pure and so naked, it was hard not to look at her. My own sadness was in a little glass smoke-filled box at the bottom of my chest, but she was almost sublime. In Hebrew school, I once learned that you were forbidden to take the eggs from a nest if the mother bird was present. Our teacher told us that Maimonides said the grief of a mother is beyond intellect or speech, it belongs to the animal world as well as the human. Watching her cry had felt like witnessing something stronger than death. I would not make him die for her again.

"No, he's not here."

"But I want him," she said simply. "I told him I would come back soon."

Her hands flew to her face in alarm, and she hid her eyes like a child does to make the world go away.

"Moshe, I want Moshe," she said behind the shutter of her hands. Then, "Andrea, I want Andrea!"

I told her that I would go find Andrea, who had said she'd be back in ten minutes, flashing two hands full of rings. It felt like it had been an hour at least. Andrea was not in the waiting area or in the lounge on the main floor, but as I opened the heavy door I saw her standing outside, leaning on the building, smoking next to some other women whom I assumed were also paid to keep the vigil that families could not or would not sustain.

"Helen asked for you," I said. "You said you'd be right back."

She shrugged and blew out slowly, blue smoke licking my face.

"Well?" I said, and she threw the cigarette on the balding

grassy margin littered with cigarette butts and turned to give a warm goodbye to the women who stood smoking away the waiting time like fates knitting the ragged ends of a life until the thread is cut, until the cigarette is finished, until they descend back into the underworld for the long subway ride home to the margins of the city where they lived, until they were summoned to another bedside. As Andrea walked past me she shoved me, softly, and it was so unexpected I had no idea if her action was on purpose. I had not been shoved on purpose since—god—elementary school, it wasn't something women did. I caught my balance and stood there in shock, too slow and too uncertain to respond, staring into the distance until I came back to myself and realized I wasn't staring into empty space at all but at the hostile fixed gaze of Andrea's three friends. As I turned and walked away I could feel their eyes on my back, could hear a ripple of laughter in my wake.

5.

The next time Persephone came knocking, I asked no questions, just put on my shoes and took her to the park. The boy was there again, as if he had never left. But this time, we forgot to leave a note.

"Persephone!" a voice called out, and a woman ran towards us. She was barefoot, thin leather thong sandals dangling from her fingers, and her face was flushed. Her hair was the same colour as Persephone's, but while Persephone's hair was smooth and shiny, this woman had wild curls down her back. She wore a thin-ribbed tank top, harem pants, clothes she might have slept in. "Fiona!" Persephone said, and ran towards her. Her mother's face was flushed, she leaned down to gather the girl into her arms. "Alice took me to the park," she said preemptively, gesturing towards me, and I stood, hesitant.

Fiona looked at me and back at Persephone. Thoughts passed, a wind over her face, and she pressed her lips together. She leaned down, dropped her sandals on the ground, and slid her narrow, dusty feet into her shoes. When she stood up, she was smiling. She smoothed back her hair—she couldn't have been much older than I was—and said, "Thanks for taking her to the park. I hope she wasn't too much of a bother." She had a British accent, and I realized I had heard that formal trace in Persephone's voice. She sat down on the bench, and I sat beside her. In the sun, her hair was every precious metal, copper, silver, platinum, gold. "She adopts people," Fiona said. "It's because she's always been around grown-ups. I worry about it, but she has good karma, I think. I came as soon as I woke up and saw that she was gone. It isn't the first time. You have to keep them safe but also, you know, keep them free?"

That explained the bare feet, the rumpled clothes, though if couldn't have been entirely true that she ran straight out, there were ropes of necklaces around her neck and red and white bangles on her wrist. She noticed me looking at them and held out her narrow, tanned arms.

"India," she said. "They're for brides. Traditionally made of ivory and worn all the way from wrist to elbow." She shook her arms, and the bracelets rang. "These ones are enamel. You know, when women used to get married they wore them for a full year? It's hard to do anything with the full set. Like handcuffs. We spent most of last year in India, they loved her there," she nodded her chin at Persephone. "Everyone wanted to touch her hair, to give her sweets. It was incredible, like having a million aunties."

She leaned back and closed her eyes against the sun. "I could use a coffee," she said, "there's a place right on the other side of the park. "Do you want one?" She sprang up, smoothed back her hair. "She'll be fine," she said. "She loves Noah, they can play for hours. And Dori's here. His nanny." She waved at a Filipino woman, one of a group huddled at the edge of the park. "Should we tell her?" I said, but Fiona was already halfway down the path, the shadows of the leaves weaving patterns on her bare shoulders.

I could see it even more now, the resemblance between the girl and her mother, because I followed her without asking any more questions to the little coffee shop on the corner of the square, just as I had followed Persephone that morning. There was a takeout window, right on the street, and a girl with long purple hair leaning on a ledge in front of an espresso machine. Fiona ordered for both of us, strong small cups of coffee with lids of foam, and then reached into her pocket, frowning. "Do you mind?" I took out the twenty, and the girl gave me back a ten and a five. I couldn't figure it out, something about the girl's face I was having trouble registering, and then I realized she had no eyebrows at all, just a smooth expanse from eye to hairline, and that made her seem expressionless.

"I'm sorry," I said. "I'll tip next time."

I fingered the five for a second, then walked away, and despite the lack of eyebrows I could read the contempt on her face.

"This is the future," Fiona said, gesturing. "Coffee shops have been opening up, bakeries. If I had the cash, I'd buy in this neighbourhood right now. You have any money?"

I was startled. "I'm a student," I said.

"NYU?" she said. We were back at the children's park, and Persephone and Noah were still beneath the bush, sitting cross-legged, facing each other. Fiona slid her hand into her pocket and drew out a cigarette, bummed a light from—well, from a bum sitting on a nearby bench, with his world's possessions in plastic bags around him, who smiled at her in brown-toothed, nicotine solidarity.

"Yes," I said. "I'm a graduate student."

"I went to NYU," she said. "For a year, then I met Hank. He was sitting in on my poetry class, he knew the teacher. Such a good-looking man. With a funny name. Like that bread with seeds in it?"

"Hank?" I said.

"No," she said, "well, yes sure he was good-looking too, but not like the teacher, every girl in that class wanted him, and next to him every boy looked, well, so immature they might as well have not even been in the room, you know, like their testicles hadn't even descended yet. He had that chin, you know. Like Gregory Peck. Manly dimples, is that an oxymoron? And he had suffered, god that's attractive. Those girls, they just wanted to wash his feet, bathe him in their youth. We used to laugh about it."

I could see where Persephone got her odd affect from, her way of talking like a child in a book rather than like a child. But Fiona was more digressive than Persephone, I could barely follow her train of thought.

"Who is we? You mean you and the poet?" I asked.

"No. Me and Hank. Hank said that was his thing, he'd always been like that, he just had this aura of sadness that was irresistible, even when they were kids. When he read out poems in class, it was like he was bringing himself to tears. *His own poems*. God, it was disgusting, like watching someone masturbate in the mirror. He never really suffered, not like Hank."

Persephone emerged from under the bush. She had a crown of dandelions in her hair, and so did Noah, who looked like her elfin consort. They came towards us holding hands.

"Don't smoke," Persephone said, and Fiona rubbed out the cigarette on the bench and threw it behind her. "You'll die."

"We all die," Fiona said. "A little soul carrying a corpse."

"You'll look old," Persephone said. "You'll smell bad. You already do."

Fiona looked into the distance, spot-lit in the sunlight, and I could see the tiny lines at the corners of her eyes and the corners of her mouth. She was exposed by the sun, not illuminated by it. She shifted into the shade and again looked young, invulnerable, shiny.

"She worries about me," she said to me. "It's nice, really. She thinks she's the mother. Why the crown?" she said, turning back to Persephone, and Persephone said, "I'm the May queen."

Fiona tilted her head at Noah, and Persephone said, "He's the May queen too." "It's September," Fiona said. "Ripeness is all. What do you study?"

She was talking to me again. She was firefly quick, lighting up right beside me as if she'd been there all along.

"English," I said. "Literature."

"That's what I did," Fiona said. "Before I dropped out. All those professors, they just wanted to pull the books apart. Me, I wanted to worship them. We had irreconcilable differences."

She had pulled out another cigarette and was waving it, unlit, in her fingers just to have something to do with her hands.

"Plus, I got pregnant. The honourable Fiona."

"How long have you been living in the building?" I said.

"Since we got back from India. Five months. You know Jack Kerouac lived in the building? In the basement. It's not bad. There's a good school nearby. I thought we could play at Eloise for a little while. Persephone could be a *city child*."

I was startled, since that was exactly the phrase that had crossed my mind when I first met Persephone. "I loved those books," I said.

"Yes, didn't we all," Fiona said. She seemed tired. "You must have work to do," she said. "Thank you for looking after her. You must have thought it was strange, a little girl knocking on your door early in the morning. *You hadn't even been introduced*." She said it in a stiff, posh accent, the way she'd said *the honourable Fiona*.

"She's lovely," I said. "I didn't mind. Better than reading Heidegger." I gestured at the abandoned book, which I still hadn't managed to finish.

"She's lonely," Fiona said. She closed her eyes, sitting back on the bench, boneless. "Late night last night," she said, "I'm going to take a little nap while they play. I'll see you later." I stood there for a minute, watching her, but it seemed she had immediately fallen asleep. A small bubble of saliva glistened, popped at the corner of her mouth. I took my book and walked back towards the apartment.

The thing about the Eloise books is that you hardly ever see the mother. She is a pair of strappy high heeled sandals on a little girl's feet, a seldom-heard voice on the end of the line.

6.

Fiona began to come by, with and without Persephone, often bearing gifts. She claimed they were things she was getting rid of, but also that they were objects that made her think of me, so her gifts had a casual and intimate frequency which made me feel singled out, but not indebted. She gave me a delicate pair of necklaces strung with tiny crystals, one black, one silver, a botanical print from the nineteenth century, thick and heavy rosewood bracelets, a pair of fur boots she didn't wear anymore. I wasn't used to such easy generosity—in graduate school, my classmates kept track of who paid for each and every cup of coffee or pint of beer—and I hadn't realized, yet, that the ease with which objects passed in and out of Fiona's life was as careless as it was munificent—prodigal, even—and that she had the same attitude towards the revolving door of people who spun in and out of her life.

Over the next few weeks, I found out more about Fiona, though she was such a house of mirrors, her story changed all the time, and I wasn't always sure what to believe. She got pregnant when she was eighteen years old, in her freshman year of university, living in New York for the very first time. She had completely severed ties with her parents, and flew over on the basis of a scholarship and a picture of New York collaged out of early Woody

Allen movies and Salinger stories. She took a job under the table at a restaurant, found a room in an apartment in Alphabet City—"A squat, I think it was, even though they were happy to take my money. I think they just pocketed it"—and she started her classes.

Mostly it was disappointing—the classes so introductory, the students so young and dumb. She wasn't sure if that was America or if it was the difference between the lives that they had lived. All these kids seemed to be best friends with their parents, their rent was paid, they went home on weekends, they still probably sucked their thumbs and slept with stuffed animals—I nodded, thinking of Brenda and her wall of bears, that much sounded familiar. Fiona needed more. So somehow, she talked herself into a senior poetry seminar. She cooked up a portfolio of poetry in an afternoon while sitting in Tompkins Square park. She wrote it in violet ink because that was the colour Virginia Woolf used. She showed up at the professor's office wearing a crazy sixties minidress that she'd found at a thrift store back home, navy with a white pointed collar and a skirt so short she had to maneuver herself into a seated position by swooping her hands behind her and pulling down her skirt as she sat. She saw him looking at her as she performed her awkward gesture, as if she was smoothing her feathers, and she thought that her skirt as much as her sheaf of violet words got her into the class.

He was famous, famous for a poet, anyway, and had that quality of seeming to draw all the light in the room to himself, as if he moved under a portable spotlight. She decided that he would be her initiation into the New York she hadn't yet found, and she came to the first class hoping to dazzle, but it turned out he had just remarried, a former student in her early twenties who had long black hair that fell like a silk sheet down her back, and who waited for him after class like a dog for her master. So, he was untouchable, for now—that glance at her thighs an old habit or even courtesy, in honour of her youth and the man he had been, and would be again in just a few years. His poems, which won the Pulitzer and National Book Awards, detailed the agonies of betrayal and separation, and the emollient of new love, though the quality of new love is to roughen with age, the cure in turn the disease. Later, Hank told her each relationship produced one book and one baby. He was an impregnator. There were a series of dazzling babies close enough in age to be siblings, a series of books that catalogued their origin stories, a series of awards built on the pyre of those failed relationships.

She met Hank in the class. He was auditing the seminar, and was a friend of the professor, with three slim published volumes that had been called "brilliant" and "luminous" by the critics. It only took her four months and a queasy unfamiliar feeling in her stomach to realize Hank was also an impregnator, though she didn't really make the connection, not even much later, when he said his next book was about an older man brought back to life by a young woman whom he named Medusa. In response she said, distracted by the small foot wedged under her ribs, "Isn't that a familiar topic?" He was so hurt he wouldn't speak to her for two days.

They moved in together, and she learned that everything was and was not what it seemed—yes, he taught poetry, but on a temporary contract with the New School that always seemed threatened with termination, yes, he came from a wealthy family, but he and his mother were barely on speaking terms, and he had no relationship with his father, barely would acknowledge he had a father and preferred to think of himself as the product of immaculate conception (his mother was rich, but his father was fuck you rich, Fiona said. He could have solved all our problems with a phone call). And he was indeed that rare creature, a published poet, but his poems were published by a friend with a publishing company who lived on Bleeker Street and printed them by hand on an old Chandler and Price Letterpress. He seemed to publish only Hank's poetry and Ayurvedic cookbooks and had gone a little mad, maybe with the smell of ink, like hatters did back in the nineteenth century. Only one critic had called him brilliant, and Hank used the same quote on the back of all three of his publications.

We were sitting at the Cloister Café when she told me the rest of the story.

"Publishing his poetry, it was almost like printing your own money," Fiona said. "Except if he did that, we would have money. Back then, of course, I was delighted, it was exactly the love and squalor I had been seeking. We would take turns caring for the baby and writing. We would take her everywhere—babies are portable, flexible—late-night parties in the Bowery, the South of France. Why, to not have the child would be to surrender to bourgeois values, the idea that you needed to be married, employed, in possession of a house of at least two bedrooms, a minivan, a yard, in order to earn a licence to have a child. No, we didn't need that. Alice, you should have seen our apartment," Fiona said, flushed with the memory of it. "All one room, and ceilings that were eighteen feet high. Under the skylights, our plants thought they were in a forest. We took a drawer out of the dresser and lined it with a folded blanket as mattress for the baby to sleep in. It was summertime, and I bought sleeveless silk dresses that stretched over my stomach, white eyelet nightgowns in the daytime, I wore unbelted kimonos as jackets when it was chilly. I went to parties, there were always parties, and I drank soda water and was content to be admired as around me people did—well, everything that they do, drink and smoke and snort and taste and swallow. I felt fantastic, my skin had never been so clear, my hair so shiny, I had incredible erotic dreams, almost a kind of lucid dreaming, in my dreams I walked through long apricot corridors on my way to have sex with strangers. Hank was happy too, his book was coming out, the New School had renewed his contract, and there was talk of a permanent position. All we needed was art, and each other."

But then everything changed. Fiona said when she hit the third trimester it was as if she had deflated. That belly she had lofted in front of her like a banner—fertile! it claimed. And his!—that belly now weighed her down. She didn't want to stand at parties and watch everyone else "deliquesce" into intoxication—she said deliquesce with a little hiss, and I admired her just for that, the words on the tip of her serpentine tongue—and her feet hurt, she was tired, high people told such stupid jokes and laughed like hyenas, she had no patience for them anymore. There was no comfortable position to sleep in, and it was increasingly difficult to get up or get down into their futon on the floor, she had to roll onto her hands and knees like a dog, then pull herself to standing. It meant that once she lay down she didn't want to get up again, and she wanted to lie down more and more.

Fiona took a long swallow of her coffee. "Too early for a real drink?" she asked, and grimaced. She beckoned the waiter over. "I'll have another one of these," she said, "but this time, with a shot of whiskey in it. Bored yet?" she said to me, and I shook my head and sat there like the three dogs in the Hans Christian Anderson tale, with my eyes as big as teacups, as saucers, as wagon wheels. It was evident to me that in comparison to Fiona, I had not lived.

Even when Fiona was nine months pregnant, Hank still went out at night. Fiona told him that he should go ahead, and then she stayed up late, hating him for taking her at her word. She had terrible heartburn, which she said was common—her stomach like a water balloon someone had stepped on, dripping acid into her esophagus, her breath short because the baby pressed her lungs into your throat, "Every bit of space she takes to grow is space stolen from the mother, believe me," Fiona said grimly, "a pregnant woman is a nightmare." Hank tried to be sympathetic but, day by day, she became more distasteful to him. "I remember the look on his face when a bead of milk appeared on my nipple while we were having sex," Fiona said. "He looked like someone who had bitten into a fruit and found it rotten. As if he would like to spit me out." They had only one desk—his, of course—and sometimes he worked late at night editing his manuscript or finishing up student papers, by the light of a lamp that was meant to spare her disruption but shone right into her eyes. She felt mugged by reality, she couldn't believe it, at the end of the twentieth century. Biology was a harder, smaller destiny than she had been told, the girth of her stomach, the number of steps she could take before she got tired, the six times she woke to piss every night.

Then Hank came home and said they wouldn't be renewing his contract after all. A misunderstanding, he called it, but he seemed less irate than she would have expected, more subdued. Fiona had stopped going out, stopped seeing their friends, or else someone—she thought, she hoped—would have told her about the misunderstanding that involved his hand and a young student's breast, by young she meant Fiona's age except not pregnant. Even if they did tell her, how could she have been surprised? That was their story too. And for Fiona, it was too late. He was the only one who could change his mind. She was in this for life, with or without him.

After Hank was fired, he was shocked into good behaviour for a little while. He rubbed her feet, brought her ice water, made up nonsense poems and recited them to her stomach, and when Persephone emerged, Fiona said his face looked almost uncauled, raw and damp with tears and hopeful, as if he too had just been through a dark and cramped and dangerous passage. As if he had himself just been born.

Fiona lifted her chin like an actress, put her hand, fingers splayed, to her chest, like those paintings of Mary at the annunciation when she has just been told she will soon give birth to a god in the shape of a man.

"As it turns out, she was a perfect baby. She loved to sit and watch the patterns of light on the ceiling. Tuesday's child, full of grace. The drawer we had prepared was useless, she slept in bed with us. She slept with us for five years."

Fiona told me that Hank's mother finally wanted to meet Persephone, after a long and petulant silence. This was only the second time they had met. The first time, her new mother-in-law said to her, in what Fiona called a soft mean tone, "You know, you're the last woman in the world I would have chosen for Hank." But then she leaned back and lifted her eyebrows in exaggerated surprise. "But you seem to make him happy!" she said. She hadn't sounded at all certain that was a good thing.

Fiona didn't want to see her again, and Hank made an unusual appeal for family, which never had seemed to interest him much before—family, for Hank, was a structure to be abandoned as soon as possible. They met for brunch at a restaurant much too fussy for a small child. Fiona spent the entire time trying to distract Persephone and to keep her from throwing the fine china plates, the glittering crystal. "I can't understand it," Hank's mother had told her. "Hank was such a quiet child. She must get it from you. And she looks nothing like him."

"Can you imagine?" Fiona said. "I picked Persephone up and left the restaurant. Perry kicked me, so hard I later had a bruise on my thigh—she was too old to be carried—and I put her down so fast she almost fell. Hank did not follow us. He came home much later, and said, you really fucked that up. She had dangled her money as bait and he had come ready to swallow any old hook. She was never going to give you anything, I said. You know that. She said Persephone was not your child! That isn't what she meant, Hank said. You have to admit that the girl looks just like you."

They had changed almost nothing about the apartment. Persephone was in the room with them, asleep on their bed that had grown too small, in a room that had no air in it, and their exchange was entirely in poisonous whispers.

"What did she say to you?" Fiona had said, and she was shaking.

"She said if I left you, I could have it all. You could have made an effort. That was your last chance."

"And Persephone?" she said. He was silent.

"She's a liar," Fiona said.

"She's getting older," Hank said. "She's quite fragile now, really. She's reaching out and this might be the last time." It was not an apology.

Fiona opened the door. "I want you to go," she said. She could see Persephone watching us from under her eyelashes, her glint of her eyes quick and then hidden. He hesitated in the doorway. She had kept her voice so quiet but her rage was a boiling pot and now rose through her throat, the roar of an animal—'GO!' Persephone cringed in the bed. He slammed the door and vanished from their lives for nearly two years.

Fiona told the story all at once, as we sat on 9th Street, in the coloured light of the stained-glass windows. Her hands were stained red by the tinted shadows, there was a stripe of green on her cheekbone. In the corner was the largest window, of Mary as queen of the universe, regal in her crown against a backdrop of celestial blue. The café had acquired the windows from a nearby church when they renovated, our waitress told us. That was where they got their name.

The windows—floor to ceiling saints and martyrs—seemed to witness our conversation, and hallow it, and after that day I assumed that we were close friends. But instead, her confession seemed to mark the end of our friendship. The small gifts, the midday knocks on the door ended, though Persephone still came to visit, even more often than before. When I saw Fiona, she looked distracted and barely took the time to say hello. She had new friends now, and I often heard the sound of music leaking from under the door of her apartment as I climbed the stairs.

7.

Graduate school seemed at once to stunt and accelerate time. It prematurely aged the students in their early twenties, like me, who cultivated interests in dead philosophers and *New Yorker* subscriptions and early smoker's wrinkles. Conversely, it arrested the development of students in their late thirties and forties, who wore band T-shirts and still had roommates. No one had children, it was a world without children.

One professor was pregnant, though. It was her first, and I was fascinated by the way she held her stomach out in front of her as if it was detachable. She reminded me of a pregnant doll I once owned, not a Barbie but one of the many knock-offs, with tan plastic skin and long golden hair. She had a removable stomach that popped out, and inside the synthetic womb the baby was positioned properly, head down. You reached in and plucked the little baby out. But then there was a problem. The manufacturers should have provided a second stomach, taut and flat, or if they were aiming for verisimilitude, sagging and stretch-marked and residually puffy, but they did not. So, you had the problem of returning the baby to the belly after it had been taken out—a regressive, uncanny operation—or playing with it, but leaving the doll with an empty bubble of a stomach, or a big open hole in her center. In general, my mother didn't let me have Barbie dolls. This must have been educational, some way to prepare me for the arrival of the twins, who indeed hollowed her out and left her with a hole in the middle.

Our professor was a star. She was first mentored by the men in the department and then hired by them. In exchange, she was their mirror. She had the same habits of speech, which are, after all, habits of mind. So even though she walked around with a banner of impending maternity on her belly, it seemed impossible that the bulge would become a child, or that the professor—so combatively intelligent, quick-thinking, ruthless—would become a mother, soggy with breast milk and boredom. When she spoke in class, her head and shoulders visible, I always forgot that she was pregnant, and the brute reminder of her body as she rose at the end of class presented itself as a kind of Cartesian riddle. How can you have a mind and a body, or more accurately, how can you have a mind and a woman's body? Perhaps there was some nursery in the Hudson Valley where intellectuals could send their children so they could be free to think and write, like George Sand did when she left her children with her mother in the countryside so she could live in Paris with a nineteen-year old law student and walk the streets dressed as a man and write brave beautiful books.

Every so often there was a breach, and someone brought a baby into the department. It turned out they existed after all but were hidden in too-small one-bedrooms and crammed studios and the back-stories of graduate students hesitant to bring them too far into the foreground in case their presence should make them seem uncommitted, less serious, ineligible for teaching assistantships and scholarships, disqualified from the life of the mind. This woman—I didn't know her, she worked on Shakespeare and was a couple of years ahead of me, and had a milkmaid prettiness that I admired, blonde and congenial and hearty—had brought in a baby as round and milk-skinned and fair as herself. It was a disaster, you could tell, there was a breakdown in the supply chain of caregivers and partners and she had to go in and meet with her supervisor in the presence of this baby, who was about a year old. I was loitering in the common area, and I said, "I'll watch her." She must have had no choice, she barely knew my name. The milkmaid thrust her warm squirming child into my arms and I spent the next hour in the odd play that has no guidebook but comes as if recollected to the surface, as if drawn out by grasping hands and expectant smiles, and that consists mostly in the repetition of small gestures, round phonemes, shifts in scenery and altitude, and engineered appearances and disappearances.

We had just been reading Freud's *Beyond the Pleasure Principle* with my frangible, brilliant, Modernism professor, who doubled as a music critic for a famous alternative weekly. We talked about fort-da, the notion of a compulsion to repeat, which Freud discovered while watching his eighteen-month year old grandson play with a cotton spool that was dropped and retrieved, disappeared and recovered, in a game that built a sense of mastery in the child's tiny world. Watching a child is not boredom, it is an act of discovery, I thought, which made the childfree environment of graduate school seem all the more useless and yes, sterile. The feedback loop felt complete with this baby, and exorbitant. My small gestures evoked blissful contagious laughter, so unlike the uncertain reception of my intellectual labour, the papers I worked on in solitude that then vanished into a professor's mailbox, only to disappear or reappear months later as a grade I could not quite parse or a few scribbled sentences in the white space left on the bottom of my final page.

I was galloping the child around the room on my hip when I realized I was being watched. I looked over to see that same professor, the Freudian, staring at me from the doorway of his office.

His mouth was soft and he was not wearing his glasses, so his face looked naked and unguarded. "Is that your child?" he said, and I said, "No," feeling embarrassed, or more precisely, caught. "You know," he said, "I've never seen you so lit up." He flushed as he said it—he was a man who mottled red and purple all over his face—then he pulled a handkerchief from his back pocket and polished his glasses, which he had been holding. When he put them back on, he seemed restored to himself. I felt like he had caught me undressing. He closed the door again—another kind of fort-da, where he had the control and I had none—and the mother came back out of the office and took her child back into her strong, capable arms.

8.

I said I was taking a class with Derrida, but the truth is that Derrida flew in for a month of weekly lectures and an ordinary professor handled the other two months of classes, the administration, the grading, all the mundane tasks the great man could not be expected to navigate.

The first day Derrida taught, I thought I'd come into the wrong classroom. I didn't recognize any faces. Chairs were set out in rows, and most of them were full. There was an elevated podium in the middle of the room, a stage for the speaker, and a chair was set in the middle but the space was vacant. I slid into a corner seat and looked around. Now I began to recognize people, but I recognized them from their author photographs and from blurry black and white pictures in the newspapers. All of the academic avant-garde had come to pay homage, and they sat in tight knots that signaled their affiliations, Deconstructionists in the centre of the room, Althussarians to the left, Post-Colonialists at the margins.

How hopeful we were in our cynicism! We thought the age of theory would last a thousand years, we thought we were at the end of history, we celebrated the end of truth and the abyss of meaning and the aporia of interpretation. We were Geryon's children. It was a lot of fun, actually, though sometimes I think that's why I have had so much trouble believing in anything, because we were told in every class and in every text and in every way that belief was something to be troubled, fractured, fissured, destabilized, until we were hypnotized by the spectacle of shifting the pieces of the mosaic rather than by the quest for some kind of sense of the absolute.

"Think about the most popular clothing store in the world," my Freud professor said in our very first class. "What's it called? The Gap." He paused, as if to insert that very gap into the classroom.

There was an odd dynamic in the lecture room, which had to do with the audience trying to ogle one another while trying to simultaneously ignore each other. The woman with the shaved head and tired eyes in the back was a famous postcolonial scholar. She wore a sari and gathered the folds of her drapery around her, straightening her back, glaring at the room. Beside me was a man with fitted trousers and narrow ankles and the most beautiful shoes I'd ever seen in my life.

"Showtime," he said, as a small door near the back of the room opened—I hadn't noticed it before, it was almost as if it was a trick door and had just appeared for this entrance. A man walked through. He wore a narrow paisley vest and a golden scarf. His white hair was combed upwards in a pompadour, a sharp contrast to the tea of his skin. He was slim and contained, and had very small feet. He walked up the stairs of the podium—stumbling on the second step, but he caught himself so quickly, it was almost balletic. The room grew still. The man sat on the stage and crossed his legs, twisting his foot to catch his ankle. He leaned over and pulled a file of papers out of his briefcase, dog-eared and messy, and then he reached into his waistcoat and found a pair of reading glasses with a grimace of self-conscious surprise, as if he could not be the old man who needed them. He waved them in the air before putting them on, like a magician showing his props to the crowd.

"To begin," he said, and then he paused and squinted at the room, which rippled into a wave of laughter. There were never a friendlier audience for a deconstructionist than a NYU lecture hall in the last years of the twentieth century. "Were it possible to begin," he continued, and there was a collective sigh, a shifting and settling back into the folding chairs the university had assembled for this unexpected, this historic event. "To begin with an ending," he went on, "anticipated but never arrived, the end that prefaces our beginnings, to begin, I mean, with the moment of my death."

The next hour passed in a pleasant ramble, and whatever it was he was spinning with his words had a hypnotic effect, like a gold watch swung between thumb and index finger. Listening to him felt something between a nap and a headache, both restful and strenuous. I was concentrating as hard as I could because it felt like every word was weighed and measured, but at the same time he seemed to say the same or similar things frequently, so it was like being caught in an eddy and circling back again to what we all knew could not be the same river.

That was how we talked back then, it was viral, our fingers notching quotation marks that called everything into question. Not ironically, but as a relationship to meaning. Crossing through the words we wrote to signal they were under erasure, prefixes in brackets, rampant puns. It was easy to imitate but hard to do well. "Do not undermine the ground where you sit," Wittgenstein said, and we should have listened to him, but we were too busy building thrones out of air.

Derrida was interested in the ambiguity of fiction and autobiography. In "The Moment of My Death," Blanchot both was and was not the young man of the story, spared the firing squad in a moment of chaos and doomed or saved to live forever beyond himself. A posthumous existence, Derrida said, and the phrase sent a shiver down my spine. That very morning, the beautiful, confident Russian student in my Freud class had quoted Hegel. "The owl of Minerva spreads his wings at the coming of the dawn," she said. "That's wrong," the professor said. Dusk, the word was dusk. Because we had such contempt for history, we thought we weren't subject to its rules. We believed our day was just beginning when everything, even the calendar, pointed to its imminent end.

9.

I was teaching my first class later that day. I'd never been in front of a classroom before, and I was nervous. The university had a mandatory year-long writing class run by graduate students. There was a small army of us, a hundred strong, and we had just undergone two weeks of initiation. The program was run by a former West Point professor, and he tried to instill in us a sense of mission, as if he was preparing us to break a siege, to storm a city. We were not teaching the correct use of commas and semicolons, he barked (that was good, I'd never understood them anyway, and proceeded through instinct and flavour, sprinkling them through my writing like sprinkling salt in soup). No, we were teaching them to understand the self. He must have been the only postmodernist at West Point, since the self, in his understanding and the understanding of the textbook for the class, was variable, self-constructed and elusive, a lava lamp of shifting possibilities. Very well. Like a deconstructionist or a drill sergeant, our job was to break those students down, to question their habitual assumptions, their suburban certainties. Our textbook was called *Ways of Reading* after *Ways of Seeing*, the John Berger essay that dilated and spun out Walter Benjamin's essay to such delirious effect.

I spent time planning an outfit that would lend me authority and had come up with ankle boots, black tights, a knit turtleneck dress. There was a hole in the calf of the tights. I didn't spot it until I was halfway to class. When I arrived, the door to the room was closed. Students were sitting on the floor, leaning on the walls. "Is it locked?" I said, and as I turned the knob the door opened smoothly into a room of fixed desks (no round tables, no group work), a chalkboard, and a view of Washington Square.

"We've already found the smart-ass in the class," one student quipped. I took a deep breath, and moved to the front of the room. I saw his head drop, like a puppet whose string has been released. A few students laughed. "Figures," the boy said. He had the uneven scruff of the newly bearded, like when you leave the yogurt in the fridge too long and it sprouts a ragged tight fur. As if it wasn't already hard enough projecting authority when I was—what—five years their senior? Those ankle boots fooled no one. And a girl in the front row was wearing the same dress as me.

"Welcome," I said, "to Expository Writing 101. I'm Alice Stein. Let's go around the room and you can say your name, where you're from, what you hope to get from this class. Starting on the left, oh, and I'll pass out copies of the syllabus right now, you can let me know if you have questions."

Fifteen students, thirty eyes. Skeptical, skeptical, skeptical, curious, eager. It didn't have to be difficult. They wanted to like me; I wanted to be liked. Most of them were New Yorkers, a bunch of Stuyvesant grads. I'd gotten lucky. They were all similar to one another, which meant they were similar to me—middle-class, bookish, whitish—except for one boy. He was Chinese and looked a few years younger than the other kids. He seemed by contrast to them unformed, unbaked. He sat in the back row and, when it was his turn, he spoke so softly I had him repeat his name twice. The third time he said it much more loudly, like a bark. Bo. He was the only one to give an honest answer to my third and ill-considered question, which was that he was taking the class because it was required, and he expected nothing from it. A few students laughed at that, but most looked at me in sympathy, I mean, that wasn't part of the social contract, to say it out loud like that. In his posture, in his placement, in the lack of expression on his face—and weren't we all such smilers, so eager to please and be pleasing—he was already outside the group. I said something stupid and affirmative, like "You'll get what you put into it," and a few students, all girls, nodded emphatically, knowing that they were of the elect. They'd been hearing slogans like that all their life. Bo held my gaze, but it was hard to see his eyes, he had thick glasses, and there was a glare in the room. Then he shrugged, and I moved to the next student with a sense of relief.

At home, later that day, I was sitting in the living room thinking about Bo, with a nest of soiled tissues around me, when I heard the rapid muffled tattoo that was Brenda in her running shoes coming up the staircase. Quickly, I kicked the tissues under the couch. I was technically allowed in the living room, though not behind the screen that hid Brenda's bed and messy drawers—for a girl who was absolutely immaculate about her manicure she was a slob in her own space, her Care Bear comforter piled at the foot of the bed, her shirts stuffed into her drawers. She had the careless overflow of a girl who had grown up accustomed to housekeepers silently, invisibly, picking up behind her. I stayed out of the living room entirely when she was home—she had a habit of chatter, and walked loudly—but when she was out I liked to read on the couch, where I could look out the window at Manhattan. My own bedroom faced onto the airshaft where I could see nothing and could hear only my neighbours fighting, their shouts rising in the narrow air well.

She skidded to a stop in front of me. "Alice!" she said. "I didn't expect you to be home!"

She was dressed in a pink velour sweatsuit, to match her sneakers. Her cheeks were pink, her hair pulled back in a thick pink scrunchie. It was an odd shade, the exact colour of penicillin that came in cloudy plastic bottles when I was a child, that tasted cloyingly sweet and left a thick bitter irritation in your throat when you were forced to swallow it.

I didn't have any reason to dislike her. She was nothing but nice. It wasn't personal, rather, something like an allergy. I couldn't help but react, be inflamed by her. I think she felt the same way, only her response was to double-down on cheerfulness which felt like a form of passive-aggression.

"It's good," she said, still breathing hard from her workout. "I have to talk to you."

She looked around for a place to sit down but we had no chairs, just the single loveseat we'd dragged in from the sidewalk, so she squatted down to face me, unconsciously stretching out one leg and then another.

"Jess's roommate moved out?" she said. She was one of those girls for whom every statement was a question. "Well, actually, she moved home? Because she had a kind of breakdown, anyway, she's going to be OK now. Soooo, Jess needs a roommate."

She finished, all in one breath, and looked up at me from her perch on the floor.

"I wouldn't ask," she said. "But poor Jess. I mean, she's pretty freaked out about her roommate. She's in a bind."

She rocked back on her heels, expectant, and I tried not show her that I was suffused with relief. Rent would be tight, but I could just about manage it if I was careful about everything else.

"When?" I said, and she said, looking worried, "Well, it's almost the end of the month. But you can have next month's rent, you know, so you have a chance to look for a new roommate. This is a Great Place—you'll have no problem." She chewed her lip as she looked at me. "And you can keep the security deposit," she said, with an air of magnanimity. If I had kept my mouth shut she might have offered me more.

"I understand," I said, with an air of gravity.

"Great!" She said, bouncing up immediately. "I'm going to take a shower!" When she wasn't in the interrogative mode, she was in the exclamatory. From the living room, I could hear her singing the Mariah Carey/Whitney Houston ballad, "When You Believe." Actually, Brenda had a beautiful voice. Of all the things, I realized, I would miss her singing in the shower.

Jess moved her out that Sunday. I met her on the way out of the apartment, and she was soft-spoken and tall, with a shaven head and a stud in her nose—nothing at all like the person I had imagined. She kissed Brenda on the mouth in greeting, so it seemed I had understood nothing about my roommate and her rapid departure. I left them to the move, heading to the library for the day, and when I came home, there was a cheque on the kitchen table, and the couch was gone—we had found that couch together—but the tissues I had forgotten about, those were still curled in a soiled pile against the wall, a rebuke. She had taken the framed inspirational quotes, and the mugs with the slogans, and all the stuffed animals except one, though I couldn't tell if it had been left by mistake or on purpose—a pale blue teddy bear with a homicidal gaze. I swept the floor and then immediately delivered the teddy bear to Persephone, who agreed that it was terrifying, and said we should offer it as a sacrifice to consecrate my newly empty apartment, so we walked over to the haunted lot in the East Village, where there was a tall ziggurat of stuffed animals washed by the rain and bleached into the realm of the uncanny, and we left the bear tucked between the rungs of the fence. When we came back, Persephone did cartwheels in the empty space of my living room, and then we spied on our neighbours—the woman who liked to drape a red shawl over her lamp and belly-dance in her bra, the man on his treadmill in front of the television—and I made us spaghetti. Fiona was—I don't know where Fiona was. It was a very good day.

10.

Persephone started coming over every Sunday morning, the day I always meant to visit my grandmother. I skipped one week, and then another, and then another. My grandmother was in her hospital bed, and I imagined her suspended there, like Sleeping Beauty grown old, until my next visit. She was in the time of waiting and I was in the rhythm of everyday life. Fiona was another kind of Sleeping Beauty. She liked to sleep in, Persephone said. We would walk over to the little bakery on 9th Street and buy two pastries: a cinnamon roll for me, and a poppy seed Danish for her. Then we took the pastries back to my apartment and I made us tea. I associated poppy seed with my grandmother, with the taste of an older generation, but Persephone loved it, loved to unroll the dough, to pick at the glistening black seeds with her finger. After we finished, we would sometimes walk to the park, or take a walk down 3rd Street to the Sunday market. When we came home, around one o'clock, her mother would just be getting up.

Fiona didn't acknowledge the time we spent together, didn't ask me or thank me. I think she took it for granted that the world would gallantly rise to assist them. She was the kind of woman who never paid for her own drink. I didn't mind. Persephone was a discovery for me: her sophisticated innocence, her subtle shine.

I had a good childhood. We lived in the suburbs. My parents kept me safe. I lolled in the familiar boredom of backyards and driveways, nowhere to go except the 7/11 on a bicycle, no appointments to keep except for Sunday cartoons and after-school soap operas. For the grandchild of refugees, that boredom was a tremendous privilege. As indeed, I was frequently reminded.

My parents were active, ambitious people. My father was a doctor, and his rhythm was determined by the urgency of the hospital. At any moment, the little black beeper on his hip could call him to away from us, to an emergency. My mother had gone back to school, and was doing a PhD in psychology. She was energized by her studies, which she had abandoned when my sister and I were born and to which she returned when we started school. The dining room table was always covered in papers. For dinner, we ate pasta and ketchup. My mother talked to her advisor while boiling water, graded papers while doing laundry, practiced oral presentations while driving me to school. I was born in 1975, and my sister less than a year later—we were almost twins. We watched a lot of television and read on the couch together, our legs intertwined.

All that reading drove our mother crazy. She hated our lethargy, kept telling us that we should do something, not realizing that for my sister and me, until we became teenagers, reading was everything. If we lay on the couch, we attracted too much attention, so we would retreat into our room and, if we were lucky, she would forget about us for a few hours as we vanished into Avonlea or Oz or Wonderland. Eventually, my mother would remember our existence, and she would knock on our door, beg us to go outside. "You girls are wasting a beautiful day," she would say. She was herself so busy, so frequently working, that she'd spend entire summers pale as a ghost, without even the hint of a suntan. We'd humour her and go outside, and take turns sitting on the swing under the apple tree with our books. The apples were not good for cooking and so they fell off the tree and rotted in the grass, attracting bees and wasps. My sister was afraid of wasps and fled indoors. I would swat them away as I tried to read, and would eventually give up and retreat back indoors until my mother noticed me again.

A year before my mother was supposed to finish her dissertation, she got pregnant with twins—an accident. After that, all the energy that had gone into her studies went into being the kind of mother my sister and I had never had: dinner at the table at six o'clock, laundry not only folded but in the drawers. It is a mistake to think that siblings have the same parents, since age and birth order and time change so much. The house was less chaotic, paradoxically, after the twins were born, because my mother had resigned herself to her role as a housewife or what Louise Bourgeois called a *femme maison,* in those strange and lovely paintings of female nudes half-trapped by buildings and houses. Sometimes I missed the young woman who sent my sister and me to lunch with a granola bar and an entire tomato because she'd gotten so distracted with a paper she was writing, her hair loosely fastened with a pencil, and a smear of blue ink on her cheekbone.

Persephone didn't seem to get bored, although occasionally she expressed a kind of ennui which expressed a philosophical consciousness entirely foreign to my own sheltered and late-blooming childhood. She had friends everywhere—the drag queens who ran the sex shop down the street, the street punks who panhandled for change and skateboarded on Astor Place, the Sri Lankan family who ran the deli on the corner. She could summon a taxi with a flick of her delicate wrist, she could navigate the subway on her own, she walked the streets with a sense of ownership. She was eleven years old.

Without Brenda, the apartment expanded. Even time dilated—I had not realized that somehow just her presence ate time, my consciousness of her company on the periphery. I bought a futon on the corner and a stranger helped me carry it up the stairs for ten dollars. I covered it with a block-printed sheet and armfuls of pillows, and made a reading corner and nest. I bought baskets of ivy and hung them in the window. Otherwise, I left the space bare. Persephone came up often to work on her homework or to read, and we were like a pair of companionable spinsters with our books and cups of tea.

Fiona was partying a lot, and there were men in and out of her apartment all the time, or not even men, boys, some of whom I recognized as the punks and skateboarders of Astor Place. One day I knocked on her door on my way upstairs to see if Persephone was home, and she was playing cards on the floor with Fiona and one of those boys, blue hair and a face scattered with small wounds and piercings. "Ratfuck!" The boy cried, throwing his cards down, and Persephone laughed hysterically and repeated, "Ratfuck! Ratfuck!" Fiona looked over her bare shoulder at me, her hair spilling down her back like snakes. "Do you want to play?" she said, and I said meekly, "I was just wondering if Persephone wanted help with her homework?" Their laughter followed me up the stairs.

That week, I got a letter from my sister, my first in nearly a year. An aerogram, the paper thin and the handwriting so crabbed it was difficult to read. Sometimes the pen had pressed right through the paper. My sister lived in a women's yeshiva in a mountaintop city that was, as Thomas Mann described Venice, "part fairy-tale, part snare"—narrow snaking alleyways, stone houses, precipitous views, a clutter of mystics and artists, a labyrinth of seekers. The walls of the city were stone, and the doors were painted blue against the evil eye. The rabbi of her program had set her up, she said. An arranged marriage—a shidduch. She was getting married in six weeks. I looked at the date on the aerogram and it was two months old. She hadn't even told me his name. My sister had already passed into a looking glass world whose rules I did not understand.

11.

I was taking three classes and teaching one. Derrida's class had become even more surreal and meditative. I had long ago lost my way through what he was saying, and he was still on the fifth line on the Blanchot piece after three weeks of classes, gleefully caught on the Cartesian opening of the sentence—*je sais*. Each class, the room was more crowded. His obscurity operated as a mechanism of celebrity and, as he became increasingly opaque, more and more people came to watch. It was a form of performance art and an exercise in endurance. I liked him anyway—his walnut face, his cotton candy hair. He had a nice smile, as if to say this was all a joke he was playing on us, or on himself, or on the history of philosophy. What I couldn't understand is how everyone took it so seriously.

The writing class I taught was going well, except that I had a heretic. In one of my classes I had learned about Ludwig Wittgenstein's brother Paul, a concert pianist who lost his right arm during the First World War. In compensation, Ravel composed a Piano concerto for his left hand alone. The loss of his arm could not stop him, but his brother? Paul claimed he couldn't practice when Ludwig was in the house. "I feel your skepticism seeping from under the door," he said. In my class, Bo played that role. He was a vacuum for enthusiasm. Every suggestion I made seemed idiotic when reflected in the black mirror of his eyes. It didn't help that I was a young, unexperienced teacher, and most of my strategies had to do with the solidarity of youth. Everyone called me by my first name, except for Bo, who called me Miss. When he did so I flinched, as if the title was a way of calling me out and exposing my masquerade. I wasn't one of the kids, I was the teacher. Miss was a way of reminding me of that, a challenge rather than a corroboration of my authority.

Video cameras had just become a little cheaper and more accessible, and in uncharacteristic extravagance my mother had sent me one for my birthday. Because we were doing a unit on memory, I had taken the camera to Tompkins Square to try it out and interview strangers about their first memories. At the scruffy periphery of the city there was a confrontational friendliness that I would miss, later, when I moved away. More people than I expected were willing to talk to me—the camera was still a novelty. Soon, video cameras would be everywhere.

A middle-aged man sitting beside a stroller that held plastic bags of shoes and clothing told me that his first memory was reading Moby Dick.

"Moby Dick," I said, not certain I'd heard him correctly.

"That's right," he said. "And you know what I learned from that book?"

His glasses had a spider web crack, and his skin was dry and ashy.

"I learned about prejudice." I kept the button pressed. Kept the camera rolling. "All those men, after that whale, just because he's white!"

He leaned back, stuck his thumbs in his belt loops, and sucked his teeth.

"That's what I learned."

A man in a newsboy cap told me his first memories were of his family farm in Poland.

"It was cold," he said, in his deliberate, hard-won English. "So. I went in the barn. And put my feet in the shit! To warm them up."

His friends laughed. The last person I interviewed was a young man.

"Yeah, yeah," he said. "I have a first memory. How could I forget it? I was molested. By my babysitter."

He held a child by the hand, a boy with silky black hair, long bangs, big brown eyes.

"That's—that's terrible," I said.

"Absolutely not," the man said. "I loved it. She made me a man."

I stopped recording after that, though without even intending it, before I turned the camera off, the lens slipped to watch the little boy by his side, our accidental witness, big ears sticking out from his ill-cut hair.

On Wednesday evenings, I went drinking with a group of graduate students in a historic pub with sawdust on the floor. The pub served only two beers, light or dark. The room was yeasty and loud. We played fuck-marry-kill with professors from the department, then with dead philosophers, then with each other. I had a crush on Kierkegaard based on his cousin's romantic pencil drawing, which was on the cover of my collected writings. Those lips, that hair, those eyes! But he clearly wasn't marriage material, having notoriously broken off his engagement because of his tendency towards melancholic thoughts. Most of the men in my program were just like that, compulsive seducers who then declared themselves unworthy and unfit as a way of escaping entanglement.

There was one boy named Jacob who came to the pub every

night, and I had a crush on him. He wore well-washed flannel shirts, and faded denim, like a uniform, every day. He was from the Midwest and vacillated between irony and sincerity in a manner that was as dazzling and hypnotic as a spinning top. His hair was shoulder-length and copper, his eyes were green and gold and mud, I often squeezed in next to him at the table and stared at the hair on his broad knuckles, felt my leg against his thigh. He smelled like cigarettes and sweat and peppermint gum, and he spoke of New York with an impressive contempt. Mostly, I came to the pub for him, but my desire made me loose-limbed and thick-tongued. I couldn't think of anything to say that wouldn't sound stupid, and he was a man who was ruthless about stupidity. He talked faster and faster as the night went on, took frequent smoke breaks in the pissoir of the alley, and eventually I would give up and go home, not a good enough drinker or a good enough philosopher to make a move.

Other nights I spent with Persephone, both of us stretched out on the futon that served as sofa. She drew pictures or did her homework, I did my reading and graded papers. I boiled pasta for supper, opened jars of spaghetti sauce, bought carrots and celery stick with a sense of duty. I kept this secret from my graduate school friends, because I didn't know how to explain it to them, and it seemed strange when I took a step away from it. But as soon as I was home it was the most natural thing in the world to hear that muffled knock on my door, to make sweet mint tea in my special new teapot that was covered in rosebuds, to settle into something that was sweeter and more innocent than the morass of intellectual rivalries and lusts at graduate school. A few times I asked where Fiona was, and Persephone said she was working. At nine o'clock, Persephone would get up, stretch and yawn, and go downstairs to her empty apartment and her narrow bed underneath the window facing St. Mark's Place.

12.

No one called me to tell me my grandmother had died. So, when I made the long underworld journey to visit her that Sunday, a month since my last visit, I found the room empty and the bed made. I stood there, in the entranceway, looking at a space that showed no trace of her presence or of her passing, as if she never had been. They must have just washed the floor, the door was ajar and the linoleum glistened, the room smelled of the sweetish chemical they used to disinfect it. A nurse saw me standing there and she looked distressed.

"Oh, my dear," she said, "Are you here for Helen?"

She must have been new, or working a different shift, because I had never seen her before. She held my hands with both her own—dry warm hands fluent in healing and comfort—and said, "I'm very sorry, she passed last night. It was a painless death."

"Her things," I said, and she said, looking panicked, "But the woman who looked after her has already taken them this morning."

That was the last we saw of Andrea. By the time I got home a message was waiting on my answering machine.

"I can't come in for the funeral," my mother's voice said, "the boys...But I am glad that you will be there to represent our family."

I didn't blame her for not coming in to town. My grandmother had been cold to her when my mother first entered the family. In fact, only my grandfather had been welcoming, and she mourned him sincerely when he died young of a stroke. Since my father had died, I knew she had very little to do with his family—blaming them, perhaps, for their absence in his illness.

My father had also struggled with his family, especially with his brother. I did not know the source of their animosity. We spent little time together when I was growing up, just the stiff, occasional, unmissable family event. When my father got sick, it took my uncle two weeks to call, but that was only the last unforgivable act in a series written in acid and revealed by fire, like a poison pen letter sent by a malicious child. Which may be an apt simile, because there was something childlike in their animosity, which had also begun when they were very young, in something mysterious that one got and the other was denied, brotherhood as a zero-sum game, a nearly biblical rivalry.

By the time my uncle finally called, my father was in a coma, past response or any chance of late forgiveness.

I went to the funeral the next day, feeling shabby in an old dress, the only black thing I owned. I sat at the back and felt like a stranger. My black shoes were worn at the heel and once again, I could not find a clean pair of tights without holes. My uncle spoke at great length about a woman of warmth and strength and character whom I did not recognize. The room was full of his friends, men in business suits and slender, well-preserved women in black cocktail dresses, bodices beaded in jet, faces carefully and immaculately made up to meet his loss and their own mortality with a mask of perfect unperturbability.

In a Jewish funeral, there is no showing of the body, but I kept remembering her as she lay in the hospital bed, deflated like a balloon leaking air at the end of a party. Though she had wasted at the end, she was still a large woman, and as the men hoisted the closed casket on to their shoulders at the graveyard I saw their legs buckle, stumble, stiffen with the unexpected weight. The hole had been dug that morning, and the gravediggers waited politely on the outskirts of our little group of mourners as my uncle's rabbi said a prayer and talked about a woman I was sure he had never met. My uncle threw the first shovel of dirt on the coffin and then handed the shovel to the gravedigger the way you might hand a used napkin to a waiter in a restaurant. I did not follow them back to New Jersey for the shiva, nor was I invited. My uncle clasped my hand before I left, and I consoled him in the familiar formula, like all the rest of us mourners of Zion and Jerusalem.

That night I dreamed I was in my apartment, but it was transformed. There were doors opening up to rooms I had never seen, high-ceilinged, capacious spaces with big windows and floor-to-ceiling curtains, and they in turn led to other rooms. As I wandered through this place, both familiar and unfamiliar, I felt relief and delight, but not surprise—it was as if the miraculous expansion of my apartment had solved a problem for me, but also as if it had been that way all along. I came to a set of French doors and I pushed them open, stepping into an enclosed garden. Persephone sat there, under a brick wall covered in honeysuckle. She was wearing the same dress she had worn on the first day she came to tea, and her feet were bare, her hair loose across her shoulders. She held a bunch of grapes in her hand, and as she held it out and offered it to me she started to say something but no sound came out of her mouth. Instead, I heard my father's voice in my ear, as if it was coming from outside the dream, to shake me into wakefulness as he had done so many times in my childhood. "It's time to get up now," he said, "You've slept too late again."

PART TWO

1.

Nov 1998

That week, the week of the funeral, I cleaned out my grandmother's apartment and found her secret treasures, the coins, the photograph, and the ring. They were a little like the dream I'd had of finding an entire new wing in my apartment: they seemed to open up a door, but I did not know where it led.

I meant to tell my mother about my finds as soon as I got home but, when she answered the phone, I knew I wasn't ready. I had the hoarder's ambivalent desire to at once display them and to keep them to myself. The ring was hidden in my underwear drawer, the most obvious hiding place, as if I wanted it to be found. The coins were in a pair of socks beside it. My mother sounded distracted, and I could hear the twins fighting in the background.

"Alice," she said. "How did it go at the apartment? Thanks for doing that."

"Fine," I said. "I mean, there was a lot of junk, but I made some progress. Hey, did Helen spend some time in an institution?"

"What?" she said. She was moving around, and I could imagine her on the other end, holding the receiver between ear and neck as she chopped onions for dinner, as one hand swept them into the frying pan, as the other picked up a fallen toy or interrupted a fight.

"An institution," I said. "I found a piece of paper. A discharge notice."

"What kind of an institution," she said. "You mean a university?"

"A hospital," I said. I hesitated. "A psychiatric hospital. Did Dad ever say anything to you?"

"Sorry," she said. "Jonathan was crying, I couldn't hear you for a second. You said a hospital?"

"A psychiatric hospital," I said.

A pause at the other end of the line, and I thought I'd lost her.

"Hello?" I said.

"I'm thinking," she said. "No, he never said anything. Why would she be in a psychiatric hospital?"

"That was my question," I said. "Do you don't know anything about it?"

"Ask your uncle," she said. "He might know something. Anyway, I'm not sure you should be looking through her stuff."

"Didn't you ask me to look through her stuff this weekend? And I have a paper to write," I said.

"You know that's not what I meant. Look, I've got to finish getting dinner ready. Thanks again, for doing that, and good luck with your paper."

Click, and the full chord of no one on the other end of the line. I stood there, holding onto the phone, then placed it gently back onto the cradle. No way I was calling my uncle. I thought of him, fat with grief, receiving his guests like the king of all mourners.

I had left *Every Woman's Medical Guide* on the kitchen table and, when I picked it up, the book fell open to a page in the middle, an accustomed crease as if it had been opened to that page many times before. My eyes were drawn to an illustration of a baby at the bottom corner. The baby was adorable, his head turned in profile, tiny nose, tufts of fair hair. One hand flung up, the other down, like the gesture Christ makes to indicate "I speak" in paintings from the Middle Ages. One sock was on and the other off, and he was wearing a cloth diaper, draped like a toga around his broad soft middle. Indeed, the effect of the gesture and the drapery was to make the infant seem imperious, imperial, the young emperor in his tiny cage, since the thickly drawn bars of the cradle behind him made him seem imprisoned. But there was no perspective in the image, so perhaps he was sitting outside the cage and the mother, invisible, was imprisoned behind it.

Why imprisoned? The caption was what led me to that conclusion, the caption and the jollity of his expression. Above the drawing was a hopeful banner heralding the annunciation—"When Baby Comes." Underneath, a smaller, sober addendum warned, "Arrival of the new baby may be a signal for the beginning of nervous tension in the sensitive anxious woman." The sentence was underlined in pencil. He did not look like a prisoner, but like an imprisoner. Perhaps with his magniloquent gestures he was pardoning her, the mother, though he was also her sentence.

Long ago, people told their fortunes by opening a book and reading the first sentence they saw. This felt like a sign. Or a clue.

2.

Since the funeral, I had been sleeping a lot. At the time, I thought my fatigue was caused by November, and the fading light, and procrastination, maybe, but now I think it was grief. I went to bed at eight that Sunday night, like a child, and when I woke up in the morning, my students' papers were waiting for me in dumb rebuke. I should have handed them back a week earlier. Instead, they were still weighing me down.

"Miss," Bo had asked in the last class, the title once again a deliberate reminder of my precarious status and the fact that his parents were not paying twenty thousand dollars a year for their children to study with graduate students. "Miss, when did you say you'll have the papers back?" I hadn't said, but I promised to have them Monday. It was Monday, and the class was in five hours.

I made myself a cup of coffee and sat in the windowsill, the papers balanced on my knees, the city stretched out before me replete with enticing distraction. The exercise was a simple one: the students were to write about a memory that held a charge for them, that seemed loaded or significant. Later on, they were going to revisit that memory and learn to poke holes in it, to question its assumptions and undermine its foundations, so that they could see that the edifice of the self they had built was full of holes and evanescent as smoke. We weren't training writers, we were breeding fucking postmodernists.

Of course, it was fascinating for the students. It appealed to their fundamental narcissism and their late-adolescent distrust. It felt like an initiation, it blew their minds.

I wasn't much older than they were, and I was also a believer. Nothing felt truer than the impossibility of truth. I don't regret it, though I do feel some sense of responsibility for having been, as Socrates was once accused, a corrupter of the youth (though I had been corrupted in my turn, and so freshly I could not yet smell the rot). No one ever said to us that it might not be a good idea to take impressionable young minds at an age particularly susceptible to crack, and convince them that their shell was already fissured beyond repair. Oh well. It was a useful time, actually, to come of age intellectually, intoxicating, even. It seems now like a folly of my youth, but like so many other things about my youth, still more formative than anything I ever learned later on.

The papers were banal. These were middle to upper-middle class suburban kids, and they were so mild and so polished in their traumas—the memories they chose to record were all traumas, since pain is sticky and joy is not. This dead grandmother, this broken friendship, this first heartbreak. A boy who sat at the front of the class with an eager, puppyish look on his face kept slipping into the present tense as he wrote about his ex-girlfriend—I happily circled every slip and wrote in red: "Symptomatic! This isn't over for you yet." Another boy wrote of the theft of his car—a red Corvette he "loved," purchased by his parents on his sixteenth birthday. "It must be what rape feels like," he recorded. I left a long and irritated comment in the margin.

Except for these exceptional extreme and sometimes humorous errors in grammar and taste—taste itself was a kind of grammar, a way of organizing the world—most of the papers felt like something I had read before. These were students who were coached in their college admission essays, who were Oprah-fluent, who had learned to hold up that ruby jewel of their pain and make it catch the light in order to gain an audience, and yet knew very little of suffering. As was true for me, dead father and dead grandmother withstanding. Never such privilege before, never before or since, in our little pocket of the West. The world and our parents had surrounded us with airbags and safety belts. Pretty soon it would all change again, the bottom would drop out of our city and our idea of safety, and Francis Fukuyama would have to eat his words about the end of history. But not yet. No wonder we had only words to play with.

I picked Bo's essay up with a sense of dread. I had started to think of him as my Bartleby, because he refused to participate in class. Everyone else was so shiny, so eager to please, and it had been easy to get them on my side. When I asked him to read out loud or to respond to a question, he would defer, politely, and look down at the ground. He stonewalled me, and I wasn't sure how to respond to that, so I started to skip over him when it was his turn in class, to try and turn his resistance into invisibility.

I wasn't expecting much from his essay but when I started to read it the voice was raw and angry and intimate, as if he was whispering in my ear.

"I am fourteen years old and I am in love," the essay began. "We have just moved to New York from Hong Kong. The streets are full of litter and the air smells like urine. In the subway, men wear no shirts and sweat on me. Our apartment is a hot concrete box, and I sleep in the living room on a fold-out sofa. My parents pass through when they come home late from work, and when they go to the toilet early in the mornings.

Back home, my mother was a teacher and my father was a businessman. We had a maid and two bedrooms and a view of the mountains. My mother was happy. She had a good job, and a nice apartment, and a little balcony garden. But my father was obsessed with emigration. You just wait, he would say. In one year, there will be war. He spent all his spare time applying to embassies in Australia, in Canada, in the UK, in the United States.

The people who stay will lose everything, he said. But it is we who have lost everything.

New York is disgusting. The noise on the streets, the filth on the sidewalks, the stench of the sewers. People say this is the greatest city in the world, and I say they have lost their minds.

My parents are afraid of everything. They double lock the door and bolt the windows when they leave the house. They tell me not to leave the house without them, but the air conditioning is broken—it drips, whines, stinks of mold—and the television has no reception. As soon as I know they are gone, I leave the house and lock the door behind me.

I see her that first day on the elevator. She is there when the doors slide open. I stand behind her and I breathe in the smell of her hair. Her hair is a golden cloud and she smells like bubblegum. She is wearing a pink tank-top, and I look at her naked shoulder blades, and at her narrow hips in cut-off jeans. She is standing on one leg, and there is a hole in the bottom of her white sneakers. She looks like an elegant stork. She is my age or younger, I think, and she does not turn around to look at me, but the boy standing beside her does, just before the doors open, and then he steps back on my foot on purpose as he goes out into the hallway, reaching towards her hand. I am gratified to see her impatiently shake him off, like an irritating mosquito. She runs to meet her group of friends eating freezies on the bleachers facing the basketball court. They say hello with their dyed lizard tongues, acid green and electric blue and stop sign red, and she turns around and sticks her tongue back out at them so I see her face. She is very beautiful—brown with long legs, and a mouth I would like to kiss.

Her name is Shauna—I hear the girls shout it. They always want her attention. They turn the name into three syllables—sha-wa-na—dragging out the middle, a wail or a whine. She is at the centre of their social group, you can tell, the girls circle her, the boys circle the group of them, and even further out, like an exiled star, so faintly visible it might not even exist, I sit under a tree that is barely worth the name, under a pathetic umbrella of shade. I pretend to read my book and watch them, and they pretend to ignore me. I try to do her the courtesy of not staring, but I can't help looking up her, and a couple of times I find her looking back at me, curious. As soon as our eyes meet she breaks the look and jumps up to do handstands or cartwheels or to steal the basketball and throw it through the net with breathtaking grace. Everything she does is simple and beautiful, and I am like fungus at the bottom of the tree, so pale and useless and spongy and stuck that I could never even hope to speak to her."

The essay ended there and I was disappointed. I wanted to know more about Shauna, about Bo, about what happened that summer. His writing had an energy that all the other students lacked, despite an occasional lack of polish. In his own way, he was astonishingly fluent, past fluent, he often used words that the careless first-language speakers didn't know, which made him seem pedantic and older than his age, perhaps one reason he was often silent. "Great," I wrote at the bottom of the paper, and then I circled the word twice. "What happens next?" I wrote. "I think you should continue with this. I love the vivid language. You make me feel like I was there." I thought another minute, sucking on the end of my pen, and then wrote, "Tell me more about why you feel so sad."

In class I kept looking over at Bo, as if to dowse for the signs of depth that his story had shown, but he did not look up, and seemed as sleepy and disaffected as he had every other class. I returned the papers, and he didn't look at his, only swept it into a knapsack stuffed with a rat's nest of papers. As he left the room I reached out to get his attention, and he flinched away from me, shuffling to a stop. "I liked your story," I said. "Why don't you come to office hours to talk about it? I think you should work on it for your final project."

"If you say so," he mumbled, but his face had no expression.

"My office hours are from one to three," I said brightly. "I'll expect you!" He looked down, which I took as a sign of indifference, so I was surprised when he was waiting at the door of my shared office as I arrived the next day, sitting on the floor as if he had been waiting for a long time. He was very slow getting to his feet, as if he were an old man and not a very young one.

What spare and enervating spaces we worked in those days! The insect buzz of the fluorescent light; the beige enclosure of the narrow cubicles; it was as if it had been designed to produce anomie and despair. My cubicle-mate had left a coffee cup on the laminate desk, still holding an inch of sludge. Someone had tacked a Klimt postcard to the partition wall a long time ago, and it was a sordid window into a vivid, dark-eyed world of lust. I saw Bo notice the postcard, hesitate, sit down, and hunch into his everyday posture, elbows on his knees. He was an uncomfortable man—or boy. He must have skipped a grade if he was fourteen in 1996. Was he even seventeen?

"I really liked your story," I said. "I thought it had a lot of energy. Why did you choose that memory to write about?"

He looked up at me then, and I realized I had never seen him without his glasses. His face looked undressed, and he had dark circles under his eyes.

"You told us to write about a memory."

"Yes," I said, "but why that one?"

He shuffled his feet on the floor.

"Because you told us to write about a memory."

I could feel the flush of excitement that I had when I read his story beginning to fade. I couldn't connect the dots between the Dostoevsky voice full of rage and passion, and the pallid, pudgy apathy in front of me. I wanted to reach over and shake him awake.

"Tell me," I said, "What do you think about university so far?"

He shrugged.

"OK, I guess."

"And how is this class going?" I asked. That made him look up, two sharp lines like darts between his eyebrows.

"To be honest?" he said. He didn't seem to have much of an accent, except that he was very soft spoken, far more so than his brash New Yorker classmates, who took noisiness as their birthright. "To be honest, it's a waste of time."

I took a breath. "What do you mean?"

"This kind of writing," he said. "It isn't what we're asked to do in other classes. It's a distraction. It's frivolous."

I flushed. Though he couldn't have known it, this was exactly the objection various department heads had voiced to the director of the writing program. They wanted his instructors to teach thesis statements, three-paragraph structures, transition sentences, summarizing conclusions. They were baffled and upset at students who spent a year working on writing with us, and then wanted to add autobiographical preludes and poetic reveries to their papers on Stalin and Darwin and the fall of the Soviet Union.

I decided to dodge it. "All writing helps you become a better writer," I said, evasively. "Anyway, I don't think your story is frivolous. I think it's important. I think you should write more."

He turned his hands up on his knees and opened them as if

he was surrendering. His fingers were smeared with ink. Then he reached into his bag and pulled out some more pages. They were crumpled, and stained with something that might have been tomato sauce. He tried to smooth them out with his hand, then gave up.

"I did," he said, and handed me the pages. "Is that all?"

"Yes," I said, and I left the pages on the corner of my desk like a wrinkled trash bouquet. "I'll see you in class." When he closed the door, I reached out and smoothed the pages with the blade of my hand. They were written, not typed, in cramped dark blue letters that crawled across the surface of the page.

Because this was my first year as a teacher, I hadn't yet learned that there were students like this, who would hurt my heart and take up more of my thoughts than all the shiny acquiescent well-behaved undergraduates who were born to be here. Bo was right. These classes didn't make sense in the structure of the university, or in the expectations of the world outside the university. Our director was a true believer and he saw what we were doing as a mission. We were double agents, working from inside the system to subvert the system, to train students to think and not to mimic, all for the purpose of true education. I was less certain, and was afraid that we were just teaching students our own values, our own formulas—questioning, discovery, revelation, which when laid out so clearly in that order can never truly be any of those things. Still, I was seduced by the power of the personal story, swore fealty to ambiguity, ambivalence, struggle, rather than boxes of received wisdom. And despite his objections, that must have seduced him too, because there he was, writing, despite his skepticism, so feverishly that the ink stained his fingers. I didn't have time to read it now, the next student was coming (this one entirely predictable: another dead grandmother, not mine, and an unveiled query about what it would take to get an A in the class).

I put the paper into my bag and I readied my smile as the door swung open.

3.

I didn't have much time for mourning. I was too busy. But mourning showed up anyway, a persistent and pestilent uninvited guest. I had trouble sleeping and developed a persistent cough and a crick in my neck so I could not turn my head from side to side. The first-year anniversary of my father's death had just passed and, in a graveyard already covered in snow, my mother inaugurated his memorial stone. She called me afterwards, her voice thick with grief. "Oy," she said, "how much loss can a person stand?" She sent me a photo of the grave, but it was taken from a distance and out of focus, so I could not tell which one was his, could not find his name in the field of stones.

I tried to focus on my classes. My favourite was with our Freud professor, though he was notoriously erratic, which he had somehow managed to parlay into a reputation for brilliance. We never knew if he would show up or not. There were twelve of us in the class, and we sat around the seminar table nervously, waiting to see if he would come and in what temper. My friend Daniel always saved me a seat beside him, which was good since, when the professor did show up on time, he had no patience for late students. I always slipped into class right when it was beginning and was grateful not to flounder looking for a seat.

Erratic: it's a noun, Daniel told me, the name of a rock that is different from those surrounding it because it has been displaced by glacial melt. The professor was like that, entering into the room with an impression of violence. He was such a different creature from the rest of us, it was as if he belonged to some distant geological stratum, despite his insistence on sitting in the middle and not the head of the table as if he was just one person in an equal conversation.

This time, the professor showed up twelve minutes after class had started—we were watching the clock, waiting for fifteen, when we would leave. He glared at the lights and turned them off, then slung his leather jacket across the back of his chair. I had once made the mistake of sitting across from him, and I was pinioned by his eyes the entire class, like a butterfly. Another time, I sat beside him and was so jangled by his anxiety I couldn't understand a word he said. Now I sat in the corner of the room, close enough to hear and far enough to hide.

The professor told us that Freud came up with the idea of the therapist's couch as a way to avoid the patients across his desk staring at him for the entire session. I could tell that he wished we could all lie down for the class, so he would not have to look at us, or worse, be seen. Or even better, that he could lie down and screen us all out. Teaching was clearly a torture for him. Still, he spat out moments of brilliance—like oil on a too-hot skillet, he could mark you even as you flinched away.

"Freud said America was a gigantic mistake," he said, by way of a beginning. "When he went on a lecture tour in 1908—the one and only time he ever went to America—he said he was going to give some lectures and look for a wild porcupine. Actually, in the opposite order. He was going to look for a wild porcupine and then give some talks."

He cleared his throat and pulled a pile of papers out of his leather briefcase, placing them, messy and bristling, on the table in front of him. He always came with a pile of notes and never seemed to refer them, instead following a stream of consciousness that mimicked the authors we studied. The one time I sat beside him, I tried to read the notes over his shoulder, thinking they might make more sense than his charismatic and uneven ranting. There is a moment in *The Shining* when we finally get to read over Jack Nicholson's shoulder. This wasn't quite that level of recursive uncanny, but still, I could make no sense of it—long looping script in heavy blue ink, with arrows and notes scribbled in every bit of available white space, and only occasionally a word legible, usually in caps and underlined three or four times—YES or, much more often, NO. I didn't know if the notes had some kind of Talmudic relationship to what was said in class, if they were further exposition or commentary, or if they were the very skeleton.

"Why a porcupine?" he continued. "We have no record of Freud being particularly interested in wildlife or indeed, in nature, except, like Nabokov, his love of mycology. There are old mycologists and bold mycologists, you know. But no old, bold mycologists."

He narrowed his lips and looked at us and we all laughed politely.

"Have you heard of Schopenhauer's porcupine? Anyone?" All of us glued our eyes to the table. The bolder students shook their heads.

"Right. What is it you learn in university anyway?"

A girl at the far end of the table, with thickly-framed glasses and straw-straight hair, guffawed, then silenced herself. He glared at her. He wore glasses most of the time, the lenses so thick it was as if his eyes were swimming, each visible through a circular porthole. When he took the glasses off, as he did now, his eyes were a pale, startling blue. He was nearly blind without them, he'd confessed to us, so my theory was that he took off his glasses when he wanted to shut us out.

"It's a parable. A group of porcupines huddle together for warmth in winter. The collective noun for porcupine is a prickle—a prickle of porcupines. So, you can see what's coming next. As they draw close to one another, they prick each other with their spikes, and they are forced to retreat. That happens again and again. It grows cold, and they draw together, they wound each other and draw back. So it is for all of us."

Now he put his glasses back on, and looked down at his notes. As far as I knew, he did not have a partner, a girlfriend or wife. Imagine living with that bristling angry intelligence, that collection of leather jackets and skinny jeans. Imagine a lover who turned off the light every time he walked into a room.

He said, "Schopenhauer writes, "By this arrangement the mutual need of warmth is only very moderately satisfied; but then people do not get pricked." "People do not get pricked," he repeated. "Though in the next sentence he says it's ideal, actually, to hold onto your own warmth and stay outside, outside society he means, neither pricking nor getting pricked. They climb trees, you know. Porcupines, not philosophers. We think of them as land animals, but they are arboreal. Arboreal rodents. Rats with spikes."

Daniel drew a rat in the margins of his paper beside me. The rat had a kind of Mohawk and the round glasses, the pointed face of our professor. He showed it to me then rested his hand on the page to hide it.

"Freud talks about that story ten years later, in a footnote about the hostility and aversion that complicates any relationship. Come here, go away. But that's not what he claimed to mean when he said he was hunting porcupines in America. He said, instead, that it's good to have a secondary goal whenever you go do something big, whenever you anticipate something that provokes anxiety. To distract you and to focus your attention. A lot was at stake for Freud in bringing psychoanalysis to the New World. But he already had intimations of failure. It may be that he found Americans, like psychotics, untreatable."

He ran his pale tongue over his lips.

"Ironically, today New York has got to be the last bastion of real psychoanalysis. My analyst, for instance. We caught the plague after all, it just took a little longer than Freud thought. Though he did get to see a porcupine. In the Adirondacks, at a place called Putnam Camp, owned by a Boston psychologist who saw him give one of his lectures at Clark. Some girls said they knew the location of a porcupine's den. It was a long hot hike, much more than he had bargained for. He was fifty-three years old. The porcupine, when they found it, was a collapsed heap of spikes, buzzing with flies. It's dead, Freud said. On the way back to New York, Putnam gave Freud a bronze model of a porcupine. It still sits on his desk in London. I've seen it."

The professor went on to talk about intimacy and ambivalence for the rest of the class. It didn't have much to do with the Freud text we were reading—which was *Dora*—except in the way that everything has to do with everything else. He gave a good class that day, and I could feel the anxiety in the room relax into attention. The professor seemed almost benevolent, though as always, near the end of the class he got edgy, shifting in his seat with the nervousness of a smoker five minutes past his window. "Go ahead, find your porcupine," he said as he rose to dismiss us.

Daniel turned towards me with an air of expectation. All term he had been edging towards me, tentatively, as if I had spikes, and sometimes cautiously edging away. He had a high broad forehead, pale hair already beginning to recede, and small teeth evenly spaced with little gaps, like the teeth of a child. This time, I went home with him.

4.

Of course, Daniel was a mistake, and I was the wrong porcupine. He was at once clumsy and too polite, and kept apologizing each time his elbow hit my rib, his nose mashed against my cheek. Afterwards, he showed excessive gratitude, and I was afraid if I stayed, I would wake up to find myself his girlfriend. I went home on the subway, although it was late, certain he was not going to continue to save me that seat.

I slept in, and woke up to Persephone knocking on my door, composed and looking older than her age, wanting to know if I would take her to the Met. She had tied her hair up in one of Fiona's scarves and was wearing eyeliner and lipstick. She looked ready for Halloween, or like one of those girls who walks in pageants and already knows how to turn herself into the most precious doll.

"We are supposed to write about a painting," she told me. "Fiona has a headache."

I bit back the something else Fiona had and instead asked if she was OK. I hadn't seen her since the card game I'd walked in on, and something had unsettled me about the scene, not just that the adults were high but that Persephone herself had seemed like someone else. "Who was that kid?" I asked.

"What?" she said, and then she blushed. "Oh, Brad," she said, like a teenager. "He's a nice boy."

He was not.

"I need to do some work," I said, and then relented. There was no need to punish her, anyway, for what? For laughing at a boy's dumb joke. For her mother's bad judgment. Someone needed to be the grown up in her life.

"I haven't been the Met all year," I said, and she said, "I never have been," solemnly, which surprised me. Persephone loved art. On the street, we had found a collection of art history textbooks—some student throwing them out at the end of her studies, no doubt—and they had pride of place at Persephone's bedside. She liked to thumb through their slippery pages. She especially loved the French impressionists, and the book fell open on the images of Monet's garden, she had looked at them so often.

"I imagine I'm there," she once told me. "Standing on the bridge."

"Imaginary gardens with real toads in them," I quoted at her, and she looked startled. "I'm not calling you a toad!" I said.

I told her about the oval rooms at the Orangerie in Paris with the curved paintings that paradoxically blurred into focus as your eyes softened. I had spent an afternoon there the previous summer and learned the water lilies were a gift to France after the First World War. As Monet painted, he could hear the canons at the front. So those hazy gargantuan flowers were war paintings, or their opposite. A refuge from the war. A place for the nation to retreat. Persephone listened politely, and I remembered something that might better hold her attention. Before it housed the paintings, the Orangerie was used for dog shows, I said, and her face lit up. We had spent the Saturday prior at Tompkins Square, watching a line of dachshunds as they sashayed in their sleek absurdity.

On Sunday morning, the entire city felt hung over. Our only

companion on the sidewalk was a thin, darkly tanned woman in a long, ripped tunic and pyjama pants. I had seen her before, and steered Persephone to the other side of the street. "I was raped by Bill Clinton," she called out hoarsely as we passed. "Tell the world. I was raped by Bill Clinton!" We were still in the middle of the Lewinsky trial, that tawdry blue dress of a scandal. Persephone twisted around to look at the woman and I pulled her forward. "That's right," the woman said, encouraged. "That's right, honey! Watch out or it could happen to you!" Why anyone would raise a child in this city. The subway stairs were sticky and the air below was foul and close.

But then—emerging into the wide boulevards, the capacious expanse of Central Park, the broad ziggurat of the concrete staircase and the tall Corinthian pillars at the top which seem to say, ascend to this temple—I remembered how much I loved about New York. Persephone was entirely awestruck. Everything delighted her. She was not—as I was so often—crushed with possibilities, she was ready to take everything in as a discovery, even the brightly coloured lapel admission pin that she clipped to the Peter Pan collar of her dress. Through her eyes, the places I had often visited became new again. She adored the Temple of Dendur, where she discovered the granite crocodiles, and added coins to the loot on the bottom of the reflecting pool, the knights posed in full armour on their high pedestals. I took her up to see the Impressionists, and she kept saying, "I know this one," when she saw the paintings, as if she was recognizing a friend.

The gallery with the Monet was too crowded, the heads of visitors clustered more tightly than those water lilies, but on our way out she stopped at a painting that everyone else walked past on their way to the celebrities of the collection—the Renoirs, Monets, van Goghs. It was a large painting, framed in gold, on a wall to itself although a little stranded between two open doorways.

The painting depicted a nude woman, reclining like an odalisque, a white sheet draped over her thighs which called attention to her nakedness rather than concealing it. It was the kind of painting I would never look at, assuming that I already knew what it was about—the shiny dishonest lasciviousness of the academic nude. The frothy peach milkshake of a body on offer for display and consumption. But now that I looked, it struck me that this painting was slippery and strange. The woman was flung back on the bed, her pose sloppy, and there was a pile of clothes on the floor, as if she had disrobed in a hurry. In contrast to her general languid collapse, one arm was held up, and a brightly coloured parrot was feasting on her outstretched fingers. Even stranger, her auburn hair uncoiled and spilled over the bottom corner of the painting, lively as a basket of eels, certainly more vivid than the bare, inert, almost boneless body. Her mouth was open in a half-smile—gleaming teeth, and a strip of suggestive darkness opening into the cavern of her mouth. I thought of the pictures of Lewinsky in the newspaper and a country's fixation on her thick lips, her big teeth. The model in the painting looked oddly familiar.

"It's by Courbet," I said in surprise. I was only familiar with his most notorious painting, "The Origin of the World," the crotch shot, belly to thigh, once owned by Jacques Lacan, who covered it in a specially made mechanical screen then pressed the button to open it up for guests like the pimp at a peep show. I leaned forward to read the rest of the wall plaque. "Oh, that's Joanna Hiffernan. She posed for so many artists. Look, it says here that they called her the beautiful Irishwoman."

Persephone said, "It's Fiona."

As soon as she said it, I recognized the resemblance. The wild, serpentine hair that she coiled and uncoiled in her hands when she was talking, or waiting, or thinking. The smooth pale skin, the seductive self-absorption, the eyes that drew you in by looking away. Fiona had this way of being fully, entirely engrossed whenever she saw an animal—if a dog was being walked down the street she would drop to her knees, she would pet it and stroke it in an ecstasy of enthusiasm. I had watched men watching her, wanting to be. That dog.

"You're right," I said. "It's Fiona."

She dropped the thread of her attention, and turned away. "I'm hungry now," she said. "Can we get ice cream?" She seemed angry, almost, to have found her mother's mirror in the museum. It was as if her mother followed her everywhere, even as she neglected her. Or maybe that was going too far. I tended to forget that she was a child sometimes. She was so patient, so adult in her habits of speech and of mind. Every child gets tired of the museum eventually. I bought her a drumstick cone in the kiosk at the bottom of the steps.

All this time with Persephone made me think about what it would be like to have my own daughter. The truth was, my body and my mind had an irreconcilable conflict. In many places, I would certainly have been expected to be pregnant or have a child by the age of 23. My mother had me when she was my age. But if I got pregnant, as a liberated woman, as a graduate student in New York at the end of the twentieth century, everyone would treat it as a tragedy. My baby-longing was a little like the flush of lust that came over me near the end of my cycle, when each man on the subway was like the world's most delicious little cake, and when I could almost see the electricity buzzing from my fingertips and thighs. A temporary madness, except it wasn't men, but babies, and it began the week of my birthday. Nothing in me wanted a child except for every non-thinking cell in my body.

Each month, an egg rolled into place like the world's highest stakes pinball game and then expelled itself in slow, bloody disappointment.

5.

When we came back from the museum, I remembered that Bo had given me his paper, and I retrieved it from the bottom of my bag and sat in the window to read it. Across the street, my neighbour had once again draped a red scarf on her lamp and was bellydancing, semaphoring seduction with her arms. There could have been an audience, hidden in the shadows of the room, or she could have been dancing for no one. Or she could have been dancing for me.

I had recently read a newspaper article about a photographer who took pictures with a telephoto lens from the window of his Tribeca apartment. The photos were like Dutch paintings of interiors. They had a voyeuristic intimacy, framed by shades and curtains, so that you, like the photographer, were looking in on daily ordinary moments in life frozen into eternity. A woman sitting on her bed, her hair turban-wrapped in a towel; a man sleeping on a couch, his T-shirt exposing a pale, bare slice of back; a woman cleaning, her skirt like classical drapery; a child's long and naked legs. In most of the photographs, the subjects faced away from the camera, or were shown in part, hidden by the opacity of the wall or the interruption of a curtain.

The neighbours decided to sue, framing the photographer not only as someone who had invaded their privacy but as a pervert, lurking in the shadows and peeping through windows with his long, expandable lens. They had paid millions of dollars for their apartments; they mentioned the value to the media, as if that price included the power of invisibility, as if buying an apartment in one of the most densely populated areas of one of the most densely populated cities in the world had not already removed that possibility. My sympathies were with the photographer; I also liked to watch through windows, though I kept my own lights low. His pictures reminded me of the Wallace Stevens poem, that the modern poem must be a finding of a satisfaction—a man skating, Stevens wrote, a woman dancing, a woman combing—and then something in the line is missing, the object of her careful attention (combing her hair, presumably?) so that what is left in shadow makes what is illuminated by language even more luminous, and more mysterious. The photographer had a similar eye for the drama of chiaroscuro, leaving his subjects half in in the dark, like a little girl holding a pair of scissors (to cut bangs? cut paper? cut skin?) lit up in a moment that felt risky. The photographer said he had inherited the lens from a birdwatcher, and that was indeed how he saw himself, capturing fauna in its native habitat, disturbing no one and nothing. I liked his insistence on his remove, *noli me tangere*—he touched nothing, disturbed nothing, just caught the momentary shift in the light caused by a body and reflected in the mirror of the camera.

Though of course, when you look in windows, you yourself sometimes get caught. It was hardly as innocent as he claimed. I kept watching through my own window as the woman across the street stretched—was she topless in the rosy light?—her hands in fifth position, or what my ballet teacher called *bras en couronne*, her arms a crown. Then she leaned forward and pulled her drapes closed. Before my view was blocked, I thought I saw a crossed pair of legs in the corner of the room and I was glad for her, that she was not alone. I had been leaning forward; I sat back now, and turned my attention to the window of the page, and to my student, the young voyeur.

"My parents leave at five a.m. each weekday morning and Saturdays," the essay continued. "They walk through the living room with their shoes off, so they will not disturb me, but from the time they wake up I hear everything—the flushing of the toilet and the endless drizzle of our water tank refilling, the buzz of the electric toothbrush, the soft click of the door. I try to sleep more after they leave, and sometimes I am successful, though in the early morning I always have bad dreams so that sleeping feels almost more tiring than just getting up. I leave the apartment at nine o'clock, I have timed it so closely that I often meet her in the elevator. She nods now when she sees me, a gentle greeting, and never giggles as her friends sometimes do if they spot me in the elevator. She has a rotation of tank tops in bright, kool-aid colours—lime-green, fuschia, electric blue, grape—colours I do not like at all but that look good on her anyway. She wears little hanging charms of butterflies and hearts, and she puts them on the same slim gold chain. She bites her nails—I hear her complain about it to her friends, and complimenting their own long shiny claws—but she paints them anyway, to try to stop biting them, in the same fluorescent colours she likes to wear. One day she smells different, like peaches and vanilla, and her friend wrinkles her nose and says, "You been in your grandma's Gucci Rush again? She better not catch you!" I like it better when she smells like herself.

Once outside, I sit under a tree at a safe distance. I hide behind my book and notebook. I watch her. Some days, she and her friends go to a movie or go shopping, and then I let myself back into the apartment and sleep, waking up only when I hear the door open and hear my mother start to prepare supper. But most days they just hang out, playing basketball, buying ice cream from the truck whose irritating jingle is on a constant loop in my brain. They gossip in the shade and tan in the sun. They flirt with the stupid boys who play basketball and show off their muscles like jerks. Some of them have younger sisters and brothers whom they have to look after in the day when their parents go to work. They complain, but they also make pets of them, braiding their hair, showing them off, taking turns pushing the stroller or swing. And some of them have older sisters who already are mothers, and often walk by the playground, pushing their own babies, chewing gum and smoking cigarettes. I am glad I am an only child.

Sometimes I write poems for her. I tell myself I am practicing English. This way, when my parents ask me what I did all day, I will not have to lie. Shauna—fauna—Madonna, which I know only as the name of a singer and not as the name of a saint, since I grew up without any religion. I am glad those poems do not survive, though I am still ashamed when I think about how I lost them.

Stupid. One day I leave the notebook under a tree when I go to the bathroom, and when I come back, it is gone. Or not gone—in the very worst place. One of the girls in the group—the loudest and meanest—is standing on a picnic table and reading out loud from my poor notebook. Shauna sits on the bleachers, twisting her hands. She is pink, but she is laughing. She looks at me then looks away. I retreat with as much dignity as I can muster, though I feel every eye in that field turn my way. I feel like a shambling monster exiled from the company of mankind, much like the monster in the book I have been reading. I feel a burning hate for Shauna.

Later I find the notebook, trampled and abandoned in the mud. I take it home and flush the pages, one by one, down our pathetic toilet, which clogs, predictably, so I have to reach in and pull out the soggy paper. My face is stained with snot and tears, my hands are stained with toilet water and ink, I cry in hideous hiccupping gulps as if my voice has been stolen and replaced with the moans of a wounded dog. Once I am done, when I stand up and look in the bathroom mirror, I do not recognize myself.

My parents come home that night with takeout dinner—a rare treat—and news. Since we moved in they have been looking and saving for a nicer apartment, in a better district. They have finally found one, and we will move in two weeks. It is closer to Stuyvesant, where I will start in the fall. Their news is a miracle. I am hollow from a day of weeping, so I feel the relief from a distance. My mother notices my red eyes and pale cheeks, and puts me to bed as if I am still a small baby.

I leave the apartment only one last time. Shauna and her family are going away for the last few days of summer—I know this from my week of eavesdropping, my hearing supercharged with love. I know from my own apartment that the locks on these apartments are cheap and easy to jimmy open. Yesterday I collected dog shit from the park and today I smear the floors and walls. I open the light. I plug the toilet with my mother's sanitary napkins and smear the counters in jam. I am careful in the wreck I cause—I wear gloves, move quietly, and soil everything I see. I leave the door closed and locked, leave the house to marinate in the filth she deserves. By the time they come home, we will be gone. No one knows us in the building, not really. Anyway, this is the kind of place where many crimes, more serious than this, are left to fester. Though even so, for a few months my heart jumps every time I hear a knock at the door.

The next year, I do well in school. I keep to myself, even though at Stuyvesant there are kids who try to befriend me. I graduate a year early. I never see Shauna again.

Of course, that is not her name."

The essay ended there, though I found myself gripping the paper, unwilling to let go. I looked out the window as if the street could give me the answer. My heart was jumping in my chest and my breathing was shallow. I had no idea what to do.

He couldn't give the class his essay, that was clear. It said too much. Though we encouraged the students to go deep, to ask questions, to tell the truth, this was more than they needed to hear. I wondered if I should contact the school psychologist, if I had a responsibility to get him help, or if my responsibility was to protect the other students. On the one hand, this had happened two years ago. Much had changed. On the other hand, he showed no remorse. If anything, he seemed proud at the end of the essay, proud and defensive at once, like the gesture he used when he pushed it towards me, as if he was not giving it to me but snatching it away.

I remembered the first cold day of school, frost on the ground, when I came to class rubbing my chapped ruby hands. He was waiting outside the door—he was always early, only his silence was recalcitrant, in every explicit rule he behaved immaculately. It was the first time he initiated a conversation with me. "You should wear gloves," he said, and I said, "I always lose them." I was milking the warmth back into my hands. "It's important if you fall in the winter," he said, "or if someone pushes you, so you can catch yourself on the ice." I felt a flicker of fear. It was such an odd thing to say, almost a wish, or a threat. The other students were arriving, I decided to brush it off, a second-language glitch.

Finally, I wrote one sentence at the bottom of the paper. "Please come see me in office hours," it said. I would try to resolve this myself.

6.

That weekend I had promised to attend a family wedding. Since my grandmother's death, my mother was insistent on our need to connect with family, and I agreed to be our representative, though I dreaded the event. The bride was my father's cousin's daughter, which made her, I guess, my second cousin—I didn't really care, in those days, I could barely keep track of my own sister. My cousin was marrying the scion of a real estate empire, and she was only twenty-four, barely older than me. Everything about the wedding was too much and too rich and too loud—the size of the hall, the spiky flower arrangements that obscured half the table, not one but three bands, still barely audible under the cacophony of five hundred guests. My best dress was a crushed velvet frock patterned in roses that looked elegant when I bought it at the flea market on Lexington but was here revealed as a tawdry, terrible mistake. I looked like a girl at her first prom. All the other women were in heels and pearls and satin.

I was seated in the hinterlands, at the edge of the hall where even the light faded, and I hid at the table, trying to figure out how long it was before I could leave. "Do you know who I am?" the woman beside me said, and I looked at her.

She wore a dress like a peacock's tail, overlapping feathers in blue and black and green. The dress changed colour as she shifted towards me. Her hair was silver and long, held at the sides with jeweled barrettes the same shades as the dress. Her lipstick was expertly red. She was sitting sideways on the chair, towards me, and her legs were wrapped around each other, the foot caught behind the calf. They were excellent legs, clad in smooth pale stockings. On the floor were a discarded pair of high-heeled silver sandals.

"I would have remembered meeting you," I said. She was extraordinary.

"I didn't ask if we had met," she said, "I said, do you know who I am?"

"I'm afraid not," I said. "Do you know who I am?"

"You're Helen's granddaughter," she said. "The spitting image of her at your age, which must be about twenty—what is that expression, anyway? Spitting image—is that against the evil eye?"

"That's right," I said. "I'm Helen's granddaughter. One of several."

"I was sorry," she said. "When I heard." Her fingers drummed on the table, each nail a separate pearl.

I snuck a look at the place holder. Bella Silver.

"She was my best friend," Bella said. "That was a long time ago. We were best friends when we were eight years old."

"She left Europe when she was eight years old," I said.

"That's right," Bella said, "1932. They were smart. Though you should never attribute to virtue what belongs to fate. They left after her father died. We stayed. My mother was so proud of being Hungarian. We gave the country the best writers, the best artists, the best musicians. She could never believe that we would be so betrayed. By a bunch of peasants who weren't even fit to scrub our floors."

Her words were angry, but her tone was even and calm. I

wasn't sure how to respond.

"Did you see her again?" I said. "When you came to America. Was that after the war?"

"After, and after," she said. "Two years in a DP camp. I could have gone to Palestine. I didn't think they'd win, you see, or else maybe I would have gone there. Then Brooklyn. And since 48, Harlem. A nice Jewish neighbourhood."

"It was," I said. Even I knew that.

"I came, they all left," she said. "There's a Jewish star on the church across the street. It used to be a synagogue. Anyway, it's home." She shrugged, narrow shoulders brushing the bottoms of her feather earrings. "I have my studio there too, you should come and visit sometime. You might be interested."

She slipped a card out of her small beaded reticule. It was thick, heavy card stock, matte black. I couldn't see anything on it.

"Hold it up to the light," she said, and then I saw an address, in narrow silver script. No name, no phone number. I didn't have a purse, so I slipped it into my bra, with my subway pass and a single damp and crumpled ten-dollar bill.

"How do I get in touch with you if I'm coming?" I said and she said, "I'm always there." She stood up and pulled a cane from behind her chair. The neck of the cane inclined into the sterling head of a swan, the eyes red glass beads that caught the candlelight.

"I get tired so easily these days," she said. "It's a gift, really. Aging. No one expects you to stay late at parties. You always have an excuse."

She stood and, even though she walked with a cane, she moved like a dancer, her head light on her long neck. She was like a performer playing an old woman in a masquerade.

"Wait," I said. "You didn't answer my question. Did you see my grandmother when you came back from Europe?"

"Of course," she said. "I told you, we were best friends. I lived with her for a while, with her and Abe. I didn't have anywhere else to go."

"Then why is it"—I started to say and stopped myself.

"Why is it I wasn't at the funeral?" she said. "I haven't seen Helen for almost fifty years. I would have come to the funeral anyway, I wanted to. But I don't know if the family would have appreciated it. You see, they thought it was my fault."

"What was your fault?" I said, but just then the bride and groom came into the room to a fanfare of trumpets, a litter of rice and confetti. Strobe lights stuttered my vision, and when the hubbub subsided she was gone, and all that I had left was the strange black card tucked between my bra strap and my breast.

7.

There was no writing due the next class, which was a relief. I was afraid of what would happen if Bo submitted the draft I'd seen to the class, though I wasn't sure if I was afraid of him or afraid for him. He was his usual self that day, only he kept looking up at me when I wasn't looking at him, then looking away, so I would catch only the sideways slide of his eyes. I was distracted.

We were talking about an essay by John Berger about the impossibility of originality, and I'd found an old TV series from before I was born that he'd done for the BBC. I reserved a VCR from the library and dragged the equipment into the classroom on a cart which dangled a dozen obstructive and mysterious cords. I hadn't watched the video before bringing it to class, and as soon as it started, the students began giggling. John Berger first appeared from the back, the original hipster, his grey pants too tight, his hair like an unkempt poodle. He must have been in his forties. He had eyebrows like unusually enthusiastic caterpillars, a deep furrow between them that he used like an exclamation point, for frequent emphasis, sensual lips, a Tom Selleck chin with a dent so deep you could lay a finger in it. And what was that shirt he was wearing? It seemed like an optical illusion, one of those seventies visual tricks meant to hypnotize you, to dazzle you into in an alternate state of consciousness. It was a slim-cut cream polyester shirt, with a pointy collar and buttons undone just one past good taste. But the most remarkable thing was the vertical pattern, in a colour I thought of as seventies shit-brown—were they locks? Checks? The camera zoomed in, and I was able to parse the pattern, lozenges linked with double diamonds framing Greek orthodox crosses, like masonic or satanic symbols, or just the semaphore of the new world order. If that makes no sense, it's because the shirt did not. That shirt hurt my sanity; I was relieved when the camera cut away to a Vertov clip.

My students watched with a sense of awe. I switched it off after fifteen minutes. "Alice, that was awesome," one of them said, a high-school football star who still wore his letter jacket, and one of the girls, my favourite, who liked to poke holes in her stockings with her pen as we sat in class, said in a hushed tone, as if she'd read my mind, "Did you see that shirt?" Bo, of course, stayed silent. At the end of class I left his paper on his desk.

I was surprised when Bo knocked on my door. I hadn't expected him to show up. He was all dangling hands and big feet and hair, and he blocked the light in the small entry until I told him to please come in. He sat down and we were both silent.

"Your essay," I finally said.

The silence continued. He was not interested in making this easier for me.

"I found the end—jarring," I said, hating myself for the word. When I took writing workshops as an undergraduate, jarring was a code word for everything anyone hated but could not or would not name, it was the queen of euphemisms, impossible to contradict, impossible to identify. He still said nothing.

"I'm not sure how the class would react to that story," I continued. "Perhaps you should consider ending it a little earlier, when the girls read your notebook. It's such an—intimate—story after that, you might want to think about the consequences of sharing it. And—"I sped up because I had to build up my courage to say this part "—you might want to talk to someone at the university who is able to—" I faltered "—process this with you. Since it sounds like a difficult experience."

He was looking at me now, and I could feel the pressure build up in him. He had a little half smile on his face, which was the first flicker of expression I had seen.

"It wasn't a difficult experience," he said calmly.

"Not difficult," I said, "upsetting perhaps. Did you never talk to your parents about it?"

"I did not," he said, "because it never happened." Now his smile was fuller, he was enjoying this flipped interrogation. I was slow, anyway, to understand what he meant.

"Which part," I said, "what are you saying?"

"I mean, I made it up. You wanted a story so I told you a story."

"I asked you to write about a true story," I said slowly. "A memory."

"Every memory is perhaps a fiction," he said. "How do we tell the story of our lives?" He was quoting my assignment. Not just quoting it, mocking it. Actually, it wasn't really my assignment, it was modelled after a template the writing program had distributed to first year instructors, as we rolled the students through that first Cartesian stage of doubt without ever getting them back to certainty.

"If you had trouble with the assignment, you could have told me," I said.

"I didn't have trouble with the assignment," he said. "I did the assignment. You said my language was vivid and moving."

"Right," I said. He had completely outplayed me. Actually, I was having trouble letting go of the whole scenario. I could still see Shawna, the narrow chain around her neck, could almost smell her bubblegum breath. I believed in Bo under the tree, eavesdropping and turning his damp loneliness into poetry. I couldn't help myself. "You made the whole thing up?" I said. "The apartment, Shawna, everything?"

"The whole thing," he said proudly. "I never lived in an apartment. There is no Shawna. My father is a doctor. We have a big house in Westchester. I'm American. I mean, we came here when I was three years old. And my mother is gone."

He stopped, as if he hadn't meant to tell me that part.

My face burned. I had just assumed he was a recent immigrant, was so surprised and pleased by his fluency. I had pointed out some common second-language errors, even before that first essay.

He had baited me, but I deserved it.

I said, "You're a talented writer. You should keep writing fiction. But that wasn't the assignment."

His eyes shuttered. He had girlish eyelashes, long and thick, incongruous in his face like ruffled curtains in a tenement window. I could imagine a mother discovering those eyelashes, exulting in them, in her beautiful new baby boy.

"What if you tried to write something true?" I said. "What if you tried to write about your mother?"

He stood up so fast his bag dropped to the floor and everything spilled out—papers, pencils, the dead clunk of a laptop hitting the floor. He cursed as he stooped to pick everything up stuffing it back into his backpack, which was child-sized and patterned in dinosaurs, as though it had been purchased for someone much younger. I stood to help him but the cubicle was so narrow I couldn't get there fast enough, and instead loomed over him, helpless, all but wringing my hands.

It took much longer to clean up than it should have because he kept dropping objects as he tried to put them away. It was excruciating. I kept reaching out my hands as if to help him. Bo finally stood up, slung the pack over his shoulder, and backed out of my office. He couldn't get out of there fast enough. I sat, feeling useless, feeling angry at myself, feeling used.

8.

That week, I found Bella's card in my laundry. The script had miraculously stayed legible, and on Sunday I decided to take up her invitation to visit her uptown.

The subway emerged from underground at 125th Street, and I got out, blinking in the light. I'd never been this far uptown, didn't even realize that the subway climbed up to emerge into the day. I was at the level of the buildings, and could look down on the street below, which was a snarl of wide lanes and highways merged with urban streets. I didn't know which direction I was going. I was predictably wrong at guessing which way to go, so much so that when I tried to outsmart my instincts I was wrong again, like a level that will always calibrate to the exact opposite of balance. I ended up in a big block of projects, tall brick buildings that lurked on the streetscape like a gang of bullies and hid the sky, and then I tracked back, but too far, until I reached the steep park that led to the river and the highway and the severe sarcophagus that hulked over the north corner of Riverside Park and held the remains of a dead president and his wife. From there, I was finally oriented; I turned left and walked two blocks upriver until I reached a building facing the water. The address was missing—I thought of the dubious usefulness of a card with only an address, when the building itself had no number. There was no doorbell, no speaker system, but I pushed the front door and it opened, revealing wide dusty steps lit by a skylight.

I looked at the card again, and there it was, the second floor. There were plants on the stairs, in lush tropical display, cascading down even as they reached up towards the roof. The plants must have loved that skylight. There were ferns and vines and flowers, but none of them seemed to belong in an industrial Harlem building. They made it feel like I was ascending to another place, another climate—Brazil, Costa Rica, somewhere that deserved to feel that lush.

The door was heavy and made of metal. Again, I knocked, and the thick material seemed to swallow the sound, but when I pushed the door it opened smoothly and silently. I was looking at an open loft, but with none of the associations of spaciousness or modernity associated with that word in real estate advertisements or magazine articles. No, this loft was massive, but it was cluttered, with books lining every wall and piled on the floor in unstable towers. There were filing cabinets bursting with paper, the wood floors looked like they had scurvy, the paint was peeling, and someone had written on the walls in pencil, strings of numbers and words in a language I did not know. There wasn't much furniture, but whatever there was had been covered in layers of books and papers. Images were thumbtacked to the walls, one on top of the other. Grand windows reached from the floor to the ceiling, but black fabric had been tacked over them, and the only light was the weak December sun that streamed through where the makeshift blackout curtains had fallen. And most strangely, there were puppets hanging from the ceiling like spiders, perched on top of the bookcases, sitting on the floor, some small and gestural—a pillow on a chair had a mouth, a button that suggested an eye—and others truly magnificent, elaborately carved and painted and costumed as if I'd found myself in Geppetto's workshop rather than in a Harlem studio facing the river at the end of the twentieth century. I turned and faced a thicket of children's doll heads impaled on posts. A soft textile sculpture of a pregnant woman hung by her gravid stomach near the windows.

"Hello," I said. The air was thick with dust. "Bella?"

"I'm right here," a voice said, and a woman emerged from the shadows. The puppets had served as a kind of camouflage—she had been there all along, I just hadn't been able to spot her among her uncanny dolls. She didn't look like the same woman as I'd met at the wedding. That woman was enameled, brittle as a scarab. This woman was draped in layers of fabric and covered in chalk dust and charcoal. Her hair, which had been drawn up into an expert chignon at the wedding and impaled with a jeweled chopstick, was long and fell around her shoulders, hid her face. Even her voice had changed, was quieter, a voice of honey and smoke.

I said, "Is this a bad time?" She seemed like all the light had gone out of her, like an extinguished star.

"Just a minute," she said. "I was working. It's always a little difficult to come out of it."

I wondered if she'd been working or had been sleeping. She had deep creases on the side of her face, and I saw that behind her was a black velvet day bed, newspapers on the floor surrounding it.

"And who are you?" she said, and I wondered if I had imagined our meeting, or if I had somehow misunderstood her invitation.

"I'm Alice," I said. "I'm Helen's granddaughter."

She sat down on the daybed heavily, and as she sat the velvet released a cloud of dust. As she looked up at me her eyes filled with tears.

"Helen," she said. "Helen is dead."

"Yes," I said.

"And we've met before?" The intonation made it a question.

"At Stella's wedding," I said. "A month ago." I saw the cane with the swan's head leaning against the bookshelf, red eyes glinting in the gloom.

"Forgive me," she said. "I'm an old woman. My memory is poor. Of course, you look just like Helen. For an instant, I thought I'd seen a ghost."

"I didn't mean to disturb you," I said. "I can come back another time. Or not come back," I added. "I didn't mean to interrupt you while you were working."

"No, stay," she said. "Helen's granddaughter."

"This place is incredible," I said. "Is this all your work?"

"My life's work," she said. "Every child likes to play with dolls. I just never stopped. Would you like some tea?"

"Thank you," I said, but I was distracted, looking at the books piled on the shelves, the faded photographs tacked to the walls. I went closer, and one image looked familiar: a black and white picture of two young girls in wool coats and berets, arms wrapped around one another's waists, standing on a bridge in front of a river. They were laughing. One of them looked just like my third-grade school picture—freckles, flyaway hair, an expression of manic glee.

"You found us," Bella said. "That was the day before she left. I thought I was going to see her in a couple of months. Instead, it was fifteen years, and she was pregnant with your father."

She had returned, with two glasses of tea on a tray. She sat once again, her back straight, and she looked once again like the woman I had met at the wedding. She had tied back her hair and her eyes were bright. She made me think of the stories of queens turned to crones, or crones transformed back into young queens, as though age were a cloak she could shrug on or off.

"She was an amazing woman, your grandmother." Bella said. "She was a wonderful storyteller. We wrote books together—she would tell the story, and I would illustrate it, or else she would write elaborate plays, and I would design our costumes so we could act them out together. She was going to be a novelist, and I was going to be an artist, and then we would collaborate together. Actually, she was more talented than I was. She always took the lead. When she left, I stopped making anything for a long time."

"I don't remember her like that," I said. "As an artist."

"Oh yes," Bella said. "She was a wonderful artist. She always had the best ideas, the best games. She told the most beautiful stories. It's heartbreaking for a child, to lose a friend like that. And distances were much farther back then. America, that was like a place in a fairy tale, I didn't really believe it existed. I didn't think I'd ever see her again. Then the war..."

"The war," I echoed. My tea was sweet and strong, just like my grandmother had made it.

"My family was very religious," Bella said with distaste. "We had tickets to Palestine. Me, my sister, my three brothers. My parents went to synagogue the week we were to leave and the rabbi told them it was a sin to send us away. Put your trust in God, he said. Repent. He said that the goal of Zionism was the annihilation of the Jewish people. My father forbade us to get on the train. My mother couldn't stand against him. Of the seven of us, I am the only survivor. "

The tea was cold in the glass. Her hands shook on her lap as she spoke.

"I owe your grandmother a great debt," she said. "After the war I had nowhere to go, and she took me in. I don't think Abe liked it too much—they were newlyweds, and she was expecting. It is a time for a couple to be alone. Still, back then everyone took someone in. It was normal. It was necessary."

"She never told me anything about it," I said. "My father never spoke of it either."

"Your father? He wouldn't remember me," she said. "But I was there when he was born, and for the first year of his life, when Helen was sick. He was like a son to me. Tell me," she said, and she caught my wrists with her cold hands, "how is he?"

I looked at her in surprise. She didn't know.

"I'm sorry," I said. "He died a year ago. He had a heart attack. It was very fast."

I said the words automatically, as I had heard them when the phone rang in New York the previous March. It was a beautiful day—false spring, blue sky, everything melting and the surge of energy that comes with the return of the sun. I was singing along to Ricky Martin on the radio—ironically, joyfully. The birds were fooled into heralding the end of winter. My mother was on the end of the line. The temperature dropped the next week and the cherry blossoms froze on the branch.

Bella dropped my wrists and her hands fell onto her lap. She fell silent, and when she spoke again she did not look at me.

"I'm very sorry," she said. "But I need to be alone right now. You can come another time, and I will tell you about your grandmother. Though I never would have thought—"

"What?" I cried, urgently. It is the forgivable narcissism of youth, perhaps, to forget that your parents, that your grandparents, had their own stories, that their dramas and heartbreaks were once as urgent as your own—no, more urgent, since they lived in a more urgent time. I could see the landscape of my past, not a series of low slopes in the mist but as a dramatic vista of peaks and valleys. Beyond that, other things, closer to me, seemed to almost come into focus: my grandmother sitting in the corner and looking around as if surprised to find me there, my father's frequent silences and rages.

"I never would have thought they would have kept that from me," she said.

9.

On Friday, I picked Persephone up from school. She had an early dismissal, and Fiona had asked me to pick her up—Fiona, who would now talk to me again, but only to ask me for favours. We saw a man wrapped in a long brown coat sitting on the front steps of my building as we came down the street, and as soon as she saw him, she dropped my hand and threw herself into his arms with a happy cry.

He was older than me, maybe in his forties, and had a loose-limbed handsomeness. His hair was grey and cropped closely to his head, his eyes were blue. He looked like an urban cowboy, or maybe like Sam Shepard playing a cowboy. The lines on his face were like the lines carved in rock through years of wind and rain. He lifted her up as if she weighed nothing.

"Hello," he said. "I'm Persephone's father, Henry."

I stood there, stiffly, feeling like the help. "Does Fiona know you're here?" I said, thinking of her story, so many months before in the café.

Persephone nestled into his neck and I felt jealous of her for a moment, jealous of them, belonging to each other. Jealous that her father had returned, and that mine never would. A moment flashed through my mind. I was fourteen years old, babysitting in a house that seemed to me a mansion, and the parents were running late. The father had picked me up in his Porsche, and now he was changing his clothes to go out. He asked me to read him the film listings as he got dressed and he left the bedroom door ajar. I could see him strip off his T-shirt, could watch him button his white shirt over his smooth dark chest, I couldn't tell if I was the voyeur or if he was some kind of low-key flasher. I don't know where his wife was at the time, somewhere in the house. He knew that he was a beautiful man married to a plain woman—a combination that always excites curiosity, unlike the reverse. At fourteen, I was every kind of ordinary.

"Of course," he said smoothly. "She asked me to pick her up. She's going to stay with me for the weekend. You must be Alice. Persephone told me all about you. Thanks for taking such good care of my girl. She adores you, you know."

Fiona had told me that Persephone had no contact with her father. She said that after he left, Persephone had nightmares about him. But Persephone didn't look frightened, she looked at home. She seemed like a little girl in his arms and it struck me how I'd been fooled by her precocity.

"I should call Fiona," I said, and then realized I didn't have her number. What kind of mother. He dangled keys from his long fingers, and said, "She's not home, but she said we should pack up a bag. Then we're going for lunch and you're welcome to join us."

"I think we should wait for her," I said, and Henry shook his head.

"Look," he said. "Fiona likes to be dramatic. The judge gave me weekends this past Thursday, didn't she tell you that? I have the papers. Do you really need to see them? You do realize, this is my child. She's supposed to be here to help with the transition, but Fiona's a sore loser. She probably asked you to look after her so she wouldn't have to see me."

I remembered Thursday. I was at the front door, fumbling for my keys, and Fiona marched past me, pulling Persephone by the hand. She was flushed and glassy-eyed, as if she had been crying. "Hi, Fiona, hi Persephone," I said, but she didn't acknowledge me. Looking straight ahead, she unlocked the door and went inside. Persephone looked over her shoulder, and smiled apologetically, but she looked pale. Later that night, I thought I heard Fiona on the street, in a dark cluster of drunks in front of the club next door. I usually avoided eye contact with groups like that—the combination of the late night and intoxication was volatile—but I thought I heard her throaty laugh, so I looked for her. I was too late. The bouncer had opened up the velvet rope, and the group had their backs to me and was crowding inside.

I turned to Persephone, as if an eleven-year old could confirm or deny his news, and she nodded earnestly. "I forgot to tell you my Dad was picking me up," she said. "We're going to the country. He has a horse." Her eyes widened at the enormity of this, as if she'd said he had a unicorn. Henry was nodding too. "Beacon, it isn't exactly in the country. But I do have a horse. She named him, right, Persephone?"

Impatient with our conversation, Persephone grabbed the keys and ran ahead, a beam of light racing up the stairs. He walked behind her, and I could see he had a slight limp on his left side. He was narrow as a boy.

I could see distaste snarl his lips as she opened the door, then he smiled again. The place was a mess, except for Persephone's tidy corner. Her tiny clothes were folded on an open bookshelf, and she placed them in her backpack carefully. She took one book, and then considered for a moment, and took a second. By the time she was done, the backpack seemed too big for her, but he slung it over his shoulder easily. "Are you coming?" he said easily, as if I hadn't questioned his right to take her. I felt uncertain about agreeing to come with Hank. On the one hand, I no longer trusted Fiona. On the other, I felt a residual loyalty, if not to her than to her version of the end of their relationship. He walked out without checking if I was following him—he was the kind of man who expected it. I stumbled as I hurried to catch up, forgetting my coat.

"Veselka," Persephone said, and he said, "Yes, my queen." I must have passed the awning a hundred times but I had never been inside.

"The kid likes borscht," he said, shrugging, "We are descended from peasants. After all."

"And pierogies," Persephone insisted, and he nodded as he pulled out my chair.

"I'll have the same," I said, though I had never liked borscht. I had trouble ordering in restaurants in the same way that I had trouble choosing my classes or structuring my day. It was easy for me to feel overwhelmed by choices. I was paralyzed in grocery stores, and a menu was enough to fill me with regret and panic.

But this borscht was different. It was the red of flesh, and smelled like sweet dirt. The waitress put a dish of sour cream on the table. I sat there with the man and the child, and I realized that we looked like a family, the kind of family I always admired when I glimpsed them from the street, sitting as we sat, framed by the glass window. For a moment, spooning the borscht into my mouth, listening to Persephone babble at her father—in his presence she was entirely different, voluble and attention-seeking when she usually seemed so mature and constrained—I realized that each of us could be someone entirely different if placed in a new context. If I were a mother, for instance, or if Persephone truly had her father back, since we each brought out different facets in each other, imagining that we are stable and solitary but in fact only revealed in relation to one another. And I couldn't imagine how Fiona could believe that Persephone was better off without her father, who seemed both courtly and protective, and listened so attentively. Was it not more likely that she was hoarding her, and wanted her for herself, or rather, didn't want her at all but just wanted to punish him by taking the thing he loved the most?

He was a man who smiled at waitresses, who tipped well and easily, who put his hand on the small of my back as we got up to leave with a firm warmth that I could feel all day, glowing at the base of my spine.

"She will be back at school Monday, Fiona can get her at the usual time," he said, and then held out his arm and a taxi pulled up with the golden alacrity of a heavenly chariot, and they vanished inside the car, leaving me feeling, well, feeling left, and chilly. A cloud had covered the sun. On my way home, I fretted about Fiona and Persephone and the dereliction of my responsibilities and the way I had become entangled in this family net not mine. As it turned out, I didn't see Fiona all weekend, so Henry must have told the truth. I was worried, in fact, that I might never see her again, but at four on Monday I spotted her walking down the street, Persephone lagging behind her, and they both smiled at me, their resemblance magnified in that smile, so I was reassured that I had not made a mistake.

10.

I woke up to a snowstorm, thick white flakes that muffled the usual sounds of the street. The roads were deserted. It was as if the entire city was under a glass drum. Everything felt suspended. A week had passed since my last visit, and I was going to see Bella again.

Ever since I'd left her house, I'd been wondering what she had meant by saying my father was like a son to her. And why, if that had been the case, had she been out of his life for so long? When my father died a year before, his death had come quite unexpectedly. His loss had sparked my grandmother's decline. He was a severe, serious person—he wore three-piece suits and fedoras, like a man from a previous era. He was a surgeon and spent long hours at the hospital, where he had a reputation for warmth and devotion that was entirely foreign to me, as his daughter.

After his funeral, stranger after stranger came up to me and told me how much his care had meant to them, how steady and reassuring he had been as their loved ones went in for anesthesia, not knowing what awaited them on the other side. I felt angry at those testimonies. My father had been distant at home, his reserve only disturbed by his rage. His moods were the weather of the house, and anything could set him off—the radio played too loud, a missing section of the newspaper. He was often at work, and then my house was as warm and casual as that of any of my friends, my mother in the kitchen cooking, the twins, so much younger than me, wreaking happy havoc in the basement. But when he was home, the rules changed and the house fell under a spell of silence. As a child, I loved him like you love a thunderstorm, in awestruck terror.

He never spoke about his childhood. His weekly conversations with his mother could be described at polite. He and his brother hated each other, and had not spoken in years at the time of his death. His childhood was mysterious to me. We didn't even have many photographs of when he was a young man, and in the pictures that I could find he looked like a stranger.

I read Virginia Woolf on the subway—the middle section of *To the Lighthouse*, and that killing passage in the brackets, when Mr. Ramsay stumbles down the hallway and reaches out for Mrs. Ramsay, who is dead. How brilliant that was! The passage travels back and forth in time—he stretches out his arms, and only then are we told that she has died "rather suddenly" in the night. It was something about keeping the loss in the second half of the sentence, as if it was an afterthought, so it comes as a surprise to the reader even as it is a surprise to Mr. Ramsay, who has momentarily forgotten that she is gone.

I wondered how long it took to assimilate grief. Sometimes when I visited my mother, I expected to find my father behind the closed door of his study—still closed, still sacrosanct, even in his absence. Sometimes I heard his voice in my dreams, and it woke me up. When I had these aural hallucinations, my father sounded exactly as he did in life, except that he was expressing love or concern for my well-being, something I never remembered him doing out loud when he was alive. Don't get me wrong: I knew that I was loved. But the same channel that gave way for his rage remained stopped up when it came to any expression of affection, except in the most formal and stilted ways possible, usually on occasions of celebration—birthday, graduation—which I trusted less than I trusted his usual reticence, even, in an odd way, trusted less than his anger, because it was so rare and felt so uncharacteristic.

Thinking of him and of Woolf, I almost missed my stop and was only called back to wakefulness by the subway emerging at the 125th Street station. More snow had fallen while I was travelling, and I had to pick and wade through snowdrifts and slush puddles, but the storm had cleared and the clouds pulled back to reveal bright blue sky. This time, I knew where I was going, but was surprised when I arrived to find the big industrial doors open and music pouring down the staircase from Bella's studio. I thought I recognized it from the movie *West Side Story*, the hectic clash of flute and drum. I was wrong. Later, Bella told me it was Stravinsky's Rites of Spring. The plants on the stairwell seemed to have grown even more robust, and the tendrils spilled down the staircase like a waterfall. The door of the studio was also open, and the room was full of light. The blackout curtains were gone, and the space had been cleared of much of the clutter. In the middle of the room was a deep and broad wooden box, the size of a sandbox in a park. The box was filled with plants, an island garden in the middle of the loft, all blooming at once though they belonged to different seasons—tulips, irises, peonies, roses. Years later, I would see a tree that had been grafted together from plum, apple, and pear branches, so that it bloomed apricot and lavender and cream all at once, and I thought of Bella's winter garden.

"You've brought the spring," I said. This time Bella was dressed in white, flowing layers that fell to the floor, and her hair was down.

"I call it the children's garden," she said. "Look closely."

I looked down, into the foliage. There was something about the riot of colour in the middle of this long winter that made me feel hungry. Among the glossy leaves were tiny vintage dolls, propped against the stems or lying in the dirt, dozens of them. They were nude, and smaller than the size of my thumb. They had big heads and eyes, luxurious shiny hair, but their bodies were tiny and vague—not boys or girls but neutered pinkish beige plastic, arms stretched out wide, their little legs spread. I couldn't tell if it was charming or uncanny—a garden of imps, or a graveyard. Once, in a museum, I put my eye to a peephole in a wooden door, and I saw a woman stretched out on the grass, hairless and naked, her face hidden. Her arm held a gas lamp over her prone body, and behind her was a landscape of Renaissance grace, the greens and blues of leaf and waterfall. It was a bloodless massacre; when I stepped back, I felt unclean. This piece reminded me of that one, except everything in the museum tableau was artificial, and these flowers were real and joyful. As I stepped back from the planter, I remembered the name of the museum piece: Étant *donné*. Given.

"It's a model, for a show," Bella said. "I should have just sketched it out and put it together at the gallery—what a waste, right?—but I needed to see it, to smell it, to feel the weight of the soil. That might have been a mistake, actually. The floors may never recover. The doors are open because I'm expecting another delivery. I'm going to fringe the entire installation in white cyclamen, do you know the flower? The symbol of resignation. I like them because they make me think of a Möbius strip, the way the petals twist around one another. They were said to speed labour, you know, but also to cause abortions if pregnant women encountered them too early."

"This reminds me of a story I read when I was a child," I said. "What was her name. She lived in a walnut shell..."

"Violet petals for her mattress, a rose petal blanket, and by day she would float in a tulip petal-boat," Bella finished. "Thumbelina. Yes, I was thinking of her, among other sources of inspiration. But really, I just wanted a winter garden. The dolls insisted on being part of it, but I wasn't planning on them. They took over. I bought them in an antique shop—that's overselling it, really, they're kitsch from the 60s and not at all valuable. When he sold them to me, the owner said they were in "played with" condition, and many had lost their clothes."

Once again, she seemed like an entirely different woman. The first time I met her she had been stunning, elegant, jeweled. The second time, frail and dark, a scorched piece of paper. Now she was a goddess, her hair loose down her back, her layers of white a sacrificial robe.

"Tea?" she offered, as she had the last time. She brought the same silver teapot, the same small glasses. I picked mine up, burned my tongue in my eagerness, and put it down again.

"I've been enjoying working with living things," Bella continued. "Usually I work with inanimate objects—dolls, puppets. The installation will be in place a month, and most of the petals—not all of them—will fall, so it will be easier to spot the dolls, I'm trying to make it transition from summer to autumn, but I'm doing this for the first time, so I have no idea if I will be successful."

She sat on her velvet couch, and I faced her, rigid on a frail wooden chair. I put the tea on the ground next to my feet. I wasn't sure where to begin.

'You were going to tell me about Helen," I said, finally.

"I arrived in New York," Bella said, as if she had been waiting to resume her story. "Your grandmother was waiting for me. At first, I didn't recognize her. Remember, we were eight years old the last time we saw each other, and your grandmother—well, she was plump, and always self-conscious about it, even as a child. Now she was tall and beautiful. I recognized her by her eyes. You have the same eyes. She was slender, but I looked at her stomach and I knew. You've got something in there, I said, and she was offended. She thought I was calling her fat, like other children did when we were young. You see, she hadn't yet realized she was pregnant. They had been married—not long. Less than a year."

She picked up her tea and held a sugar cube between her teeth as she sipped it. The record had ended, but it still spun, the needle hovering above it in the air. The room was very quiet.

"We didn't know each other anymore, to be honest. But still, there's a special bond when you know each other when you are young. Back then, we had been closer than friends. We were like sisters. If someone saw one of us in the street, they would ask about the other one. We both loved to read, loved to write. We kept diaries, even as little girls, recording everything we did. And even though her family had left, even though she hadn't seen what I saw, been through what I experienced—I resented her that, I resented everyone, it wasn't so much that I wanted it not to have happened to me as that I wanted it to have happened to everyone so that they would see, they would see what I saw when I closed my eyes at night."

The cup shook in her hand and carefully, gently, she placed it on the wooden table.

"Anyway, we were from the same place. We remembered the lilacs in the spring. She'd been in America much longer than I had. She was luckier. But both of us had lost most of our families, our home."

Her voice grew stronger again.

"That little one in her stomach, that was your father. And it was good, after all, that I came when I did. Not just for me, but for her. She was very sick when she was pregnant. She was vomiting all the time. I took over for her job at the garment factory—to hold it for her, so they wouldn't give it away. And everything else I took over too. Shopping, cooking, cleaning the house. Abe worked late, he was never home. In the evening, I would put his dinner in the refrigerator, then I would go to bed on the couch. After a week of that he told me I should sleep in the bedroom with Bella, so he wouldn't disturb me when he came in, and he would take the couch. Later I found out she couldn't sleep next to him anyway, he'd been sleeping on the floor. Her sense of smell had gotten very sensitive, and she said it made her sick to sleep beside him. Back then, he worked on the floor of a butcher shop early in the morning before he started at the factory. He always washed very well, he was very clean. But she said she couldn't get it out of her nose, the smell of blood, of raw meat. Your grandfather was a simple man, he didn't know what to do with her. So, he gave me the bed and he went to the couch, and then he was a shadow in the early morning and late at night, someone I would pass silently on my way to the toilet or kitchen.

I was always tired. I woke up and brought her breakfast, dry toast and tea, that was all she could keep down. Every day, I made myself a sandwich for work, and one for her. Then I went to work, on the factory floor, ten hours straight. My fingers and hands were covered in small cuts from the needles and scissors. I was clumsy. I shopped on the way home, and made dinner, and straightened up the house. But once I had cleaned up and came to bed with Bella, she was kind to me. She usually felt better at night, and she was lonely. We played Mahjong. It isn't a very good game with only two players, but it passed the time. We sang to the baby in her belly, songs from our childhood. Sad songs about men lost in the forest, about birds that cannot return home. It was good for her, to have the company. It was good for me, not to be alone. Your grandfather came home later and later, sometimes not at all. She didn't even seem to notice. She didn't notice much, it was like she was sleepwalking through her pregnancy. She was a good-looking woman, but she stopped getting dressed, stopped putting on lipstick, stopped washing her hair. Every few days I would run her a bath and then I would walk her over to it, like a little child. She didn't have the energy to resist me. Sometimes I would sew at night, funny little creatures out of the scraps from the factory."

"Once, when I was going to work, Abe startled me. He was usually out of the house by then. It was winter, and still dark outside at seven. He hadn't turned on a light and was just sitting there in the shadows. What's wrong with her, he said. It was as if the voice came out of nowhere, I spilled the Nescafé all over the counter. Or is she just lazy, or what? he said. He sounded broken. She doesn't want to speak to me and she doesn't want to sleep with me. Bella, she won't even look at me. It's as if I did something terrible to her, but Bella, I didn't do anything terrible, did I? I swept the coffee crystals off the counter with my hand, we were out of clean dish rags. I was tired of cleaning up everyone's messes for them. The crystals stuck to my hand and automatically, I put my hand to my mouth, sucked it clean. Funny that I remember that the taste was so bitter. I think it's just the pregnancy, I said, it hits some women like that. Just you wait, when the baby comes, she will be back to herself again. I may be gone by then, he said grimly. And if I am not here, someone needs to look after her. I need you to make me a promise. You owe us—we took you in. Anyway, there's no one else. What do you mean, you may be gone, I said, but he had pushed past me and was out the door. He was wearing the same clothes he had worn the night before, and he smelled sharp and acidic, like machine oil. I realized it was not that he had gotten up early, but that he had never gone to bed."

"I was wrong about Helen. She did not get better. One day I came home, and she was sobbing in a puddle, her housecoat wet. Her water had broken but she had felt rooted to the ground, she hadn't been able to move or call for help. For once, Abe was nearby—I had passed him on the way home, smoking in a doorway with men I did not know—and I ran to get him after I pulled her by the arm and found she would not budge. He took her to the hospital, and I stayed in the apartment, mopping up her water and cleaning the countertops. I cleaned that apartment until it shone, while I waited—I did not know if I was welcome at the hospital but I couldn't sit down, I had a nervous energy that only spent itself scrubbing counters and floors, on my knees. Now I think that I was doing the nesting that she could not, the impulse some women have, to get their house in order before the baby comes home. It was two days before anyone came home. I had sent a message to work that I could not come in, even though I meant I could lose my job, which really was her job. I had a terrible feeling, that she would need me and I would be gone. Then on the third day I heard the door open, heard Abe's heavy step, and the thin wavering cry of a very young baby. Where is Bella, I cried. I thought she was dead. Abe looked terrible, he hadn't shaved for days, and there were deep shadows under his eyes, as if he were peering out of the abyss. They took her, he said, and he thrust the baby into my arms. Then he left."

"How is that possible?" I said. It sounded like an accusation. As Bella told me her story, I had forgotten that she was talking about my grandmother, that this helpless infant was my father. It occurred to me that this all might be invented, like Bo's story in my class. Perhaps rather than something true, this was just something I wanted to hear. No one had ever told about my father's childhood. It occurred to me that I had never asked.

I remembered the drawing of the child in his cage of a crib, the underlined words below the picture. The sensitive anxious woman. Her silence, his rage.

Bella grew quiet then, and I heard footsteps on the stairs. "The cyclamen," she said with relief. "Just in time. You can come right in," she said, and a man staggered in, his arms full of flowers. Their smell was watery, transparent.

"I need to get these into dirt," she said. "You'll have to excuse me again."

"Of course," I said. "Only—"

I felt like a little girl who didn't want her bedside story to end. And it was hard to believe that these people, their stories, they belonged to me. This was my story too, only I had never known about it.

"I'll leave you my address and number," I said, finally. "In case you'd like to get in touch." I left a scribbled page on the wooden table, where it seemed to vanish instantly into the mess of other papers, camouflaged by the havoc of Bella's infinite archive.

11.

I was eager to hear the rest of Bella's story, but she never contacted me, and I didn't seem to have the time to return to her studio. I also wasn't sure what to do. There was no reason to trust her, though my impulse was to believe her. I kept her revelation from my mother, like the ring still in my drawer. And then I kept it from myself, though now it seems an impossible thing to repress or forget. I had a bunch of school deadlines, and classes kept me busy. I was the white queen, running as fast as I could to stay in place. By the time I finally made the trip out to Harlem, the magnolias had begun their louche display, white petals like pale tongues lolling on the narrow branches, and a froth of green had returned to the tips of the trees.

Spring was a filthy time of year in the city; the humid air unlocked the odours that winter restrained, and the sidewalk was covered in food wrappers, dog shit, loose papers, dirty puddles. The weather was inconstant and treacherous. When I left my house, the sun was shining, but as the subway rose to the surface around 125th Street, the rain covered the windows so that the view of the brick buildings was blurred and pointillist, and the neon signs were the only blaze of visible colour. My umbrella broke at a gust of wind on Riverside, lifted and inverted so violently that the metal ribs poked through the black fabric. I ended up pulling the fabric off the frame and wrapping it around my head like a babushka. Under the elevated highway three men huddled on damp cardboard, and I tried not to look at them although their eyes on my legs were like heat. I thought they were hissing at me, but as I passed them—eyes straight forward—I could hear the word, pussy pussy pussy, whispered as if it was some kind of a summoning. By the time I came to Bella's building, I was jangled and damp and furious at the rain, at the city, at myself for having left the house so ill-prepared.

The door to the building was open. The entrance had been freshly painted, and the plants were gone. As I stood there, gaping up towards the skylight, a worker pushed past me, holding a pile of lumber over his shoulder like a cross. I followed him up the stairs. The loft had been stripped bare and the walls stripped of the peeling paint, the cryptic notes and calculations, the pictures and papers tacked to the walls. Books gone, pictures gone, puppets and dolls gone. Bella. I stood there in the open doorway, clutching my stomach, watching two workmen scrape and paint the walls. They didn't even turn around, it was as if I was a ghost.

I drew a deep breath and said, my voice echoing in the empty space—so much emptiness now, and how completely she had filled it, I flashed on that folly of a sandbox full of cyclamen, a garden in the middle of winter—"Excuse me? Could you help me?" A question and an apology at once.

They turned in unison, in their workmen's coveralls splattered in white paint, their faces also smeared, and both shook their heads mutely as if this was a pantomime and they were forbidden to speak. But then one walked towards me and broke their choreography.

"No English," he said, mournful. "You wait. Soon. Yes."

He pointed up at the ceiling as if I was waiting for a voice from the heavens, but soon I heard the footsteps heavy on the stairs and the same man who'd passed me earlier with the lumber now descended, unencumbered, his hands on his hips.

"Yes," he said, his tone not friendly. "Did you need something?"

"What happened to Bella?" I said, and my voice sounded more quavering than I had intended, more feminine.

But as it turns out that was a lucky accident; he relaxed into chivalry. I was no threat.

"The woman who lived here?" he said. "Well, I'm very sorry to have to tell you. She died. Was she a friend of yours?"

And, of course I knew. I knew as soon as I saw the empty stairway streaming with light and that gap where the plants had been, but still I gasped, and the painters, who had now stopped their work and sat on their buckets, looked at me like a pair of sad clowns. They nodded at me in silent sympathy.

"How?" I said. "When?"

He shrugged. "I heard it was a fall, down those stairs right there. I don't know anything else. We started work two weeks ago. Have to redo the whole place. If you don't mind me saying, your friend was quite the hoarder. I've never seen anything like it."

"Oh my god," I said. "She wasn't a hoarder. She was an artist. Where did it all go?"

The warmth in the man's voice turned off as if he'd closed a tap.

"Where it all goes," he said.

"It's as if you killed her yourself," I said bitterly. I didn't recognize my own voice.

"You're trespassing," he said, and then turned to the men behind me. As I descended the stairs my knees were water and my gut was fire. Outside, the rain had stopped, and the sky mocked me with its bold blue eye. I sunk down on the stoop and buried my head in my hands, thinking of Bella, and of my grandmother, and even of my father in his three-piece suit leaving his shoes at the door so that when he woke up early in the morning for his rounds, he wouldn't disturb us with his footsteps, and I wept like a child.

Gone, I thought. Everything is gone.

But that very day a package was waiting for me. I almost missed it. It was too large to fit in the slot, so the mailman had balanced it on the top of the narrow metal tenant's mailbox. As I turned the key it fell at my feet, literally at my feet. I picked it up and saw the package was wrapped in brown paper and covered in the strange unearthly drawings I had seen on Bella's wall. I opened it right there, standing in the doorway, and saw a slim book. Those faces in the vines were as good as a signature, and her writing, which flowed like water on the page, had the same quality as her artwork, which seemed at once both ephemeral and substantial.

I flipped it open, and the writing was in pencil and in script, so that it had almost vanished into the worn texture of the page. In the margins were fantastical creatures, drawn with the same pencil, like an illuminated manuscript--fiends, cupids and beast faces peeking out from the flowers and vines. And, inside the cover, was a letter with my name on it.

Dear Alice,

I started to write this story a long time ago. I thought that I would give it to your father so he would understand. I wrote it many different ways, first as a letter and then almost like a testament. Finally, I decided to write it as a diary. Even though it was long ago, it is still happening for me. I wanted him to understand. I kept trying, but I couldn't finish it. I kept thinking I would send it to him, only now it is too late.

Since he is gone, then it must be for you.

Bella

I opened the book. I began to read.

PART THREE

Bella

There was a wedding in the DP camp yesterday. We all came out to watch. Somehow, the couple's friends had managed to get the groom a suit, the bride a long white dress, and the members of the wedding party held bouquets of ferns and roses. The lilacs were blooming, and the sun was shining, so even these bare barracks were festive and beautiful. The bride and groom smiled and held each other by the hand. Their smiles were not haunted. They only had eyes for each other and for the future. Forgetfulness is a great thing, and the faster you forget, the faster you come back to life.

Palestine or America, Palestine or America, that's all anyone can talk about. A group has formed, they sing songs in Hebrew, and they dance in circles and they hector everyone else. The only safe place for a Jew, they say, and what fools you are to think any different. The more they talk, the less I listen. I decide that New York is the best place to disappear.

When they interview me, they ask if my parents are alive. No, I say. If I have any siblings. No. A husband. No. Any children? The woman looks up at me, hesitates, puts her pen in her mouth. I see her mark the box. As it turns out, there is a space, but just for one. How lucky I am.

On the way back to barracks, with my papers and my ticket, I put my face in the lilacs and swoon over their delicate rich fragrance, the silk of the petals tickling my cheeks. The petals of the lilac bruise easily, and their season is brief. Soon, they will wither and fade on the vine, but I will be gone even sooner.

In spite of everything, I am alive and even living with intensity.

★

On the boat, everyone has bundles, clothes and candlesticks, pots and dishes, bread, sausage, whatever they could save and carry. I have one extra skirt and blouse, a change of underclothes, a pad of paper and pencils. The women in my bunk are critical. Whatever are you going to do with that, they say. The first day, I take the paper and pencil up to the deck and I set myself up on a chair protected from the wind. Portraits, I say. I will trade for food or take money. It takes a while to get my first customer, a girl who seems almost a child, with soft brown curls and a tremulous, timid lip. She has a heel of bread for me, and a piece of cheese not yet gone bad. As soon as I start to draw, a crowd begins to form around me. The girl shifts in her seat, flushed and pleased at the attention. She scratches and picks at the numbers on the soft underside of her arm. I make her more beautiful. With feathery strokes, I capture the tremor of her lips, I put the light back in her eyes, with every movement of my pencil I fill her with life. Behind me, it is as if the crowd is watching a play—they gasp, exclaim in delight, look down at the page then up at her face. A few appoint themselves my protectors, and they stand guard, keeping anyone else from jostling my shoulder or elbow, from spoiling the line. When I give her the picture, she presses both hands against her mouth in delight.

I sketch a handsome young man, his cheeks shadowed in stubble. I sketch a woman with a silk ribbon in her hair and lavender eyes that I cannot capture in black and white. I sketch a boy with a shaven head who will not smile, and whose eyes seem to take up half of his narrow face, only when I hand him the photograph, he grins like a storm breaking, before he swallows his smile and looks up at me through his long, feminine eyelashes. As she slips into the crowd I realize she is a girl, dressed in trousers for comfort or safety. There is no time to wonder about her. In front of me a line has formed, and I draw all day long.

★

There is little to do on the boat—play cards, watch the cruel and endless ocean. By luck, I have chosen one of the best spots on the deck, shielded from the sun and the wind, and when I get up to stretch my legs and cramped fingers or to go to the toilet my fans guard my seat and wait for me to resume. I don't know if the people who wait in line are more eager to be recorded or to be seen. I sit across from them, no more than four feet away, and gaze at their faces intensely. Sometimes they cannot hold still, and shift in their seats, restless and uncomfortable. Sometimes their eyes fill with tears and their cheeks flush with blood. I have to stop when it is dark, and my arms and hands are sore with the day's labour. In the morning, when I come up to the deck, the chairs are waiting for me, and the line has already formed.

And so it is that when we arrive at Ellis Island—waving our handkerchiefs and crowding against the rail, all of us roaring and weeping in relief at arrival in the promised land—my pockets are heavy with coins, and I have bills stuffed into my bosom and my waist. I have used all my paper and my pencils are worn to nubs. I took anything offered me—even, from one child, a plain dull button—but still I am richer than I was upon departure, I have enough money for a single month's rent, for a new hat and dress.

We can see the crowd waiting for us on the shore, and as we disembark we are almost a riot, pressing against the guard rails and the policemen in our eagerness to be welcomed. But somehow, a peace holds. On the other side of the fence, I watch men embrace, women fall into each other's arms, I watch a man take a woman's face in his hands and draw her lips to his lips with a hungry delicacy, all this while I wait. By the time the last of us is processed it is dark, dirtier and colder than I had expected.

Helen is waiting for me on a bench. We would not have recognized each other, only I was the very last one. She does not embrace me and I do not fall into her arms. Instead she rises to her feet, slowly, carefully. I can see that she is pregnant and that realization punches me in the gut, I stagger and when I straighten she is watching me with a neutral and impassive gaze.

When the sponsorship letter came from Helen, I was surprised. I had written to everyone I could think of, cousins and great-aunts. Each time, no reply, or a weak apology. There was always someone in line ahead of me, with a stronger claim. Helen's letter to me was careful and generous. Her immediate family had left before the war, but everyone else was dead. Like me, she had nobody else left to save.

Still, as she looks at me now, I'm not sure that she wants me here. I am nothing but problems—an extra body, an extra mouth to feed. I have money, I blurt out before I have said anything else and I can see her flinch and turn her face away. It is exactly the wrong way to begin but when she looks back at me, her face is composed. You look exactly the same, Bella, she says, and it feels like a rebuke. I am not the same: I am a hundred years old, I have been through the furnace and survived, I have lived past my proper death. Still, the customs agent who interviewed me called me a young lady. Helen looks different, but I do not tell her so. It is as if that spark that animated her has been so submerged it is no longer visible. She seems wearier than I am, even after my long voyage.

As I walk away from the water, towards my new life, I am charged with energy. The new world, the new world, I hum, despite the broken sidewalks, the burned-out streetlights, the low, ugly, brick buildings. Helen stumbles and I offer her my arm. Now it is as if I have rescued her.

Helen's husband is out, and she leaves me to make up my own bed on the couch, in the dim lamp-lit living room. She goes to her room and closes the door. It is very strange. The apartment looks nothing like the girl I remember. It is fussy and adult in a way that seems like a pretense. The couch is long and narrow and covered in a silk brocade that is slippery and sticky, even beneath the sheet. There is a glass case full of painted china figurines of shepherdesses and sheep. I cannot sleep so I count them, I cannot sleep and then I cannot sleep, and then I dream of the faces I drew on the boat, and other faces that I do not recognize, each look at me in turn with haunted eyes and beg me to record them, I cannot keep up. I am woken by the sound of the door. A man walks into the room, a silhouette in the darkness. He pauses over me and I can hear him breathing. He smells of cigarettes and engine oil. When I open my eyes again it is almost noon. The apartment is full of sun and I am alone.

*

The first morning I woke up in this apartment, I was afraid to even leave the house, I wasn't sure if I could find my way home. I was starving, but unwilling to take food that did not belong to me. I ate a single slice of bread spread with a greasy yellow smear I found in the fridge, and that was my introduction to American bread, American margarine, so soft it nearly choked me. After that I cleaned the house—the sun put a spotlight on every dust bunny, every surface that needed polishing. Even the air was thick with dust, illuminated gold like flecks of mica. At least that surprised me not at all; Helen had always been a slob. I tied back the curtain and opened the windows. I wiped down the glass of the display case, the wooden coffee table. Under the sink was an array of cleaning products I'd never seen, yellow rubber gloves, a sponge and pail. So many products, and most of them unopened, untouched. I guessed at their functions and mopped the floor on my hands and knees. The house smelled of lemon and bleach.

Helen opened the door at five o'clock exactly and stood still in the entranceway, assessing the scoured, tidy space. Then her eyes widened and she threw both her hands up towards her mouth and ran for the bathroom. I could hear the heaving from behind the closed door. I boiled the water and made a weak cup of tea, with milk and sugar. I brought it to the bathroom and knocked. The door was unlocked and when I came in she was still on her knees on the tile, her nylons ripped, her hair in her face, her red lipstick smeared as if she had been vomiting blood. There's chicken in the fridge, she said, and the words brought her to the edge again, she gripped the seat of the toilet and leaned back over the bowl. I went to the kitchen and made three pieces of chicken. At some point, she moved from the toilet to her room, and lay down with a wet towel over her eyes. I ate a piece of chicken and called her, but got no response. I wrapped the other two pieces in plastic wrap and put them in the fridge. I called her again and when I got no response opened the door. She was lying on the bed on top of the covers and seemed to be asleep.

At night, once again the shadowy figure came in late. This time he went to the kitchen, turned on the light, and ate both pieces of chicken.

In the morning, Helen asks me to fill in for her at work. It's ok, she says, you don't need to know anything. I mean, you already know how to sew. They'll show you what to do. My clean clothes, washed in the tub the night before, are still damp. Helen sits on the couch that is my bed and smokes cigarettes as she watches me prepare.

I'd offer you clothes, she says, but they'd swim on you. She has a habit of smoking the cigarettes only halfway, and then rubbing them out in the glass ashtray on the coffee table that I had washed and polished the day before. Already, there are five cigarette butts, arranged like petals in a circle, each marked by the red bite of her lacquered lips.

*

Something is wrong with Helen. She is pale and silent and even as her stomach expands her face grows thinner. In our village they would say, one child, one tooth. The women who had many children walked around with smiles full of black holes. The baby takes what it needs. It is eating her from the inside. As I leave the house in the morning I can hear her retching in the bathroom. When I come home she is usually lying in bed, the curtains down. The bedroom smells of sour vomit and cigarette smoke. I long to clean it out, but she is never out of bed long enough for me to get a chance.

It is piecework at the factory and Helen is right, it isn't difficult. The girls are only a couple of years younger than me but I feel ancient beside them. Yiddish is our common language, and their lips move faster than their fingers. On the first day, they asked me lots of questions, but I felt too exhausted to answer, and now they talk around me, weaving bright ribbons of conversation in the air. What can I tell them? I am a Pandora's box of monsters and ghosts and grief. If I open my mouth, they will possess you all. It is fascinating to watch these girls in their innocence and their ordinary unhappiness. They glow.

I feel the most kinship with the janitor, Leo. Like me, he is a recent arrival, the cousin of the owner, which explains how he has a job at all. I see him when I go outside to smoke. When I asked him where he was from he said Sobibór, as if he had no home before it. Then he would not talk to me for the rest of the day. He sleeps in the coal cellar, and sometimes when he comes upstairs he is covered in black dust. After he wakes up he will not use words, only bark like an animal in response to my conversation. Sometimes he is covered in bruises. In one of his lucid periods, he tells me it is because he often feels the need to walk in the middle of the night. He never has a plan, only goes where his feet take him, and always they take him to dangerous neighbourhoods. Sometimes he is beaten. He laughs as he shows me his new lacerations, the technicolour bruising around his eye, the scraped skin on his elbows from when he was pushed on the sidewalk. It's hilarious, he says, that they think they can hurt me. When he is tired of talking to me he walks away without saying goodbye. He is a monster—he frightens children, he seeks out pain, and none of the other women will talk to him. I feel more like him than I do like them, with their gossip and hair ribbons and silly crushes and pricked fingers.

*

I am tired and thin from working all day and looking after Helen, looking after Helen's husband. But all the activity invigorates me; every minute of my day is accounted for, and when I lie down to sleep I black out completely. Helen invites me to move into the bedroom, and I insist on cleaning it first. She lies like an invalid on the couch, wrapped in a crocheted blanket, and I do as much as bleach and fresh air and elbow grease can do. I cannot completely obliterate the sour smell—now partially concealed under the smells of Clorox and Lysol. Helen's nausea seems to be passing. She is settling into a peaceful apathy. She shows no signs of wanting to return to work, and I do not ask her. I have figured out how to be indispensable.

★

The days pass quickly. It is winter now, and Leo the janitor has disappeared. Helen is round and heavy, her features lost in flesh. She eats all the time—she claims it prevents the nausea—so I follow her around and pick up sandwich wrappers, napkins, fruit peel. I don't understand her relationship with Abe. They seem like strangers. Sometimes I catch him looking at her with an expression of hurt, dull resentment.

The other night I came home late from work, wrapped against the cold, and I was surprised to find him sitting on the stoop, drinking beer, without a coat to keep him warm. I tried to step past him, and he caught my hand. His hand was warm—he must have just come outside, and his cheeks were flushed though that might have been the drink. Tell me, he said. You knew her when she was a girl. Was she like this? I disengaged my hand, and remembered Helen's mother, Rachel. She was always wandering around the town, looking for one child or another, in a state of sloppy distraction. She always wanted the children to come home, even when the rest of us were allowed the full range of the forest and the river for our wanderings, from morning until dusk. When Helen and I saw her, we would run away, and she would stumble after us, but she was heavy and clumsy, and we were weightless and immortal.

Helen said that her mother was always afraid that something terrible would happen to them. She wouldn't let them near the stove to cook, or to the water to wash clothes, which meant that when she wasn't chasing them, she was working her fingers to the bone keeping them fed and clothed. For that, they laughed at her and ran away when they saw her coming. Despite her hypochondria, they were all remarkably robust children, never sick. Somehow, she understood that they were in danger. Maybe if my mother had been crazy like Rachel we would have left Europe in time. I do not tell him about Rachel. Instead, I say she was a normal girl. Which is exactly the wrong word to describe her. Neither of us ever wanted to be normal. I can smell danger on his breath, so I insist on going inside.

★

Abe is gone almost all the time now. He comes home to sleep, or not at all. Helen is underwater. I do my best to look after both of them, but I am also planning my escape. A girl at work has a spot opening up in her rooming house, and she has agreed to introduce me to the landlady.

One night I hear voices in the living room. I listen at the door to the men talk about the coming war. My boss from the factory is there, and his voice is the loudest. He says they will cover the guns with stockings headed for Hungary. From there, the guns will go to Palestine. They are going down to the pier that night. I want to go with them. I am tired of being a woman and wiping crumbs off kitchen counters. I want to smuggle guns under cover of darkness. I want to ride in the belly of a ship. I want to be shot from the barrel of a gun and bring death to my enemies on arrival.

I cannot sleep that night. Instead, I watch Helen. A string of drool reaches from her mouth to the pillow. There is no comfortable way for her to sleep anymore, and she takes up almost all of the bed. Her belly moves like the ocean. I sneak an arm over her, and I can feel a curious nosing through the skin against my palm. It recedes, then reaches out again—an elbow or a foot. Helen said when she sleeps the baby is most active. She claims that's the reason she is tired all the time. It feels like it is reaching out to me, playing with me, through the barrier of fluid and flesh. It feels like we know each other already. I finally fall asleep that way, spooning Helen's back, my arm flung across her, and I wake up only when she shakes me off. What are you doing? she says, and I don't have a real answer for her. I was asleep, I finally say and she bites her lip and looks at me, her hair falling over her eyes. Any day now.

★

The apartment has been empty for three days, ever since Helen's water broke. I have found somewhere else to live. In three days, my new room will be ready and I am longing for four walls and a door to call my own.

I have been taking home remnants from the stocking factory, the discarded remains of gussets and toes. I started putting them in my pocket before leaving, fingering the silky material with guilt as I walked down the street, but no one ever stopped me. This seems neither permitted nor forbidden. I stitch them into small puppets, stuffed with toilet paper, neither representational or abstract. Some have a single eye, or a scarlet slash of a mouth. They keep me company. I hide them in my suitcase even though no one is there to see them. It is late at night, and I am working on a new one, sitting on the couch, when I hear the key scratch in the door, and the door swings open, dramatically, like a stage prop. There is Abe in the yellow pool of light from the bare bulb in the stairwell, he is unshaven and gigantic, his shirt untucked from his pants, his shoes unlaced. A child is swaddled against his chest. I drop my needle and stand up. He hands me the child and stands still, his arms are empty again. They dangle against his body as if something in him has broken. The baby is so light and so hot that I am afraid to hold him, he is like a burning flake of ash. He's hungry, Abe says. He turns around and slams the door, leaving me alone with this damp new creature, this half-formed person, this clinging ball of appetite and need. This gift.

I don't even know his name. I don't know if he has a name.

That first night is a blurred dream. I walk out of the apartment into the night, holding the baby, that warm almost-no weight, in my arms. I knock on doors until I find a mother willing to give me a pile of soft folded clothes, a handful of pins. The baby had cried out when Abe held him out to me but as soon as I put him on my chest he falls asleep. His eyelids are two corrugated purple shells, and he sucks on his lower lip in his sleep. In the morning, I will have to find a bottle, and formula, I will have to find someone to tell them I can not come to work. I will have to give up my dream of a solitary room. I lie down in the bed, my head propped on the pillow, and let him sleep on my chest. In the middle of the night, he wakes up and exhales a scrawny cry, weaker than the cry of a cat. His eyes are blind and panicked and his curled fists pummel my chest, pull at my hair. Hungry. I walk him back and forth, singing every song I can remember, and then making up the words when I can not. I am crying too, and my breasts feel a heavy longing. I feel a kind of pinching, a compression. Finally, I pull down the neck of my nightgown, I hold him to my beading nipple and with a hiccupping shudder, he begins to nurse. Everything changes. His face, which had been so wrinkled and furious and red, relaxes and softens. His eyelids close. He isn't just sucking, he is swallowing. His whole body releases into my arms and I realize, this was the reason I had ended up in this apartment, and maybe this was the reason I had lived through the war."

A miracle. Or not a miracle. Restitution.

In the morning, there is money on the kitchen table, enough for a month's worth of groceries. A note that simply says, His name is Moshe. I am in a sleepless twilight, but very calm. I put on my nicest dress, bought with my first paycheck—the buttons already straining at the bosom—and my most comfortable shoes. I have a long list of things I need to buy.

As I walk onto the street I find myself conspicuous. Like so many of the rest of us—the new arrivals, the refugees—my presence had been a kind of stain, something shameful. That I was living with Helen and Abe seemed scandalous, and then there was the deeper scandal of my suffering. They had rescued us too late, and now we needed everything, had broken accents, mysterious ailments, bad dreams. The community didn't know what to do with us, now that we were saved but not grateful.

But everyone must have heard about Helen, and the baby is a pass into their world. Women who had never given me the time of day rush out of their doorways, and I am given for free what I had ventured out to purchase. A blue carriage with a quilted white interior. Armfuls of soft tiny clothes that nonetheless looked like they would swim on him. Swaddling clothes and a knit blue and white blanket. Caps to cover his bald head, and socks to keep his feet warm. He still looked peeled and raw, he was so new. He smelled of baking bread. His hands like starfish, opening and closing.

After the long night, he is tired, and as soon as I put him in the elegant carriage, he sleeps. I walk to work, but the owner, Abe's friend, already knows. He tells me Abe would be gone a little while. He had left money to take care of me, if I needed more I could ask him. He isn't sure how long Abe will be away. Of Helen, he says nothing. I think of her, bleeding and bereft in a hospital room somewhere, her post-birth bedlam, and her weeping breasts. Or not frantic at all but sedated, a white body in a white room. I sit in the park under the star-shaped blossoms of the linden tree, breathing in the smell of lemon peel and honey, and I rock the carriage with my feet. It is as if a little piece of my wandering soul has settled back into the hollow space at the bottom of my neck, right where his head rests when I pick him up.

★

Moshe is a placid baby. He wants to be held all the time, but as long as he is in my arms or in my bed he is perfectly content. He also likes to walk in the stroller and watch the shadows of the leaves as we pass below the trees. He started smiling recently, a hesitant flicker like a bubble bursting. When I pretend to be his mother, I am happiest, but often, when I walk down the street I remind myself that I am his nurse or his surrogate, and he is not mine for always.

His eyes are moonstones, his eyelids heavy, like a crack that holds the light.

Helen knew about me, but I don't think she told Abe. Once, when I was undressing for bed, I saw her appraise the silver snail trails on the sides of my stomach, the faded brown seam that still runs to my bellybutton. She didn't ask me any questions and I like to think that it was tact, not apathy. I wonder if she named him Moshe because she knew she would give him away.

The other mothers seem like children to me. Their babies cry, and I comfort them. Everyone remarks on what a happy child Moshe is, though they think it is strange that I hold him all the time, not understanding that is the reason for his calm. How will you teach him to be independent? one mother says to me. Her child spends his days in different containers and harnesses, lifted from crib to high chair to stroller. She has on a full face of make-up, and her red lipstick has smeared onto her front tooth. I lift my shoulders and drop them. The world has a hundred ways to keep us from one another. From me, this child will know only love.

★

On Moshe's six-month birthday—the birthday of when he washed up on my doorstep in the ark of his father's arms—the door opens, and Abe returns to a different child. Moshe now sits up by himself. He plays with his hands and reaches for objects. He babbles liquid vowels and plosive consonants. I sometimes hesitate to smile at him because he smiles back so fully, so compulsively, that it seems coercive, as if I have forced him into joy.

Abe is thinner and browner. I do not ask him where he's been, where Helen is now. He rolls a little on one leg as he walks over to look at Moshe asleep in my arms, and without meaning to, I clutch the baby to me more tightly. The baby stirs and wakes up, batting towards my breasts. When he starts to cry, it is with a hiccupping incredulousness, since I know what he wants and have never before hesitated to provide it. I take a bottle to the park, though usually I feed him at home. The mothers around me seem to think breastfeeding is disgusting, low-class. Like a cow, one said to me once, nodding at a woman on the other end of the park who had retreated into a kind of cloth tent to feed her child. And then, there would be the obvious question, since they know he is not my child, even if most seem to have forgotten. Moshe is now bright pink, he is beating at my shirt with his fist. Abe catches my eye and nods. It is almost as if I have never seen his face before, he has always been in the shadows, turning his eyes away when I pass him in the hallway, coming home late at night and leaving early in the morning. I thought he didn't want me there so he refused to see me. It was an easy, crude solution. His eyes are like Moshe's, and as I look at him, his pupils dilate as if to take me in. Slowly, I unbutton my shirt and the room is now completely silent.

★

We have no words for this. Now I leave Moshe in his lordly carriage to sleep, parked in a corner of the living room. I lie in bed and wait. Sometimes I drift off, and he never comes home. Sometimes he slips into the sheets beside me and lifts off my nightdress, we swap our skins for some other, better substance, slippery with each other. He smells like sweet mulch rotting in the woods. It was never like this for me before, liquid and ravenous. I was a wife but not his wife. I was a mother but not Moshe's mother. I was and now I am, and the three of us are something more than family.

I say nothing, but the women at the park can smell it on me. They stop talking to me when I walk Moshe underneath the linden trees. I start to wonder what it would be like if Helen never comes home. I start to visit other parks, farther from the neighbourhood, where no one knows my name.

★

Moshe wants to stand up all the time, on his fat and sturdy legs. It is a compulsion. If there is a ledge or rail, he must pull up on it. He strands himself, clinging to his support, since he has not yet figured out a way to sit back down, and so I must let him down gently. He will even walk, if I hold him by his hands, like a marionette, thrilled with the illusion of autonomous movement. His babbling constellates into the stubs of words. When Abe hears him call me ma, Abe looks mutinous, but says nothing. One day, I say to him, do you have a plan, and he slams the door and does not come back for two days.

I wear Helen's clothes, belting them because they are loose. I use her perfume and her red lipstick. I start to coil my hair back from my forehead in the style of the young women in the neighbourhood, to roll it at my neck. I speak in English, not in Yiddish, slowly and deliberately, so I can control my accent. The days belong to Moshe, the nights to Abe. Sometimes when Moshe naps, I take out my pad and pencil and draw again. I draw his face, the feathers of his eyelashes against his cheek, the indrawn pucker right below his bottom lip. My little puppets lie neglected at the bottom of the suitcase. I have something else to play with now.

If Helen never comes home.

*

When we arrived in the camp, I was so thirsty I was half out of my mind. I had found a little corner in the train, against the wall, and sat there on the floor, hovering over the baby to protect him. I nursed and nursed so that he would not cry and I was like an exhausted saddlebag, an empty well. When we came out blinking into the light three old women were standing by the tracks, like the fates. Quick, one of them said, and held out her corky arms.

PART FOUR

1.

Bella's notebook was a gift, but one I did not know how to receive. I kept trying to puzzle over her, my grandmother, my father, and it was like the labyrinthine lines she drew in the margins of the pages, they all looped into each other like a dream that dissolved once I tried to figure out what it had to do with waking life. Finally, I put her notebook on the bookshelf next to my novels and philosophy texts, and decided I would return to it once the term was over.

I kept looping back to an image of Bella falling down the stairs. I imagined her stepping out into a vast darkness, as if she had fallen down a well. Was it really an accident? Her note felt final, as if she knew, a way of settling her affairs. E.M Forster once described the difference between story and plot. The king died and then the queen died is a story. The king died and then the queen died of grief is a plot. The queen died of grief, of grief, of grief. I went over it in my mind again and again. The expression on her face when I told her that my father had died. How the last time I visited she could not wait to get me out of her house.

The night I finally slept with Jacob—it just took not leaving the bar early, it was that simple, and surprising I hadn't figured it out earlier—I came back around one in the morning. I walked home from his place on the Lower East Side. He was the kind of guy who had embraced feminism because it spared him the inconvenience of paying for my taxi home, or offering to accompany me. In theory, I agreed with him, but in practice I felt abandoned as I trudged up Houston Street.

I passed a young couple pushing a stroller, and I wondered at them, out so late at night. They were dressed identically, baseball hats, baggy jeans, sweatshirts. From behind me I could hear her voice, loud in the still of the night, because even New York got quiet if it was late enough, those broad avenues bereft of traffic.

"Are you looking at that girl?" she said. "Why are you looking at that girl? You want to give her the chlamydia, too?"

I walked faster, and as I finally stumbled up my staircase, I was startled at a pale figure sitting on the floor in front of my door. Persephone had fallen asleep like that, in her thin white nightgown, her knees drawn up against her chest, her cheek pressed against the wood. I stood over her and put the key in the door, gently. I leaned down and picked her up, light and leggy in my arms, and placed her on my bed. She swatted at her face, still mostly unconscious, and then opened them and looked at me, her eyes in the dark like almonds dipped in chocolate. Her eyelids sunk closed again and she grunted—a surprisingly loud, indelicate sound—and rolled over on the bed. I went to the futon and covered myself with a towel. I didn't think I would fall asleep, but then I woke up, and the room was full of sun. Persephone was gone. She had folded the blanket at the foot of my bed, but otherwise she left no trace.

Fiona had lost her job again, though she didn't tell me that. She was often at home in the middle of the day. I'd hear loud music through the door as I walked up the stairs, would smell the piney, skunky smoke. I bumped into people going in and out of her place, mostly young men with skateboards under their arms, snarled dreadlocks, and blue tattoos on their pale skin. They sometimes left the front door propped open, and among the tenants of the building, there was a growing rumble of discontent, only no one could get a hold of the landlord, a hippie who had bought the place quite cheaply in the seventies and now spent most of the year in Mexico. I could hear the bass from her apartment under my feet, a steady and sneaky invasion.

I tried to ask Persephone, but she didn't want to talk about it—they're my mother's friends, she said vaguely, and when I asked her if they bothered her she shook her head. I gave her a key, and she spent more and more time in my apartment, which was often empty, because I was spending more and more time at Jacob's apartment. His indifference was an aphrodisiac. Because he was so critical about the world, a reflexive response to his general disappointment and heartbreak (every cynic a mugged romantic)—it was intoxicating that he had chosen me, wanted me, even if I wasn't sure if it was a choice or if I had just rolled into his lap and would one day roll off again, unmissed. He was so passive that sometimes he would skip a meal rather than get up and get something out of the fridge. Without intending to, I started to mother him, laundering the grey sheets, sweeping the dust bunnies from under the bed, washing the fucking dishes. I didn't even really notice I was doing it until it became a habit, and then an expectation. Anyway, our bodies were built for each other, my head fit right into the crook of his neck, our feet wrapped around each other on the end of the bed.

Because I was there more often, and home much less, Persephone spent a lot of time alone.

For the last day of class, I organized a party and printed a little zine of student writing from the semester. I told my students it was important to think about themselves as artists, and in order to do so it was helpful to see your work in print. I was bluffing. I'd never published anything myself.

I had barely heard from Bo since his final visit to my office hours. He kept skipping class, and his assignments arrived in my box without explanation, and often late. I couldn't figure out who owed whom an apology: I felt stupid that he'd tricked me, but guilty for the assumptions I had made. I had my grades ready to file, polite A minuses like debutantes all in a row, and for Bo an ambivalent B minus, what could I do?—based on the requirements of the syllabus, I should have failed him. I didn't think he'd submit anything to the zine, but he dropped something off the night before I printed it, a handwritten poem.

> The sky is blue this morning, so blue. I want to eat the blue. I want to paint my body blue, and to rise into the big blue of the sky. I want the edges of my body to vanish so all that is left is a sunny day and a bright blue sky.

I liked it, enough that I went back to my grade sheet and erased the "minus." I knew how it felt to want to disappear. Instead of typing the poem up, I pasted it on a page, handwritten as it was, and took the whole package to the copy store on Astor Place where a bored clerk with a long earring that connected his septum to his earlobe handed me a pile of stapled zines that were still hot and left my hands black with ink. I brought Entenmanns cookies and baby carrots, big bottles of soda and plastic cups. I had told the students to invite anyone they want, and a few brought friends, mostly for the free potato chips. The students had also brought food, especially the girls, I realized with consternation, and we were arranging the treats on the tables when Bo walked in. I wasn't expecting him to show up. Behind him trailed a middle-aged couple, smiling and neatly dressed. Of course, no one else had brought their parents.

"So cute!" I heard my student Stephanie trill behind me. "He looks just like his mother!" Which was true, except he had told me she was gone. Bo kept his head low, his eyes down. The parents headed straight towards me.

"You are the teacher?" the man said. His wife stood nodding and smiling beside him.

"Yes," I said, and my stomach was like an elevator whose ropes have been cut.

He had an accent, though his son did not. Bo would still not meet my eyes. His mother smiled and nodded so intently that I realized she probably didn't track the conversation at all.

"Thank you for inviting us to your party!" he said. "And for teaching my son!"

He ducked his head, and his wife smiled even harder.

"Of course!" I said, and my stomach began to settle. "A pleasure!" I felt compelled to echo his enthusiasm. Teaching Bo had been many things, exciting, frustrating, confusing, but not in any sense a pleasure. "It's so nice of you to come all the way from Westchester!"

"Westchester?" he said, bewildered, and Bo pulled him by the hand to the snack table, and then out of the classroom, and then to vanish into the bright blue sky. I mean, of course I would never get an answer.

And even now, his essay, true or invented, is the only one I still remember from all my years of teaching composition.

I walked right past Fiona on my way home that night, at around 11. I didn't realize it was Fiona at first, just another girl on a stoop, her hair in her face, dressed in a tank top that left her too exposed for the weather. She was nodding off, her head slumping towards her shoulder, then snapping upright again. "Fiona," I said, "are you alright?" A silver trail of drool stretched from the corner of her mouth to her shoulder. "Fiona?" I tried again, and reached down. She was so thin, her elbow was like a jumble of sticks, her clavicle a hollow scoop. She shrugged me off, hard, which was reassuring in a way, it meant she wasn't as far gone as it seemed. I left her there, sitting with her head in her hands, and went to look for Persephone. She wasn't in my apartment, and I hoped she was in her own apartment, asleep. I didn't want to wake her up by knocking on her door, but I was nervous for her. I would have to see her before I could feel settled. I would have to try to talk to Fiona. I didn't know what the next steps were, didn't have anyone to call. I could parse a sentence or write a paragraph or summarize a deconstructionist while standing on one leg, but I had no skills for this, no experience, and it wasn't my business, anyway. I thought of Persephone's face, how serious it was behind the smooth curtain of her hair. I thought of the feel of her hand in my own as if I was someone who could be trusted.

2.

As Fiona dropped out, Hank stepped in, coming over in the afternoons to help Persephone with schoolwork and taking her home with him on weekends. It wasn't that I had forgotten what Fiona had said about him, but Fiona seemed so unreliable now, her relationship to the truth casual and instrumental, something you might feel bound to or not. Anyway, did people not change? Hank seemed to have settled into his role. He was starting to fill the space of parent even as she vacated it, because somebody had to take care of that child. I often followed them to the park in the afternoons, playing hooky from grad school and the sheaf of papers on my desk.

Anyway, the weather was irresistible, New York's famous tulip spangled Spring, that brief respite between slush and sauna. The colonnades of cherry blossoms calling me outside, Persephone's knock on the door, the feel of the grass in the park under my bare feet.

"Bare feet in Tompkins Square?" Jacob snorted when I told him. "You're braver than I am." The warm weather lulled me into recklessness.

One afternoon at the park, Hank said, "You should come to Beacon with us." He was pushing Persephone on the swing, and the movement had long ago become hypnotic. I was sitting on the swing beside her, shuffling my feet back and forth on the wood chips.

Swinging helps develop proprioception, a sense of the shape and place and weight of the body in the world. When children swing back and forth for hours, or spin with their arms held out to catch the wind, they are working, even though it seems like what they are doing is the very opposite of work. But at certain point, a switch in the mind flips, and those circling, whirling, swinging motions no longer intoxicate, they nauseate. I remembered swinging like Persephone all afternoon, when I was a child, higher and higher until my feet flew over my shoulders, until I almost flipped the swing. I remembered the moment of suspension when I leapt from the highest point and felt like I was flying, not falling. I used to love that feeling. Is that what it meant to get older—learning that what you loved now makes you sick? I hadn't been on a swing in a long time, and the discovery of my vertigo was as vertiginous as the physical feeling in my stomach. But I didn't get up. I was not comfortable but I still wanted to stay.

"Come with you," I said. Like stupid Echo in the myth.

"Why not?" he said. "We're going up this weekend. It's an hour on the train—well, a little more. That's how I found the place, you know. I drew a circle around New York City to mark about an hour's distance, then I starred the train stations, then I visited the towns. Well, just the one town. I saw Beacon first, and I stayed. It spoke to me."

"Towns don't talk," Persephone said, her face hidden behind her hair. She was sometimes stubborn about the literal.

"Brooks babble," Hank said. "Like the one that runs behind the house."

"And engines roar," Persephone said promptly. "But they don't talk." She jumped off the swing.

She was objecting to something else, I realized, something that was not language. She liked to have me close, to have Hank close. It was possible she did not like the idea of us getting too close to each other.

"I liked it," Hank said. "Am I allowed to say that?"

Persephone shrugged, and dropped backwards into an arch on the grass. She lifted one leg and pulled herself over from a backbend to a standing position, careless and graceful. In this light, her hair was like her mother's hair, many shades of fair: maize, flax, champagne, amber, lemon. Women on the Upper East Side paid a hundred dollars every three weeks for hair like that.

"Beacon," I said.

"It's changing out there," Hank said. "They just started construction on a new museum, in an old biscuit factory. The town needs it, well, it needs something. Don't get the wrong idea—it's not a pastoral village. It's an old factory town, only the factories all shut down. But the town is right in the middle of the Hudson Valley, and right next to the river. During the Revolutionary war, they lit fires on Fishkill mountain to let the Continental army know where the British troops were stationed."

Continental army? I nodded as if I knew what he was talking about.

"My horse's name is Black Beauty," Persephone said.

"I keep him at a friend's farm down the road," Hank said. "That was the idea, when Fiona and I decided to move out there. That it was good to raise kids near the country, but we wanted the city too. Then she changed her mind."

"What?" I said. I'd never heard about a move to the country.

Persephone had wandered off and was picking dandelions in the grassy verge of the park. Hank lowered his voice.

"I don't know what she told you," he said. "But that's what happened. My mother died and left me some money—not much, most of it went to the Tibetan friendship society, I wasn't expecting to get any of it at all. You see, she lived off family money, but she told me she felt no need to perpetuate the inequality of inherited wealth. She also didn't want Fiona to get her hands on it—she didn't trust Fiona. Turns out, about that she wasn't wrong. As soon as I bought the house, Fiona announced she had no intention of moving out there, that she never had intended to do so, that we hadn't been happy for a long time and she needed some space. Then she vanished. That was when they went to India. I heard from her two months later. I didn't know what to do."

"That's not what she told me," I said. "She told me you left."

Hank shook his head. "You know me, Alice," he said. "Would I leave?"

I nodded my head like a dutiful student. Though of course, I barely knew him at all.

"I knew she'd be in touch when she needed something. I settled into that house by the Hudson, and I guess I went a little crazy. It was the middle of the winter, and it felt like I was the only person in the town, it was like a place that had been abandoned in a post-industrial apocalypse. It was a very cold winter—it's a little higher up than New York, and north, February is just bitter. I had a little more money left over after I bought the house, and I decided I'd hunker down and wait. Work on this book I had to finish. I wouldn't see people for days, I forgot how to talk to them. I didn't come into the city for months. Then one day, I looked down at the river and saw the ice was breaking up. The light had changed, and even though it was still frigid you could see the spring was coming. I came home and there was a message from Fiona, she said they'd be back in a few months. But she was already here, she just hadn't decided to tell me yet."

"I don't understand that," I said. "She had your daughter."

"You don't know Fiona," Hank said. "It has to be on her terms.

She is capable of anything." He stopped speaking, because Persephone was back. She had twisted dandelions into a crown on her head and she offered us each a ring of the cheerfully bedraggled flowers. Hank dipped his head, and then took the second crown from her hands and held it out to me on open palms. I nodded as he anointed me his dandelion queen, and then I forgot that I was wearing it until much later in the day, on the subway, when I noticed I was getting curious stares for my snarled and wilted crown.

3.

On Friday, I took Fiona to Grand Central, where Hank said he'd meet us. The train station was an entirely different place, depending on your perspective. If you looked up, you saw the famous vaulted dome, the turquoise and gold grandeur of the constellations, an indoor heaven. But if you looked ahead, the train station was hell, a saturation of the worst of New York, hectic urgency and anxiety, people moving like a swarm of angry bees, so that if you did stop to look up at the ceiling or the marble arches, you were in danger of being plowed right over.

I had the wind knocked out of me by a teenager's enormous backpack, and had despaired of finding Hank when he found us, slung Persephone's pink backpack over his shoulder, took my bag, and led us through the crowds in a serpentine slither that opened up space in the impenetrable halls. We were just on time for the train—no sooner had we boarded than I heard the double chime of the doorway closing and the siren sound of acceleration.

The train was full, but not with the kind of weekenders I'd expected, headed out to their country places on a Friday afternoon. I saw families, mothers and children, looking strained. They sat in tight clusters, plastic bags around their feet but with no luggage. Hank followed my gaze. "There are two prisons right outside Beacon," he said. "Fishkill and Downstate. It's visiting day on Friday."

I looked again, and the woman across from me stared back at me, so fiercely I lowered my gaze. Whatever I had to offer—pity, curiosity—she was having none of it. Persephone had opened a book of crossword puzzles and was oblivious, slotting letters into little boxes. "What's a six-letter word for a new world vegetable," she said. "Potato," I said, even as Hank said "Tomato," and we both laughed. "Tomato, tom-ah-toe," I said, and then I felt flooded with sadness. My father used to sing that song to my mother, grabbing her around the waist and waltzing in the kitchen, when they were young, long before the twins came along. "Potato, pot-ah-toe," Hank said, "we better call the whole thing off."

He was older than Fiona, certainly closer to my mother's age than my own, but age was just a patina on his beauty. As we sat in the train, I saw women noticing him.

Persephone looked up, from my face to his, suspiciously. "Why do you both know that song?" she said, and I said, "Well, everyone knows it."

I was sitting beside Hank and she was opposite us, and I realized that she felt like an outsider. We were the adults and she was the child, she had been put in her proper place, when so often she was surrogate adult, friend or sister. She was her father's confidante, her mother's caregiver.

I shifted over in the seat beside her and said, "Look, it must be tomato, since that's toenail across," and her shoulders relaxed as Hank looked out the window to the river.

The outskirts of New York were ragged and industrial—a city shows you its backside as you leave it, every periphery a rubbish heap. But then, as we headed towards the Hudson valley, the landscape turned pastoral, fields, ponds, low hills that rose the farther we went from the city. Persephone finished her crossword, and we played tic-tac-toe though she was far too old for it, patterning o's and x's in endless stalemate. Hank fell asleep, his head thrown back against the seat, his hands loosely open on his knees. When the train pulled into the station, he was momentarily wild-eyed, dissociated. Persephone reached out her hand, and pulled him into wakefulness.

What had I expected? Quaintness; a church with a steeple; miniature houses held in the cup of the valley. And indeed, the hills rose around the town in protective beauty, and the town opened up onto the quicksilver of the river. But the railway station was derelict, the main street we walked down full of shuttered buildings. There was trash on the sidewalk, and people standing on corners looking lost, sometimes leaning on grocery store carts full of duffle bags and old coats, though there was no grocery store nearby. "Welcome to upstate," Hank said, and Persephone picked her way over the broken glass of bottles delicately, as if lifting a floor length ball gown. "This is what happened when the factories shut down. The big industry up here is prisons. At least, until the museum opens."

I averted my eyes—was it more respectful to look or not to look? A man smiled at me as I passed, and the inside of his mouth was a black wreck of rotten and missing teeth. He had sores on his face, and was wearing two coats, one over the other, though it was a warm afternoon. I heard people whisper to each other as we walked by, and quickly, needles were hidden, and illicit activity backed into alleyways—it was as if the street was a stage set, and theatre curtains dropped as we passed, masking the illicit backstage activity and preparing the route for Persephone. Hank walked quickly, without looking from side to side. "It's just Main Street that's like this," he said. "It's because they've all been pushed out of New York, they have to go somewhere. When the museum opens, just you wait, it's all going to change here."

He turned, and we followed him to a block of little cottages. His house was sandwiched between two others. One was well kept-up, with a row of begonias—those vulgar waxy show-offs—and an American flag planted like a stake. The one on the other side was derelict, unpainted, windows hung with sheets, and the yard full of old lumber and abandoned, sun-bleached toys. Hank's house was somewhere in between, the lawn full of dandelions but cheerful, the porch needing paint but swept. A shiny new lock had been put on the door, and he needed three different keys to open it. Persephone waited impatiently, shifting from foot to foot, and as soon as it was open ran inside and scooped up a tortoiseshell cat. The cat squirmed in her arms, and I noticed it had only one eye. "Darling," she said, "have you been good? She is a very good pussens."

Hank pulled tomatoes out of a basket and started chopping them, the movement of his hands fluid and assured. Persephone was on her knees, talking to the cat in a quiet and serious voice.

I thought of Fiona's kitchen, the sticky counters and floors, the fridge full of beer or nothing at all. I had been feeding Persephone for months, I realized, but I hadn't been doing a very good job. For four years, when my mother was in graduate school, I ate the way I'd been feeding Persephone—spaghetti and ketchup, tuna and crackers, the occasional afterthought of a bowl of baby carrots and "Russian" dressing made with mayonnaise, and yes, more ketchup. She also made meatloaf and burgers, mashing egg and breadcrumbs and onion soup mix into the mealy red ground beef with her hands—but when I was six it occurred to me that the meat looked like raw red worms, and after that I refused to eat it, my disgust extending into the slimy skin of chicken, the glaucous eyes of fish, until I had exiled myself from the entire animal kingdom. I also refused to touch those limp carcasses, so I never went into the kitchen. My baby brothers, those twin carnivores, ate chicken greedily with their fingers, devoured hot dogs and burgers, made a mash of their meatloaf, and then shoveled it into their ravenous little boy mouths, so after they started eating solid food, mealtimes became a test of my nerves and stomach, and more often than not I retreated into my room with a jar of peanut butter, a granola bar. The ways we damage our children as we protect them—my mother grudgingly let me ignore the kitchen, and accommodated my squeamish vegetarianism, if minimally. And so, I became an adult who could not cook.

Neither had it occurred to me that knowing how to cook was desirable until I watched Hank pour olive oil into a saucepan, fry garlic with fresh tomatoes and pull oregano leaves right off a plant in the kitchen window. I thought of the last meal I'd eaten with Jacob, a can of tuna scavenged from the pantry with day-old bread. He couldn't find a can opener, so we used the beer opener, notching the can all along the rim. I cut my finger, and he didn't have a Band-Aid. I couldn't remember when my last tetanus shot had been. We ate while sitting on the bed.

Each of Hank's movements, small as they were, seeded themselves in me as full of possibility. I would start to buy food, not jars; I would fill my windowsill with pots of herbs. I did have one cookbook, the first Moosewood, with its unappetizing taupe cover and long lists of ingredients that defeated me before I began. I would buy others. It's odd now to think how revelatory this was for me—the tomatoes sizzling in the cast iron pan—except I was still unwrapping myself from my childhood, when everything your parents once did when they raised you is like a veil that filters your perception of the world. I was just starting to look around and pilfer the habits and rituals of other adults, like a magpie thieving to build its own nest.

And perhaps it wouldn't have impressed me as much, if I hadn't started to fall under his thrall, his profile lit by the window, his hands confident and strong. Boys, I had been surrounded by boys. I didn't know exactly how old Hank was, but he was a man, and I realized the appeal of a person who was already at home in the world, and not in a protracted process of adolescent becoming. He opened the lower cabinet with his foot to toss some scraps. In the gloom, I saw bottles lined up like soldiers under the sink. He shut it quickly, then looked over his shoulder at me as if to check if I had noticed. I turned, not quite fast enough, to the bookshelves that lined the wall.

Mostly literature and poetry, some philosophy, arranged by genre and alphabetically. Auster, Baldwin, Bellow, Bowles, a lot of Burroughs. David Foster Wallace, of course. Had I really been paying attention, that bookshelf could have told me a lot about the man standing at the counter. A little brass figurine was lying on the bookshelf, and I picked it up. You could tell it was a woman—she had a marcelled hairdo, and distinct globular breasts—but she was split down the middle below the shoulders, her legs splayed, jagged teeth on either side of her stomach. "Do you know what that is?" Hank said, and he took it from my hands. There were walnuts in a wooden bowl on the table. He placed one between her legs, squeezed, slipped out the dry, cranial nut. "It's Dutch nineteenth century, I think. But it looks a little like a Henry Moore, doesn't it? Form following function." I didn't much like walnuts, but I took it from him and put it in my mouth. Persephone came inside with a handful of wildflowers for the table. Hank put Nina Simone on the record player, and we sat down to eat, man, woman, and child around the wooden table, like an advertisement for paper towels or family bliss.

4.

Persephone knocked on my door early the next Sunday morning, as was our custom. But this time, I was asleep—I had stayed up late at Jacob's apartment, as he tried to break up with me. I kept trying to talk him out of it, but then at a certain point I gave up, and was overcome by the sheer bachelorness of his apartment—the dust bunnies under the bed and in corners, the unwashed sheets, only three mugs in the whole house, one with a broken handle, and books stacked on the floor in the absence of shelves, each—Foucault, Barthes, Derrida, Habermas, Levinas, Deleuze, Virilo, dear God, Baudrillard—a kind of an alibi for a life in which everything else had been neglected or expired, like the milk in the fridge which I had tried to pour into my tea. To think I had initially been attracted to that unworldliness, the blinking, bespectacled eyes which seemed to see further than the ordinary demands of the world. As soon as I reached that clarity, he flipped and started trying to talk me back into staying the night, it was so late, giving it, giving us, another chance, though he had initiated the break-up himself.

The more he begged me to stay, the more I needed to leave. As I walked out into the chilly night air at two in the morning I felt righteous, then relieved, then cold and foolish as I limped home in my stupid, too-tight shoes. So, I was confused and discomfited when I heard the persistent knock on the door and when Persephone stumbled inside—she must have been leaning on the door, trying to hear if I was coming. I just wanted her to go back downstairs and leave me to my hung-over self-pity and remorse, the nausea over what I had and had not done.

Persephone wore a sundress covered in daisies and a straw hat topped in sunflowers. Her sandals revealed that each toenail was painted a different colour, a rainbow. She put her hands on her hips and looked at me in disappointment.

"I'm making you coffee," she announced, and bustled towards the kitchen, I was clearly not her first grown up with a hangover. I followed her into the kitchen and sat down heavily.

"You forgot," she said, boiling the water and spooning the coffee into my French press. "But it's ok. We don't have to go."

She spoke with the resignation of a child used to the failures of adults.

"Your birthday," I said, and I stood up so quickly I had to sit down again. "But I didn't forget. I have a present for you. It matches your dress. And we're going to Coney Island."

She smiled then, cautiously. "Really?" she said.

"That was the plan," I said. "I wouldn't let you down," I said, very nearly having done exactly that. Had I stayed at Jacob's. Had he been even one iota less disappointing. Had she given up knocking on my door.

I was glad to have a gift, at least, wrapped in tissue paper and hidden in my underwear drawer. I had found the purse in a thrift shop, and it was made of silk brocade, with a delicate pattern of purple heliotrope. The gold clasp was in the shape of a butterfly. She tested it with a fingernail, opening the purse and peering inside.

"The woman at the shop said it's very old," I said, aware how little that must mean to a girl near the beginning of her second decade. "They made purses out of the silk of kimono sashes, from Japan. You could put your allowance in it."

I stopped talking, feeling foolish. And she was suddenly on my lap, her hair tickling my face, smelling of honeysuckle and jasmine—a scent I had noticed on Fiona, she must have borrowed a little bit of her mother's perfume before heading out that morning.

"I absolutely love it," she said. "It's the nicest present anyone ever bought me."

I was so pleased and a little uncomfortable to be embraced, and I still felt sticky and unclean from the night before, having collapsed into bed as soon as I got home—Jacob's smell on my fingers, a wet stickiness between my legs (and a lurching realization, had we used something, I couldn't remember). It was almost unbearable to have Persephone so close to me, the gold down on her arms, her glowing, poreless skin.

"I should take a shower," I said, gently detaching her limpet arms. "Thank you for making me coffee. Would you like to wait for me here or downstairs? I'll be ready in ten minutes."

She was still entranced by the purse. "Look, there's a secret pocket," she opened it up and stuck her pinky finger inside.

One of the best things about the apartment was the shower. The water pressure was hard and the water was always hot. I stayed under as long as I could stand it, and then turned the hot water tap off completely, blasting myself back into sobriety. I brushed my teeth and spat red into the sink, then got dressed in the bathroom. Persephone was reading on my window-seat. She had found a copy of *Great Expectations* on my shelf and was already immersed in it. "You can take that," I said, but it wouldn't fit into her little bag. Walking down the street with Persephone made me feel the grimness and grime of the street—the trash and empty bottles left from Saturday night, the sour smells that rose from the sidewalk, the men sleeping on cardboard under the awnings—but none of it seemed to bother her, she picked her way through the trash in her delicate sandals, impervious, untouched. Even more: she seemed like the queen of the block, everyone knew her, and she had a wave and a smile for each of them, even the dogs waved their tails as she approached. Just by walking down the street she turned it into a neighbourhood. I had lived there just as long as she had, nearly, but there were people I had passed a dozen times without ever saying hello to them. Persephone knew them all by name.

I had never been to Coney Island, though I had seen black and white photographs from the fifties, beachgoers packed so closely together that there was no sand visible between their towels. We took the F train all the way, and the subway was quiet, with only a few pale partygoers making their way home from the night before. You could tell because of the way they were dressed, and because they were sleeping, their heads against the hard seats. "How do they know where to get off?" Persephone whispered to me loudly, but somehow, infallibly, they did. At each stop one or two shambled out like zombies until we were the only two left on the train as it climbed out onto the elevated track into the sunlight. Persephone was fascinated by the roofs of the houses and the unusual, birds-eye glimpse of the neighbourhoods of Brooklyn. "Look, a garden!" she said, every time we passed a shabby patch of green.

I was still hung over, nauseous from the rocking of the train, and I looked outside to calm my stomach and to keep her company. I felt a new sympathy for Fiona. It was exhausting, rising to Persephone's interest, her immaculate enthusiasm. One wanted to respond with wonder at the site of a patch of grass from the subway window, even if it was clearly a shithole, littered with old tires and an exhausted laundry line.

At Coney Island, my spirits lifted. There were the few odd

blocks towards the beach—old garages turned into suspicious antique shops, furniture with a fallen-off-the-back-of-the-van quality, diverted rather than acquired. Though I sometimes spent time by the muscular East River, from Manhattan I was used to thinking of the water as the navigable parameters of the city rather than its open spacious limit. That is, I wasn't used to tracking the waves until they reached the permeable ever-shifting horizon, not sea nor sky.

It was still early, and only a few families were on the beach, though fishermen already lined the pier with white plastic buckets of bait and lobster traps. Persephone pulled me by the hand. "Look," she said, and there was the dreamscape of the amusement park, brightly coloured roller-coaster cars and the cycle of the Ferris Wheel where the cars hung, suspended, against the backdrop of the sullen grey Atlantic. We were the very first inside.

Persephone held my hand, and once again I felt a strange awe in the face of her childish trust. She wanted everything: the tall drinks in neon colours with arabesque straws, to ride the comet and the dragon and the pirate ship and the tea-cups, to play the midway games, fish bowl and duck pond and whack a mole and milk bottle. We were both hopeless. When I swung the large mallet to ring the bell, the chaser barely deigned to lift to the second measure on the tower, then sighed and descended. The carnival barker who had taunted me into a first try felt so sorry for me that he let me go again. And in the meantime, Persephone had dissolved in giggles, her hair was messy and undone, there was a purple stain on her delicate dress, and her face was dirty. I hadn't ever seen her so utterly childlike, which made me realize, not for the first time, how unnatural her usual composed maturity was, as if she was left to carry adulthood in her mother's dereliction. On the Ferris Wheel, suspended at the very top for that extra beat that always makes you imagine you are stranded, she turned to me and said, "This is the best birthday I have ever had," which was such a cliché that it shouldn't have had the power to puddle my heart and force me to look into the distance so that she wouldn't see me tearing up.

Only later it occurred to me that there was something sinister about a child compelled to be so constantly, unremittingly charming, as if it were a kind of camouflage. Not sinister about her, I mean, sinister about the world, which could not otherwise be relied on to protect her.

My own parents had been busy and protective and cheap, in about that order. I had no memory of ever going to an amusement park, and the pleasures of my childhood were carefully doled out and fenced in. The park was full of dangers—I had to sit down at the top of the slide to watch out for sharp edges, territorial wasps, wild children. And when I was young, there wasn't quite enough money—my mother in school, my father in his residency—so that when we went to the ice-cream store or bought a hot chocolate, I would watch her carefully count the coins into her palm, would watch her lips move and her brow furrow as she measured out the consequence for our monthly budget of my moment of greed. I watched her almost always go without. I always offered her a bite or a sip, and she would take a tiny bit, a tremulous nibble, and then smile at me widely as I ate the rest. She was hungry for me to have treats rather than to eat them herself, and she would ask me if it was good at least twice in a tone of expectation and excitement so that, despite my sweet tooth and innate greediness, I always felt a sense of obligation as I licked the ice cream into oblivion or swilled the thick dregs at the bottom of the cup, a compulsory enjoyment which slightly attenuated the pleasure. As I grew older, and money got easier, we stayed in the habit of thrift, and I internalized their protectiveness. By the time the twins were born, I was sixteen. We were now wealthy, but they were very busy with these two young cubs who had a childhood so different from mine. It wasn't just that I couldn't recognize it, it was also that I couldn't recognize my place in my family, and so I slipped out, unnoticed, into stranger's homes and parties in squats and clubs that shouldn't have let me in.

Which is to say that being in an amusement park with a child was like recovering a piece of my childhood that I hadn't realized had been lost, and I didn't say no to anything, even when the fairground food and the rides made me sick to my stomach. We retreated from the fairground onto the boardwalk and, as the day went on, it was as if we were watching a parade or carnival. The passersby were ever more costumed and spectacular—two bodybuilders holding hands, her leopard print bikini the same pattern as his Speedo, each muscle on their body picked out as if they were those flayed anatomical drawings modeled on Marsyas, as if their own skin was thrown casually over their arm like an overcoat. A man with a toucan on his head and a woman with a boa worn around her neck as a scarf, a boy who had a seagull perched on the handlebars of his bike like the figurehead of a boat as he pedaled past us, the beak his prow. An entire phalanx of rollerblading dwarves. We stayed late to watch the sunset, and I quoted the Langston Hughes poem to her—"The sun, like the red yolk of a rotten egg, falls behind the roller coaster" and she pointed out, sensibly, that a rotten egg had a greyish or greenish tinge to it, not red, and then cracked herself up giving alternate similes—"like a bloodshot eye," "like a blushing ping pong ball," "like a bloody tooth." While none of them were very good, or even came close to Hughes's not entirely accurate gut-punch of an analogy, I couldn't help but be utterly delighted by her love of language. "You have the soul of a poet," I said, and she ran off with that too, claiming that she also had the feet of a drag queen, the ears of a wombat, and the eye of the tiger.

She fell asleep on the way back, and I wrapped her in my sweater—it was large enough on her to seem like a shawl.

As we stumbled home, groggy and sunburnt, Fiona was waiting for us on the stairs outside the apartment. Her cigarette flared bright red, like a stop light, and as we approached she stood up. She was shaking with rage.

"How dare you," she said, grabbing Persephone by the shoulder, pulling her away from my hand.

My sweater fell off Persephone's bare arms onto the sidewalk, and she stood there, shivering and blinking in the streetlights. Fiona's hair was wild, like a thousand snakes lit up in the sulphuric light. Her eyes were red, her face was pale, and her face was distorted into a mask of rage.

"You're hurting me," Persephone said, and Fiona loosened her grip, marginally, red half-moons on Persephone's white arm. Then she let go so that Persephone stumbled, Fiona had her that off balance.

"Upstairs now," she said. "I'll deal with you later." Like a wraith, Persephone dissolved into the dark of the staircase.

"I thought she told you," I said. "We had a plan. I took her to Coney Island, for her birthday. I thought you knew. She said she left you a note. She said you were working today."

"Working," Fiona said bitterly. She seemed much more composed now. Her face had smoothed out and her breath was even. She sat back down on the stairs, pulled her knees up to her chest, and now she seemed like a child and not a mother, as if the departure of her rage had left her deflated.

"I cancelled work. Got there, told them I couldn't stay. It was my daughter's birthday. My daughter. I came home, and she was gone."

"The note"—I said, and she said, "Yes, I got the fucking note." She seemed exhausted.

"It isn't your fault," she said, as if trying to convince herself. "But you need to understand that you took that from me. My daughter's twelfth birthday. I'm never going to get that back. I came home, and she was gone, and for a moment I thought I'd lost her forever. And I thought, this serves me right. This is my punishment. But it wasn't my punishment at all, was it? It was you. You and your shitty good intentions."

She stood up again and her shawl slipped off her narrow shoulder. For a moment, I could see what looked like puncture marks on her arm in a constellation like the big dipper, curving towards her heart. She grabbed the shawl as it slipped and covered herself again. She looked me straight in the eye as if she had nothing to hide. And the truth was I wasn't certain what I'd seen. I broke eye contact first, looking down at the sidewalk and at my sad collapsed sweater, I bent to pick it up, and by the time I stood up she was gone.

5.

The next time I went to Beacon, Hank promised we would go on a hike. He kept an old truck out there, and we piled in to visit the waterfall, Persephone sandwiched between us. She wanted to go see her horse, and he compromised, saying we could see the horse after we went swimming. The way to the waterfall was a green shady climb on a muddy path, and then the woods opened up to the cascade tumbling into a clear pool.

"And pore upon the brook that babbles by," I said, trying to impress. I had taken a class on eighteenth century poetry the year before, with a professor who dampened any possible interest in his subject with his grey pin-striped suits and deliberate monotone. All I remembered was Thomas Gray's "Elegy Written in a Country Churchyard"—"the most loved poem in the English language" our teacher intoned, unlovably—and the first lines of the epic poem "The Fleece," which I would recite sometimes if I was drunk enough, stepping onto my chair unsteadily and throwing back my head. "The care of sheep, the labors of the loom, and arts of trade I sing!"

"Full many a flower is born to blush unseen." Of course, Hank knew it. "I always thought that poem was insufferable," he said, "As if he believes the flowers only exist because he has written about them. There was a romance about rural life in the eighteenth century, mostly on the part of people who didn't have to live out the consequences. Like Marie Antoinette with her hermitage of perfumed sheep." He was sitting on a flat rock untying his shoes.

"We didn't talk about that in class," I said. "We talked about heroic couplets." He shrugged and pulled off his shirt.

Persephone was already in the water, dressed only in her underpants, her chaste white chest still flat, her nipples pale pink dents. "It's very cold," she said. Already, her lips were cyanide, though she waded in further, towards the falls. Hank leapt to catch up with her and as he splashed her, cold droplets brilliant in the sunshine, she shivered, hugging herself with her arms. I lagged on the shore, shy and uncertain, and then resolved to strip and get underwater quickly. I was wearing the wrong brassiere, stretched out and an unerotic shade of taupe, old cotton underpants. But then the rocks were too sharp to walk on quickly, so I hobbled, near nude and unnoticed, trying not to shield my body with my arms. The water was a knife. I held my breath waded in further. They were already underneath the falls, half obscured by the veil of water, laughing and shouting at each other to be heard over the roar of the falls.

Afterwards, we lay on the rocks in the sun to dry off, and Persephone fell asleep, or seemed to, her dress her pillow. We were still all alone in the grove.

Hank said, "This is why I moved up here, away from the city. I need to be in nature. Those skyscraper canyons, they're beautiful, but so unnatural. Each one a tower of babel, a challenge to the divine. I need to feel the grass under my feet, not interred in a tomb of concrete. Even in the middle of Central Park you can hear the city. All those tall buildings, they block the sky. I couldn't breathe there."

"I've seen the most beautiful sunsets of my life in New York," I said. I was thinking that the countryside often made me paranoid and anxious—all of that teeming, undomesticated nature—and that the city was the first place I had ever felt free, walking down the street in the middle of the night as if the sidewalk belonged to me.

"That's the pollution," he said.

It didn't occur to me until later that Beacon was—in a way—like Gray's country churchyard. Hank belonged to the tradition that Gray seeded and Wordsworth tended and Thoreau brought to the New World. Thoreau, who didn't even do his own laundry but carted it to his mother's house once a week. Thoreau, who burned half the woods down in his carelessness. And here Hank was, smoking and extinguishing his cigarette butts on the rocks like any litterbug. I felt angry at him, but I wasn't sure why—for insulting the city, and by extension, those who lived there, for being such an inconstant presence in his daughter's life, while presenting his choices as unassailable. I mean, the cognitive dissonance was maddening for me.

We stayed until dusk, when the mosquitoes swarmed our ankles and inner elbows. Persephone was bitten particularly badly—one of those girls whose blood is sweet—and she had a ring-a-rosy of red bumps on her wrist, like a bracelet. Hank said it was too late to visit her horse, and she cried wildly, her face a wet mask of misery. I'd never seen her like that, so undone. Her hair was knotted and wet, she had an angry burn on the back of her neck, and she scratched at her wrist until it bled. The sky grew dark very quickly, as if someone had dropped a blackout curtain over the sun—it was the mountains, Hank said, blocking the light, on the other side it would be day for another hour. Rounding the corner, a white truck rose apparitional, high lights blinding, and we swerved to miss it, breaking branches on the side of the country road. Hank leaned on his horn and Persephone covered her ears.

"Fuck," he said, hitting the wheel.

"You need to slow down," I said mildly, and he looked at me with such hatred that I had to turn away, staring intensely into the black tangle of the woods.

He pulled into his driveway and slammed the car door, unlocked the house and left it open. I opened the back door for Persephone—she was floppy, tired out from crying and all that sun—and led her inside, where I helped her wash her face, and found calamine lotion to dab on her poor wrists, a wet towel for her sunburn. She had a room at Hank's place, an austere camp bed and a dresser, a vase with a single peony in it, white and blush at the center. I thought of Hank preparing for her visit, cutting the peony from the bush in front of the house and putting it in water, and my heart softened towards him again. I hadn't been able to see, before, that he was fragile, a man whose daughter had been kept from him. So much was riding on these weekends. He was, weren't we all, doing our best.

Persephone had fallen asleep, and I tucked her in. Her long hair on the pillow, the soft curves of her face, were like a Victorian illustration of childhood innocence. When I came back out, Hank was sitting on the couch, holding a glass of wine. He was calm, so calm it seemed impossible that he had been so angry. He had lit a candle, which was our only illumination. He nodded at the bottle, and a second wine glass on the coffee table. I poured myself a glass and sat across from him.

"She's asleep," he said, and I nodded.

"It's difficult," he said. "I want to give her everything. But I get so little." I looked up, and he added, "Time with her, I mean. So, everything is magnified."

"You could talk to a lawyer," I said.

"She'd disappear again," he said. "Fiona would take her. If for no other reason, to punish me."

"That's abduction," I said. "That's a criminal act."

"So what? Let's say they found her. Let's say they charged her. Then I send my daughter's mother to jail? I can't do that. No, this has to be on Fiona's terms, I'm checkmated. There's no good move for me to make. Believe me, I've thought of every possibility." His shoulders collapsed towards his chest. He was on his second glass of wine. I was drinking to match him without realizing it, my glass already empty, my body settling into a sloppy, legless warmth.

I got up and went to the sink to fill a glass of water. Flirting with Hank was a bad idea. But what had I come out there for, anyway?

When I came back, I sat on the couch beside him.

"How is—your poetry going?" That was the stupidest question that had ever come out of my mouth, probably.

There was a secretary desk near the window, a typewriter, though we were well over a decade into the era of personal computers, an Abe O'Hara collection nuzzled up against Wallace Stevens nuzzled up against William Carlos Williams, a piece of paper half-through the carriage, something written along the top that I was dying to read. But he perked right up.

"It's a long poem," he said. "I hesitate to say epic. And about a loss, not a homecoming. Too much American poetry is about plenitude—Whitman with his endless catalogues, Ginsberg's shopping lists. I wanted to write something haunted, something empty." The flames of the candle guttered in his eyes.

"Loss of what?" I said, and he said, "Loss of a child."

Then he leaned forward, and his mouth tasted of wine and tobacco, his cheeks were rough, and I drew back without intending to, and then bent to meet him. Nonetheless my mind rose out of my body and watched us from the ceiling, saw the two wineglasses and the half-finished bottle, the flickering candle, like a tableau of seduction, saw him lift my shirt and unhook my bra with one hand, put a pillow under my hips and pull a condom from his pocket—so practiced and insulting, expected—saw myself, flushed and pliable underneath him.

There was a line in Wallace Stevens that taunted me when I was having the kind of sex that makes the mind unhook from the body, "if sex were all/ then every trembling hand, could make us squeak like dolls"—and then a little cry, like air escaping from a balloon, anticlimactic even as a climax. Hank collapsed on me on the couch then lifted up almost immediately, rolled off, went to the window and opened it, lit a cigarette. The air was cool.

"Don't tell Fiona," he said, looking into the dark yard.

I pulled down my shirt and sat up, pressing my legs together, groggy and guarded.

"I wouldn't," I said, like a kid promising to keep a secret.

"She has no claim on me," he said, defensive. "But still, she doesn't need to know. We're all adults." As he said it, I remembered that he was, in fact, twice my age. Forty-six. And Persephone had just turned twelve. We divided into each other, a simple math problem about a young woman who had lost her father and an aging man with a growing daughter. The great betrayal of bohemian rebellion is that it is very predictable. I was exhausted.

"It never would have occurred to me to tell her," I said. "I'm going to the bathroom," I said. "Where do you want me to sleep?"

He flicked the cigarette butt out the window, and nodded towards the same couch.

"Fine," I said.

There was only a small hand-towel in the bathroom, and a tub, but no shower, so I squatted down and wash myself off, scrubbing hard, with an impulse towards self-mortification. Stupid stupid stupid.

When I came back out, a sheet was thrown across the couch, a folded blanket at one end. His door was closed. On the ceiling there was a water spot that looked like a bear or a large dog, the stain kept shifting shape, like Wittgenstein's duckrabbit, until it was chasing me down a corridor in a dream, breathing hard and hot on my neck, until I found a room and slammed the door against it, Hank was in there, lying on his side, odalisque-like, in his underpants on a bed, we started to have sex as the bear slammed against the doorway, it's fine, he kept saying, it's fine, she's asleep, and then I realized that Persephone was lying beside us, her eyes closed, as silent and as still as the princess in the fairy tale whose long sleep is a kind of death and who is woken with a kiss, which, if someone has ever done that to you, you know is a really terrible way to wake up.

The sun rose at six, and there were no curtains in the living room. I woke to a sour mouth, a throbbing head, a nauseous feeling of regret. I found coffee in the drawer but no filters, and made a muddy cup cowboy style and drank it black, grains sticking in my teeth. There was no sound from Hank or Persephone's rooms. I rolled my clothes into my backpack, brushed my teeth with a finger—I hadn't been prepared—and walked back to the train. I knew they ran on the hour. People were asleep on the sidewalk, on beds of cardboard, rolled into sleeping bags that covered them as completely as cocoons. No one stirred. Hank could figure out what to tell Persephone for himself. Hank, Fiona, even Persephone. I was done with all of them.

6.

May already felt like August, the heat a wet dog breathing down my neck. I couldn't sleep. I slid open the kitchen window and climbed up the fire escape to the roof in my bare feet. It wasn't much cooler up there, and as my eyes adjusted to the darkness I saw a figure like a ghost at the edge of the roof, in a gauzy white gown, wreathed in smoke.

I must have gasped out loud because she turned, and as she turned became ordinary, as ordinary as Fiona could be, in a nightgown that looked Victorian, just like the one her daughter wore, with a cigarette clasped between the fingers.

"What's the matter?" she said. "Oh—I'm not going to jump! You weren't worried about me, were you? No, I never would kill myself—you see, I'm worried the world will disappear without me. And that would be a shame." The tip of her cigarette flared red, then faded. "I'm just looking at the whistle guy down there. Do you see him?"

I walked towards her, carefully, on the black tar roof that still held the heat of the sun. For a second, I imagined that when I joined her, there at the edge, she would grab me by the arm, push me off.

"Afraid of heights?" she said, and she pointed a toe like a dancer over the side. "Just kidding," she said. "Here, sit with me."

She sat at the end, with her feet dangling over, and I joined her, holding onto the gutter. The whistle man walked the streets at every hour of the day and night, blowing a rape whistle on a string around his neck at intervals of three, a crazed urban birdsong. Many a time I'd wished him dead. A man was lying in the middle of the road, and it could have been him, but I wasn't sure. He was face down. Cars swerved around him, honked impatiently.

"I like how they don't even slow down," she said. "Such coordination. Oof, that was close."

Squeal of brakes, angry honk, the smell of burnt rubber all the way up to the roof.

"How long?" I said, and she kicked her heels against the brick like a child whose chair is too short for her heels to reach the ground.

"I don't know," she said. I just looked down and he was there. "Maybe he's been there all night. We should take bets."

"We should help him," I said, but I did not move.

The man stirred, a heap of clothes with the memory of a person inside it. He rolled onto his side, got up, staggered to the curb and out of sight. We heard the tripartite salute of the whistle, heard it fade as he wandered toward Alphabet City.

"You would have really left him?" I said, and she echoed, mockingly, "You really would have left him?"

"I just got here," I said.

I had backed away from the edge of the roof and was standing again. The moon was full that night and cast a cold light. She rose to her feet in a single movement, her silhouette a shadow under the pale gown.

"You can't take responsibility for anyone else," she said. "You're an adult. You know that. He made a decision."

"You're a mother," I said, and she looked away, her fingers holding the cigarette and shaking at her lips, her inhale so long I realized I was waiting for her to exhale. She threw down the cigarette in a shower of sparks, and then realized she was barefoot, spat on her fingers, kneeled down, and pinched the butt to extinguish the flame. She lifted her hand and drew a cross on her forehead with the ash.

"You don't know anything about being a mother," she said. "You don't know anything about having a daughter. You're in no position to lecture me about responsibility."

"I didn't mean to"—I started, but she was shaking her head.

"You think I've taken her away from Hank. You think he's the victim here. He's good at that. Getting women to want to save him. Wounded warrior, blah blah blah. He's not a victim, honey. He's a predator. And you're a slut. I know about last weekend."

She said to me, "You want to steal my life. But you can't have it. I never want to see you again. Oh, and stay away from my daughter."

As she walked past me she leaned in as if she was going to kiss my cheek but instead moved to the left, her breath in my ear.

"Your cunt stinks," she whispered.

I drew back, but she had a half smile on her face, her forehead unconcerned. Had I heard it wrong? Could she possibly have said that to me?

She opened the door, and let it slam hard behind her. I was alone. I sank down and sat there, leaning against the closed door.

"I would never hurt her," I said to the no one standing there.

A week later, I got a postcard from Berlin. "Travelling man," it said. "Had to go. Look after her for me." Hank's signature was barely legible. There was no return address.

7.

My grandfather's prize possession was a beige Cadillac Eldorado convertible. I remember him driving with the top down, my grandmother beside him in her oversized sunglasses with a scarf around her hair. When he died, she left the car parked in their space in the underground lot. I don't know why she didn't sell it, except that it was a kind of totem. He loved that car, and everything you love holds a piece of you. As long as it was parked below her, perhaps she felt a little less alone.

But like so many women of her generation, she had never learned to drive. In fact, that was the only advice she had ever given me. "A woman needs to learn to drive," she said. "It's your independence." I think by the time she realized that, it was too late—she was too old and too afraid, and then later, her eyes were too bad to take her own advice. In her later years, she rarely left the house. She was not much for gifts, she never remembered a birthday, but she had paid for my driving lessons.

It was nearly summer before her estate was settled. When my uncle called me, he sounded furious.

"She's left you the car," he said. "I can't imagine what she was thinking. You live in Manhattan. That goddamn thing is eighteen feet long."

I had never heard him swear before. That was one of the many things that had divided him from my father, who had been intransigently obscene in all contexts, including parent-teacher meetings in elementary school.

"That car is a fucking classic," he said, and again I heard the shock of the word in his mouth. "If you sell it, you sell it to me. You better get it this week, the co-op wants the parking space back, and I'm not paying for another month."

"Will it start?" I said, but he had already hung up.

I picked the car up from the lot under my grandmother's building. I drove the city streets like a tugboat perilously navigating a canal. The car revved aggressively when I touched the gas pedal, and it felt like I needed to brake for miles. I turned more heads in that car than my body ever did.

When I inherited the car, I decided that once the term was over I would visit the address on the envelope. Helen's mystery man. I would go on a real American road trip, away from Fiona and all the rest of it. The truth was, I hated the Beats. But even as I squirmed and laughed at their bogus bohemianism, their predictable misogyny, I found their vision sneaking under my skin, that rolling film spool of the open road.

Jacob laughed at me when I told him I wanted to go to New Mexico, to see what I could find out about my grandmother. "What makes you think he'll be there?" he said. "It's been—what—forty years? He may not even be alive. You know, you can just write him a letter." After Beacon, we had started to see each other again. I had planned to ask him to come with me, but after that I decided to go on my own. Of course, it was more sensible to write a letter, or find a phone number, or give up on the idea of this absurd quest to find out more about a woman he would likely not even remember. But the idea had sunk little hooks into my imagination and would not let go.

"You don't even drive," Jacob said, throwing up his hands—his father had him circling empty parking lots when he was twelve, and he had a manly disdain for city-raised and car-shy Easterners.

"But I do," I said. My father had taught me to drive. Those lessons were the only time we ever spent alone, without the insulating layer of my mother or the distraction of other children. True, the lessons were a disaster. He was nervous and angry, and I was hysterical and pathetic. Once he grabbed the wheel from my hands and swerved us hard to the side of the road while I hit the brake in terror.

He kept slamming his foot on the floor of the car, which alarmed me, of course, and when I asked him what he was doing he said, "I'm slamming the emergency brake!" At least we both laughed at that.

Despite the fact that he was a terrible teacher, and I was a terrible student, I managed to pass the driving test at the end of the summer—my instructor, casual and lazy, even let me repeat my attempt at parallel parking. I had driven very little since then, but I kept paying for my licence, so I would never need to take that test again. And I had spent the last couple of days practicing driving, mostly because I had to constantly move the car for street-cleaning, and it was nearly impossible to find a spot for that giant chrome albatross.

"Your ass is much bigger than you think," one stranger called out after my third time trying to back into a spot too short for the car, and I didn't know whether to curse or thank him as I pulled away.

The end of term was a predictable blur, I had to give in my papers, I had, now, two men to avoid at school, who met me in hallways with hurt and accusatory glances. I had my own work to do, and I was in no mood to think about Hank, to navigate Fiona, to worry about Persephone. Besides, I was drunk on spring.

I walked home, one soft night, in such a springtime reverie—all my work for the term was done, and I was free of encumbrances, I almost danced down the street. As I ran up the steps I saw that Fiona's door was covered in papers. I stopped and peered at the papers in the dim light. Eviction notices, beginning days earlier—how long, then, had I not been paying attention? The door was padlocked and chained. They were gone.

I lurched up the stairs, as if I was falling and not climbing, as if the dimensions of the building had changed, and each step was too tall or too short. My heart felt peeled open. I stopped at the top of the staircase to catch my breath, and then I saw something that looked like a soiled heap of white laundry on my doorstep. I gasped when the pile stirred: a ghost in a long white dress, a thing that goes bump in the night, an apparition with bare and dirty feet. A sleeping child.

8.

Just like the first day she came to my door, I made her mint tea in a glass. In the beginning, she did not want to speak. She hunched over her cup and kept putting in more and more sugar until it was undrinkable. Her hair was in her face, her face was in her hands. "What happened?" I kept asking, until I too fell silent, watching her stir her tea into a little whirlpool, looking at her dirty fingernails, the bruises on her knuckles where she had knocked and knocked and knocked.

She had gone to the park that morning, as usual. Fiona was sleeping, as usual—"At least, I think she was," Persephone said, hesitating, biting her little finger. "Her door was closed." She came home when she got hungry, and it was then she found the locks on the door. She would have let herself in to my apartment, but my key was also locked inside. She'd been all over the city, to the sinister black diamond on Astor Place, to the bars on St. Mark's, to Union Square, to the Lower East Side. Not only did she not find her, she didn't find anyone she knew at all. It was as if she was a ghost, people looked right through her. The strap of her sandals broke, she said, she dropped them in a trash can and kept looking until it got dark. Then she came back to look for me. "But don't you have a phone number, a friend, anything?" I said, and she looked like she was going to cry. "I am so hungry," she said again, and that shut me up. The fridge was nearly empty—I was leaving the next day—but I found two eggs and the heel of a loaf of bread, scrapings of jam and butter. I flashed on the day I came home to find her eating uncooked spaghetti dipped in ketchup because no one had thought to feed her. She ate everything I put in front of her, she ate the cupboards bare, and then she curled up in my bed and fell asleep.

I lay awake for a long time, thinking of her father, who was a postcard from Berlin without a return address, thinking of her mother, with her serpent's nest of hair and her dead eyes, remembering the violaceous nebula I once spotted on her thigh. Thinking of Persephone's fallen body, like an unwrapped gift on my doorstep.

Around three in the morning, I realized I had no choice. I would have to take her with me.

We went to breakfast at a diner because there was nothing more to eat in the house. Over burned bitter coffee and runny eggs, I told her I was going away, and she bit her lip and looked away. "You could come," I hastened to add. "Road trip!" My fork flew out of my hand and by the time I had retrieved it, she was nodding her head, like a student who knows the answer but is too shy to raise her hand. Where else would she go?

9.

Once we decided to leave, it was an adventure. Persephone had no clothes except the long dress she was wearing. They were all locked behind the door, and no potion would allow her to slip beneath it.

We went to the Salvation Army on Fourth and bought two sundresses covered in daisies and roses, a few worn, soft T-shirts in violet and aquamarine—she had a child's tastes, still, drawn to bright colours and floral motifs—a pair of jeans, though they were difficult to find, since she was suspended between the girl's sizes and the women's sizes, a pair of sandals, a pair of shorts. She tried each on in their little changing room, and came out spinning, as if every outfit had a skirt fit for twirling. I noticed that her breasts were starting to poke through the thin fabric of the T-shirt, but I would not, I could not, ask her if she needed a bra. She must have grown two inches in the last two weeks, it was uncanny.

Next, we went to the Diamond District, that single block in New York whose generic ugliness hides untold treasure. We took a bird-cage elevator up into a hall of locked doors—my neighbour had given me the address. We pressed the buzzer a few times before someone came to open it, a small man wearing a jeweler's loupe and, a long black coat and a high fedora. He had a blondish-brown, whiskery beard, and short, pert peyos almost like mouse ears. He barely looked at us—one eye magnified by a circle of glass, the other half-closed—and he shuffled back to a table in the cover, where he resumed examining a pile of glittering rocks so luminous and out of place in the windowless room. There were two folding chairs against the wall, so we sat down, waiting.

The office door opened, and a woman came out, with the sheitl that was standard issue for Chassidic women—heavy bangs, straight shoulder-length bob, a helmet as much as a hairstyle. She, too, seemed barely to notice us, looking at her feet as she set a pile of papers on the jeweler's desk—he twitched when she came near him, and did not otherwise look up. Hunched over his pile of jewels, he seemed to be drowsing rather than studying them, and every so often would rouse himself with a little shudder.

"Dormouse," Persephone whispered in my ear, and I nodded.

Pausing at the entrance to the office, the woman finally turned around to look at us. She was wide and almost filled the small doorway. In that room, we were both so naked, with our bare knees and arms and necks and wrists, and I could see her noticing and—not exactly judging us for it, since to judge would mean that we were inside her world, but confirming our insignificance.

"You're waiting for Mendy?" she said, in a manner that made it not a question. "He'll be ready for you soon. Maybe you want something to drink?"

"Yes, please" Persephone said, and the woman leaned into the office, and called to someone I could not see in Yiddish. We heard a muffled, guttural response.

My father had once described Yiddish as German spoken with a Southern accent. It was his parents' first language. He didn't speak it, but understood it. And, in the fallen pattern of generations, I didn't know it at all.

She swished back through the door—wide hips, long rayon

skirt—said, "We don't have anything to drink, " and closed the door.

Persephone turned to me with wide eyes. "Well, that was *rude,"* she said.

The jeweler's loupe clattered on the desk—he had taken it off to examine one of the diamonds more closely, and had nodded off while holding it. He looked up, his sleepy eyes finally open, and glared at us in accusation. But then the door opened again, and this time another man was standing there, tall and dark, in a sweeping coat and high beaver hat, the majestic costume of a Galician aristocrat from the eighteenth century.

He looked at us with great curiosity.

"What's your name?" he said to me.

"Alice Stein," I said meekly.

"You know Hindy Stein?" he said.

I shook my head.

"You know Etsy Stein?"

I shook my head again.

"Maybe you're related to Alte Stein?"

This time he shook his head, those heavy fat curls swinging against his cheeks like a watch chain. Stein had to be one of the most common Jewish surnames in America. It meant "stone," and once I'd been told that it might have come from the profession of jeweler or stone-cutter. The Diamond District in Manhattan was a creation of these displaced European Jews, who fled the Nazis with stones sewn into their long hems, their heavy silk linings. Three generations back, his people were probably my people. And behind a blue door in a mountain city, my sister was married to a stranger dressed in the same anachronistic finery.

"Never mind!" he said. "So, what do you have for me?"

He walked over to the jeweler's desk and slammed his hand on it, making the diamonds shiver in their little pile, and startling the jeweler awake. He put a calming hand on the smaller man's head, then he nudged him out of his chair and sat down. The jeweler opened a small door I hadn't noticed and vanished behind it. I took the coins from my pocket. He sniffed at them, weighed one in his palm, then picked up the loupe and squinted at it.

"Not worth much right now," he said. "Better to hold onto it."

"Yes." I said. "But I need the money."

I had come here—rather than the many places on the Lower East Side with the neon signs blinking on and off, "We Buy Gold"—because I heard they asked no questions.

"Not for you I do this!" he said. "For Alte."

He had already forgotten that I claimed no family tie.

He counted the coins with a pianist's long fingers, then pulled out an old-fashioned metal cash box, tried to unlock it with a key hung around his neck.

"Ach, it's the wrong one!" he said. "Hindy, Hindy!"

Once again, the muffled reply behind the door.

"She's coming in a minute." He said. He sat back in his chair, so I thought the narrow rungs might break, and rested his palms on his spread legs. "You know the story of Reb Isaac of Krakow?" he said.

I shook my head. When my parents turned their backs on Yiddish, on the dull weekly ritual of synagogue, on all dietary prohibitions on shelled and swarming things, they had also abandoned these tales.

"Reb Isaac of Krakow," he said. "A poor but very righteous man! One night he had a dream of buried treasure, under a bridge in Prague. At first, he didn't pay any attention. But he had the dream every night, again and again. So, of course, he decided he must go."

He said "of course" with a talmudic dipthong—"of koo-worse"—a gliding insistent vowel which claimed necessity when a choice was arbitrary. It reminded me of the brief period my parents sent me to Hebrew school after my grandfather's death during a mourning period of regret in which they worried they had robbed me of my Jewish education. My sister and I had weekly Saturday afternoon sessions with a rabbi whose sterling side curls shook as he told us stories of heavenly retribution and miraculous reprieve. We sat there patiently waiting for our earthly, not heavenly reward—strawberry licorice and gummies cunningly shaped like pieces of fruit—which he tossed at us from across the table, but only after we'd joined him in a rousing chorus beseeching the messiah to come, come now. I sat now as I did then, my eyes unfocused, waiting for a treat. But Persephone leaned forward. She loved all stories.

Hindy came from the office with an entire ring of keys, and as he spoke he pressed one after another into the locked box, looking for the right fit.

"When he came to the bridge," he said, "he found it was near the castle, and guarded by soldiers, all the hours of the day and night. Oy-vey-zmir! How would he dig under the bridge when the guards were always watching! He came to the bridge, watching, day after day after day."

His hands found the right key and opened the cash box. As he spoke he counted, automatically, twenties and fifties in a neat pile.

"The soldiers grew curious. Why are you here every day? So, he told them about the dream. They laughed. "You came all this way because of a dream!" the one guard said. "You know, I had a dream that a Jew, Reb Isaac of Krakow, buried treasure under his stove! But do you see me chasing it like a fool!"

"A treasure," Mendy said, "of gold coins." He palmed one, opened his empty hand, then pulled it out from behind his side curl. Persephone chuckled appreciatively.

"So, Reb Isaac went home, and sure enough, there it was, under his stove the whole time! A chest of gold!"

He slammed the tin box shut.

"10 coins, I give you for each three hundred dollars, three thousand dollars," he said. "Mazel und bracha." He did not shake my hand.

Our Saturday afternoon rabbi had once told us many stories like this one, stories about fate. Often, they were complicated and elaborate, and involved illness, torture, or mutilation, then compensated by a heavenly redemption. They all ended in the same way. "And so, we know," the rabbi would say, "that Hashem has a plan for all of us!" Hashem just meant the name, and the name was God. His stories gave my sister nightmares, and when she told my mother why, we were pulled us from those gruesome weekly sessions which were somehow intended to illustrate God's benevolence and charity.

But I could see that Persephone ate it up, young enough to still believe in fate—that our suffering has a recompense, that our virtues are rewarded, that someone somewhere has a master score which makes the random strumming of the universe into one grand symphony.

10.

How do you disappear?

It helps if no one is looking for you. Hank was gone, Fiona gone. The school term had just ended, and there seemed to be no other person who cared enough to ask where in the world this young girl had vanished. Though Fiona had been careless in so many ways, she was canny about keeping off the radar of social services, so no one followed her file or checked up on her parenting. Fiona had parents, I supposed, somewhere in England—I imagined a country lane lined with roses, a thatched cottage, I had never been to England—but they rarely spoke. Her disappearance would leave less impression, even, than a stone skipped on the skin of a lake which disturbs the surface only momentarily before the water turns back into a silver mirror.

I told my mother I was taking a road trip with a friend before heading home. She assumed I was going with a secret boyfriend, not with a pint-sized Thelma to my Louise. Though Persephone was less pint-sized every day. She'd entered a period of exaggerated adolescent growth, which seemed unnatural though nothing in the world could be more natural. When we walked down the street, she was nearly my height, opening up like a telescope, and it was clear she would soon be taller than me.

Her character was also changing. Her voice, so bell-like and clear, had become mumbling and hesitant, and even her curiosity seemed to have retreated behind a cotton-wool layer of adolescent indifference. She shrugged more often than she spoke, and despite her new height, seemed to want to shrink into herself. When I was her age, I remembered hunching my shoulders to hide new breasts—it took a while to learn how to wear them, took a while to figure out how to be a woman and not a girl. I tried to be patient with her, though I understood, for the first time, how excruciating my own teenage years must have been for my parents, when I was all sulk and swoon in a world adolescent, technicolour and extreme.

And Persephone had far more to contend with than I ever did.

Persephone had gone through a period of being fascinated with butterflies, and she told me that during the period of metamorphosis, inside the cocoon, the caterpillar goes through a sort of dissolution. In this fallow time, it digests itself, disintegrating into a kind of primordial soup from which the butterfly is reborn. It looks more like death than change; indeed, if the process is interrupted at any point the insect will die. The caterpillar has something called "imaginal discs" which survive the metamorphic process. They hold the blueprints for the butterfly, and from them spin out the adult form of the creature. A little insert in the *National Geographic* article that she was reading explained that these imaginal discs had been discovered by a seventeenth century naturalist named Jan Swammerdam, one of the first to use a microscope in dissections. He saw the intricacy of the insect world as a proof for the existence of God, whose omnipotent finger, he wrote, can be seen in the anatomy of the louse, miracle heaped upon miracle.

I was thinking of the other metamorphosis, in Ovid's version. In the poem, Persephone does not transform. She just goes underground. Instead, the world changes: in her rage, Ceres curses the earth, blights the crops, destroyed by too much sun and too much rain. Her daughter returns, but she is not fully restored, changed by the seven pomegranate seeds she ate in the underworld, and doomed to spend half the year in hell. The cycle of the seasons mimic the manic glee of the original empty nester: bereft when her daughter leaves, and giddy with bud and blossom every time she comes back home.

It was natural for daughters to leave one day, unnatural for mothers. Though Persephone had been left.

She asked no questions about where we were going, and it was this that broke my heart: she seemed to take for granted that the world would move her like a chess piece, and she would follow those cues. We packed our bags in the exorbitant trunk, large enough for a whole troop of little girls.

We drove west, which in American journeys is always the direction of discovery even as north is the direction of freedom.

11.

New York was a different city for drivers than for pedestrians. Persephone sat beside me, in a straw fedora she bought in the Salvation Army for a dollar at the counter, the window rolled down, her feet on the dashboard. Houston, a street which makes no sense when you're walking—so wide, so shadeless—was a piece of cake in a car, though I was already flustered getting onto the ramp at the Holland Tunnel. And then we were leaving the city, through that shiny lavatorial passage, once the longest underwater tunnel in the world, beneath the grey and gloomy Hudson River.

We passed the world's most irritating airport, and flew onto the smooth blacktop bordered with scruffy trees already exhibiting a late-summer fatigue—overgrowth, droopy leaves—though it was still only spring. We drove sections of the roadway sponsored by the Boy Scouts of American, by the Veteran's Association of New Jersey, by the Knights of Columbus, by Weight Watchers, by Alpha Kappa Alpha and Omega Zeta Omega and Delta Omega Ro.

Persephone fell asleep, her head resting on her own bare shoulder, and I struggled to keep my eyes open, because the road was like a swung watch on a hypnotist's chain, it lulled me as the car ate the miles and the miles appeared, ever renewed, on the highway before us. We drove through New Jersey, past Warren and Tewksbury, and Lebanon and Bethlehem and Allentown, which had a life-sized replica of the Liberty Bell, and Harrisburg, where Persephone woke up and announced that she was starving. When we stopped for lunch, we saw a sign for Hershey Park, and detoured there to eat crepes drenched in chocolate syrup. The measurements for the rides were all named after Hershey products—both of us were Cookies 'n' Creme, tall enough for all the rides—and people wore tinfoil hats shaped like upside down apostrophes after the famous candy.

Persephone begged to ride the Sooperdooperlooper, but I couldn't join her, those crepes heavy in my stomach, so I stayed in the line as long as I could, and then joined the loitering parents at the exits, waiting for her appearance and for her unsteady drunkard's dismount. Every two minutes, a car careened down the slope, flash-bulb of a face frozen in ecstatic terror. I watched one person after another streak through fear and glee and be greeted by an earthbound chaperone, and still Persephone did not come. Now it was my stomach doing unsteady loops over the abyss—if I had lost her—imagining hardened Pennsylvania carnies with the entire Bible tattooed on their bodies, men in trench coats, loose iron bolts and safety bars that did not lock—and then she came, flying down with a look of stoicism on her face, sitting beside a family of three who looked absolutely green with nausea.

She didn't even stumble getting out of the car. "That was fun," she announced. "But the line was too long, and they kept holding me back until they had a single seat. Where to next?" But the truth was, I didn't know. I had an end point and I had a vehicle. And I had a travelling companion-cum-kidnapping victim, whom I had almost just lost again. I wanted to turn the car around, three hours back into an East Village sunset. We had been in the park for longer than I realized, it was already getting late.

If we went back, where would she go? While we were on the road, the problem seemed suspended. It was almost as if, when we moved through space, we were outside of time, or even travelling backwards—this park amusingly retro, as if I'd stepped into an amusement park from my own childhood. And as we walked out of the park, we seemed to move even farther back in time, to a cobblestone street with a fountain, an old-fashioned big-top striped the colours of the American flag, and an old-timey painted carousel that circled to the music of a fairground organ.

12.

To cross the country, we had chosen the dreariest road trip possible, where the reward for finally getting through endless Pennsylvania was Ohio. I thought we could make it to Indianapolis for the first night, but I was cross-eyed by Columbus. Persephone had put on her headphones and was in her own world, listening to Hanson and Spice Girls and the Backstreet Boys. Her musical taste was the only age-predictable thing about her, and it was just as well there was no tape deck in the car. We found a motel right off the highway for fifty dollars a night, and as soon as we were let into our room—twin beds covered in orange blankets rough as horsehair, a beige carpet with a faded brown stain, a microwave balanced on the mini-fridge, and the lingering, baked-in smell of cigarette smoke—Persephone sprawled out on her bed and turned on the television.

"Come on, Persephone," I said, "let's get some fresh air."

I was nauseous from the chocolate crepes, from the amusement park rides, from the long drive, from the smell of smoke and the colour of those bedspreads. There were forms of warfare fought with acoustic weapons, outside of the audible spectrum, which produce nausea, dizziness, disorientation. I wondered if colour could work like that, or if this queasy feeling was dissonance catching up with me from when I drove out of my life.

"I want to watch TV," Persephone said, mulish as any teenager. "It's the real world." I didn't know what she was talking about. On the screen, two teens too attractive to be ordinary but not quite as luminous as movie stars, climbed into a Jacuzzi while having a rambling conversation, full of odd pauses and first-date non-sequiturs. The camera lurked like a voyeur. Persephone said, *The Real World*? You know. It's in Seattle this year."

I opened the door, paused, thinking again to invite her out, but she was laughing at the TV, now three new people in an exercise room. Or were they new? It was hard to tell, they looked nearly the same, like dolls who swapped wigs and outfits and now played entirely new characters.

And Persephone, who looked the same, seemed like a different person. I didn't know how to reach her, where the girl had gone.

She still hadn't said anything else about Fiona, and mentioned Hank only once, while I was driving and I thought she was asleep. "Now tell me the truth," she said, and I was startled. I thought she was addressing me, in a coy, intimate tone. "Tell me the truth, Hank," she repeated, "Do you really like poor Alice?" She laughed, then closed her eyes again, and I realized that she had been talking in her sleep.

Poor Alice? That stung me for a hundred miles, though maybe she hadn't been talking about me at all.

I thought I'd find us something to eat, or perhaps to cook in that dismal microwave. I wanted to see the river we'd just crossed, that looked cool and muscular from the window of the car, to explore the streets, to let the wind wash the tedium of the drive from my skull. But I realized that I was walking through a kind of wasteland. There were wide avenues, nearly carless, empty shops with plywood nailed over the windows, abandoned grocery carts full of trash bags, like empty snail shells. Where was I? Two men haunted the corner ahead of me, ducked into a doorway as I passed. Across the water were the blue towers and spires of downtown, but here were only empty windows and shotgun shacks, sometimes with a lone person on the front porch, or a barking dog untied and circling the yard in a frenzy of hectic barks.

What had happened to this place, and not only here, to all the stretches of abandoned roadway and deserted downtown? They were like the billboards abandoned on the highway, bleached by the sun and torn by the wind, that showed a happy family eating dinner around a kitchen table, say, or playing baseball in the park, as a way to advertise a product that had long ago ceased production, or a business which had—and not lately—closed its doors. There was no there there.

I walked back to the hotel, where Persephone was asleep again, fully clothed and shoes on the bed, and the television was still on. I went to bed feeling empty though I didn't think I was exactly hungry, not really.

Hallelujah, when we woke up, we were saved by the sugar cereals and waffle maker of an unexpected continental breakfast (which continent? Persephone snorted. Wafflania?). I hadn't even realized the hotel included breakfast. Sometimes the smallest mercies are the ones that redeem you. We were both in better spirits when we hit the road.

We ate ice cream in Indiana.

We played mini-golf in Missouri.

We went kart racing in Kansas City.

We averaged about seven hours of driving a day, and it was only when we hit Colorado that we remembered America was also called the beautiful. Then New Mexico put Colorado to shame. I thought it was here our journey should have begun, and I wished we could keep going.

"Where are we going?" Persephone asked somewhere near Taos. It had taken her that long to pose the question.

"We're going to see a man who knew my grandmother," I said, "There was a year, about fifty years ago, when she sort of disappeared," and then I stopped. That was one possibility I had not even considered, that Fiona might not have left on purpose, might have been taken. I could have checked. I should have called emergency rooms and psychiatric hospitals and in-patient rehabs. They wouldn't have wanted to tell me, but if I told them there was a child...

Persephone didn't seem to make the connection. "Oh," she said indifferently. "Look, there's another duck," she said. We had been tracking roadside architecture, ducks and decorated sheds in Venturi and Brown's terms. And here, mirage in the desert, was a building in the shape of an enormous sombrero in the distant haze of the morning.

"Let's go there!" I said, grateful for the distraction.

Though in the grandeur of the state, it was, like everything else, much farther than we had expected. We must have driven another hour before arrival, and when we did, it turned out to be a decorated shed after all, the happy sombrero—big eyes, wide grin—just a façade on an aluminum shack, and the shack not just closed, but abandoned. The windows were boarded up, and the lights were off, though in the gloom we could see the tables and chairs, still waiting for a long-departed clientele, the sugar canisters left for ants on the tables.

"Isn't that just typical," Persephone said. "I hate it here."

"We're almost there!" I said. "Next state, New Mexico!"

"We're almost nowhere." Persephone said.

I stopped. There was no shade anywhere, and our shadows were shrunken and pinned to our feet, squat caricatures of the people we had been.

From a phone booth on the roadway I made a call. We got tired before we found a motel, and slept in the car. It was like camping, we had never seen so many stars. "What is that?" Persephone said, pointing at a diffuse alien glow I'd never seen before. "Oh, wow," I said. "That's the Milky Way. There's so much light pollution in the city, it's never visible. But it's there all the time. This is what people used to see when they looked at the sky."

"So, one day, when the lights go out and the people are gone, the sky will look like this everywhere," Persephone said in a sleepy voice. "It will be so beautiful."

13.

The address we had was just a scratch off the road, and we missed it twice before finding the turn. The car had no shocks, so we rode like the settlers in the covered wagons of old, feeling every stone, every rut. The silver trailer was hidden between two rocky mounds, and in every direction stretched desert. It was a lonely place to grow old.

I hesitated at the door—I couldn't do it—and Persephone reached out a capable fist and knocked three times.

I had expected the man in the linen suit to answer, as if I was opening a door back in time. Indeed, this trailer was old enough to have been new when they were young, it could have been their honeymoon home if this man had indeed been her lover, had he tempted her into fleeing their lives. And Bella my grandmother? Or would I have ever been born? The future forked, and the roads ran to vanishing points. But of course, that young man did not answer. Instead, a woman came to the door. She was the one I had spoken to the day before. She was all bosom, and segmented at the waist by a belt that pinched in flesh rather than defined it, in a floor length dress whose tropical profusion was the opposite of her desert home.

"Isn't she darling!" the woman said, and reached up to pinch Persephone's cheek. She was a head shorter than her. "Oliver's grand-niece! I'm Brenda." she said, turning to me, because of course I had lied when I spoke to her.

"So, you're on a family history tour with your daughter? That's so nice. You know, the apple doesn't fall far from the tree. She looks exactly like you."

I looked at Persephone, and our faces mirrored only perplexity.

"You must be thirsty after your long trip!" she said, ushering us to the sofa. My thighs stuck on the plastic cover. Her large eyes were cloudy, and as I saw her move confidently but carefully around the small trailer, her hands always extended at her side like feelers, I realized she couldn't see very well, if at all, even though she carried a tray of lemonade over to us without spilling a drop. There was a plate of chalky cookies, and she gestured at them.

"I remember having teenagers, they are always starving," she said. "All good things come to those who wait!" Persephone pincered her fingers, and lifted up a cookie to take a delicate bite. Her face wrinkled in disgust and I saw her palm the cookie and put it in her pocket. I did the same. "One man's meat is another man's poison!" Brenda said cheerfully, and I didn't know if that meant she'd seen us discard her cookies. But she seemed unconcerned as she rustled around the trailer like a grounded bird, all bustle and wing.

I looked for the paintings, looked for evidence of a man in the house—it was a feminized environment, all crystal trays of potpourri. Framed cross-stitch quotes in pastel colours—"You're Never Too Old to Learn" and "You Can't Teach an Old Dog New Tricks"—faced one another in the small seating area, duelling maxims. I perched at the very edge of the sofa, shifting my legs to unstick from the vinyl. The lemonade tasted like urinal pucks smell, chemical and acrid.

“So where is Oliver?” I said.

“Ah,” Brenda said. “I wanted to talk to you before you saw him. I think you’ll find him quite changed.”

That would be a feat, since I’d never known him at all.

“But what do you mean?” I said, and she said, “Well. Oliver is the sweetest thing. I’m sure you remember. But he’s carrying an empty Easter basket, if you know what I mean.” I looked at her in confusion. “The chimney’s clogged,” she said. “He’s surfing in Nebraska. He’s all of the notes, none of the music. For goodness sake, his clock’s ticking but it’s not telling time.”

“You’re saying his mind’s not right,” I said slowly, and she said, “Well, you’re not the freshest egg in the carton either! Eat up, sweetheart,” she said to Persephone, who was laughing at the both of us. “And close your mouth, you’re catching flies. I couldn’t have told you on the phone. It didn’t seem right. And he couldn’t have told you himself, you’ll see, he’s simple as a fence post. But a nicer man you’ve never met!”

She started to clean up, putting the lemonade back in the fridge, wiping the cookie crumbs off the table and onto the floor. A small dog I had mistaken for a furry cushion on the edge of the couch roused himself and jumped to the floor, lapping the crumbs with doggie fervour. Persephone slipped to the ground too, to play with him—she never could resist a puppy.

“I was his housekeeper,” Brenda said. “And now I’m just his keeper! And Rothko takes care of the crumbs. Dumb name for a dog, I know. He was a painter, you know, and back in the day, before,” she drew a little loop over her ear, “he used to say that Rothko was a fraud, so he liked ordering the dog around. That’s enough, Rothko!” she said. He was in a shivering muppet ecstasy. Persephone had his ears and was tickling him with both hands, neither of them inclined to stop.

“She can stay,” Brenda said. “Give that dumb dog something

to do." She opened the door and led me around the house.

"He's always somewhere around here," Brenda said. "He's making something—well, you'll see. That's all he cares about, really."

I had thought the trailer bookended by hills, but it was an optical illusion. When we rounded the corner, I could see a vast expanse of copper earth and sandstone hoodoos, like giant chess pieces stranded in the landscape. Brenda was less confident here, and I could see her stumble on the rough ground.

"Do you see him?" she said and I did, a distant scarecrow in the hot sun. "Well, I'll leave you to it," she said, "I'm not much for the sun or the desert. Funny that I live here! But we never know where we'll end up."

She turned back to the house, and I walked towards the red rocks.

If he saw me coming, he didn't bother to lift his head or wave, until I got much closer and saw he was hunched down because he was working, drawing lines on the sand with a long stick. He was near the centre of a spiral labyrinth of lines. I stood outside it, not sure where to enter or how to begin. Of course, I could have walked right through, but that seemed like a transgression. The spot was sheltered by a cliff, but still, the wind must have effaced those lines every day. He was out here, carving them once again. This was what Brenda had meant.

I thought of the monks who rake Zen gardens, of the sand mandalas of the Buddhist priests. Once Fiona had told me that when she and Persephone were in Dharamsala, they saw a sand mandala on the day of ritual destruction. It was particoloured and intricate, and had taken a team of monks weeks to construct, first on a geometric grid of chalk, and then with bright crushed grains of stone, applied with long metal funnels that she said were like the piping nozzles used for icing cake. When the monks circled the mandala and brushed the brilliant pattern into a dull mound of sand, Persephone was so upset, and Fiona could not calm her down. A nun sitting beside them, spinning her wheel, put her hand on Persephone's shoulder in consolation and spoke in perfect English. "Don't be alarmed," she said. "It is meant to demonstrate that everything is impermanent. Everything passes, everything changes, everything dies."

And here was Oliver, drawing those lines again and again.

"Who are you?" he said, and I was relieved. Brenda had prepared me for worse. Maybe there were answers here after all.

"I'm Helen's granddaughter," I said, and waited. I had not come for confrontation. I didn't know which questions I should ask.

"Well, that's very nice," he said, and he turned back to his slow work. He walked backwards, between the lines of the spiral track, and he shuffled to rub out the traces of his footsteps. In either hand, a stick, for each stick, a line, for each line, a trail that led no place. I realized what troubled me about the labyrinth. There was nowhere to enter it. It was open only to the sky. There was no way out. Here was a man who knew only inner convolution and entanglement.

I waited, and once he'd completed a circle and was facing me again he looked up. "Who are you?" he said and his voice was full of as much startled innocence as the first time he'd inquired. "Bella's granddaughter," I said, my heart tight against my ribs, and then I realized what I had said. "Helen's granddaughter," I amended. "Well, that's very nice," he said again, and resumed scratching in the sand. "Who are you," I whispered. I stood there for an empty minute before turning back and going inside.

Persephone was on the telephone, an old rotary number in mint green. Brenda whispered, "She wanted to call her father. But it's long distance!" She pointed to the wristwatch she wasn't wearing. Persephone handed me the phone.

"You're back," I said.

The phone was silent and for a moment I thought there was no one there.

"Hank?" I said, and I heard him clear his throat.

"I'm going to fly out tomorrow," he said. "You're not far from Albuquerque. Can you get her to the airport for two o'clock?"

"Yes, of course," I said, and swallowed. "Is Fiona alright? Do you know where she is?"

"How about neither of us ask questions," Hank said, and hung up the phone. I stood there, holding the receiver. Persephone started at me with a gaze that was half plea, half defiance.

"He's going to come get you tomorrow," I said. I was very, very tired. Her face broke into a smile so brilliant I was ashamed.

No, she was never mine.

Brenda followed us out, waving. She held Rothko in one hand, and he wagged his tail as if also trying to say goodbye. "Now, drive safe," she called. And remember, the middle of the road is where you get run over!"

We turned to each other and started laughing. Say it was a road trip and not a kidnapping. Say we had come to the end of our journey and found not what we were looking for but what we needed. Say we were loved by the people who were born to love us.

We stayed in a forgettable motel, had a forgettable meal, and watched television that made no impression until we both fell asleep.

I thought Hank might upbraid me at the airport, but he barely even saw me. Persephone ran to him, and when he picked her up she looked like a girl again, his girl.

I waited for her to turn around and say goodbye. I waited for a long time after their backs had vanished into a crowd of fellow travellers. Sometimes I think I'm still waiting.

14.

Years later, I would look for her. I would spot her in the blurred face of a teenage girl walking down the street, in the blown-up tragic eyes of a model on the roof of a building, in an airport on the other side of a pane of glass, at a restaurant table in a laughing group of friends, all alone sitting on a street corner with no shoes.

It was not her. It was never her.

They walked away. Time is an arrow and moves only forward, and with that motion everything is lost. But time's arrow is also Zeno's arrow, and as Kafka once said, Zeno's paradox suggests that only an arrow is ever at perfect rest. Borges also loved Zeno's paradox. He first learned it from his father, so in a strange way when he wrote about Zeno's paradox he was also remembering his father. Which is to say, he was stopping time.

On the lonely drive back to New York, I did not think of Persephone. Instead, I kept thinking of my grandmother, and of my father. I could not picture his face since he died, it was like that riddle when you imagine the flame of a candle once it has been blown out.

When I was a little girl, and my father planned to go away to a medical conference or lecture, I savagely missed him in advance, perhaps even more strongly because even when he was in town, he was so rarely home. One night, I was howling in muffled misery, pressing my pillow against my face, when he heard me and came into my room. The surprise was enough to make me stop crying. I sat up in bed and stared at him, clutching the pillow to my chest. I had forgotten he was not already gone.

"Why are you crying?" he said, and his voice was gentle.

"Because you are going a-wayay," and saying it aloud made me start crying again. I must have been about six years old.

"But I'm right here," he said, and the shame of it made me sob even harder.

"But you're going soon!" I wailed, well past all reason.

"I'm here now," he said, and he touched my shoulder. He was not a man comfortable with much physical affection. "You lie down now," he said, "and I'll stay until you fall asleep."

I lay down in a state of utter perplexity. This was never his role. My mother was the late-night comforter, the chicken-soup bearer, the early pick-up, the end-of-the-night carpool. I don't know where she was, but she must have been out.

And because she was out, he was, miraculously, home.

He stroked my hair as I fell asleep, and when I woke up in the morning, my face sticky and my hair snarled, he was gone.

I was a child who learned mostly from books, and often poorly. For a long time, I thought the word Procrustean referred to a geologic era—I think it was the "ean" of the suffix and the trace of "crustacean" in the centre. I imagined it—and here, Proustian also played a part—as a stratum in the earth's crust that preserved the forms of the world as it had been. Even after I learned the true meaning of the term, from Procrustes and his mutilating bed, I still envisioned a layer of clay, this time with fossils missing limbs, reduced and curtailed, frozen into the rock. Beckett said we cannot escape the past because the past has deformed us. Driving alone was like entering a long, long, tunnel, and sometimes, especially at night when the yellow lights blurred to red, I had the impulse to twist the wheel and throw myself off the road.

When I packed the apartment, I could not find my ring. It was as if it never had existed. I emptied all the drawers, pulled apart my socks in a riot of anxiety, swept the floor and poked my fingers into gaps and crevices. It was then that I remembered the little purse that I gave Persephone for her birthday, which had been stashed in the very same drawer. Was it possible the ring had slipped from my designated hiding place into the cheap gift bought for a little girl? I tried to remember if I had seen a glint, a gleam of opal or gold, some hint as to whether or not it had slipped from my life into her own.

Finally, I decided I would rather she have it than have it lost forever. Persephone, wherever you are, I hope that ring brings you better fortune. Wear it in good health.

I did find a wood chip in the bottom of the drawer, and it took me a minute to place it. I rubbed it between my fingers, trying to remember the origin of that dull token. A ticket. To take me wherever I wanted to go.

I left my apartment empty, broom clean, key left in the landlady's box. I sailed through the jagged waves of the Adirondacks. I went home.

Right before the city limits of my home-town, I pulled the car into a rest stop by the side of the road and opened the door. I put my head between my knees, and in the whispering company of the pines I said, in a low and quiet voice, "I want my Daddy." There was nobody there. I lifted my head and bellowed to the indifferent woods, "I want my Daddy!" I waited for the trees to echo back my emptiness.

The trees said hush, hush, hush.

There is only so much crying you can do without an audience. Eventually, I recovered myself, my face wet, and my hands and knees so cold in the evening air.

15.

My mother seemed different, as if she had emerged from the fog that had surrounded her while she was in mourning. Still, in the last year she had gotten old. I went straight to my room, which remained unchanged since I was ten years old—a Princess comforter on the bed, Proustian albums of scratch and sniff snickers on the bookshelf. I slept. The world felt far away. My mother brought me glasses of sweet milky tea and chocolate milk and tall glasses of coke with ice, as if I were a child, and like a child, I sucked it down.

My brothers came into my room sometimes and played on my floor or bounced on my bed, they patted my hair as if I was a large stuffed animal, comforting and inanimate. One day, I got out of bed and played on the floor with them. They loved lego and their games were all construction and destruction. They only had a certain number of pieces so if something needed to be built something else had to be taken apart, and they did so without drama or grief.

One day they took my hand and pulled me outside. The apple tree had been cut down, and the grass was no longer full of a soft minefield of rotten fruit. Instead, there was a new climbing gym, a fort and slide that they pretended was a ship, or a rocket, or a time machine, or a car, anything that would take them far away.

My mother didn't ask me what was wrong, but I often caught her looking at me. Sometimes I heard her on the phone, and by the tone of her voice, quick and low, I knew she was talking about me. I did not leave the house and yard until my brothers pulled me by the hand to the park on the corner, to the ice-cream store down the street, and then one day I got up and felt like leaving the house, all on my own. I also started to read again. I started with books that I had read as a child. The stories felt familiar and soothing, like wrapping myself a soft blanket that had been washed many times. Once I had exhausted the familiar books, I looked for new ones. Some of my grandmother's books had arrived in a box, and as I pulled them out, one by one, I found a composition book at the bottom.

So, there it was, waiting for me the whole time.

I opened it up. The writing was in black ink, and block letters. Sometimes Helen had pressed so hard the ink blotted the page, and sometimes the nib of the pen had ripped through the paper. There was writing on every page, but often only a few paragraphs, except for the last two pages, which were covered in a dark scribble. I held the page up to the light to see if the scribble was trying to obliterate something, some record or name or event, but it could have just been a scribble for its own sake, like a child colouring on a piece of construction paper who is not satisfied that he is done until all the white space is obscured by a labyrinth of marks.

I took the notebook to bed and closed the door.

PART FIVE

Helen

When the baby was born I woke up and saw him lying in his crib. He was crying. I cannot stand the sound of crying. There was a window in the room and the window was open.

What are you doing? the nurse said.

Everything is black.

★

They took me for my first treatment today. It takes four women in their little white hats. One to hold my arms and one to hold my shoulders. One to put the paddle to my head and one to hold my hips. And it takes one man in a white coat to turn the knobs that shoot the lightning through my skull.

★

Am I crazy? You only come here if you are crazy. Is it my fault? If not my fault, whose fault?

★

My mother always told stories about foolish women who made idiot mistakes and were punished forever.

Eat a radish and lose your first-born.

Pick a rose and lose your freedom.

Often the stories began like this: Once upon a time there was a stupid girl.

I keep thinking of her because everybody said she was crazy. We were always embarrassed of her. We ran from her when she called for us. We imitated the clumsy, dumb way she walked. We stuffed rags down our undershirts to mock her enormous breasts, her soggy, fat, so many times pregnant stomach.

When my breasts came in, my father said, you're starting to jiggle, and poked at the chubby, alien bumps. You're going to have big ones, like your mother. I would not talk to him for a week.

I never wanted to be like my mother. But even she did not end up in a place like this.

★

Today I told my roommate I just had a baby. She said, "Another one?"

Most of us are here because of woman problems.

Meals are at noon and at six. Lights out is at nine. So far, I have had three treatments. They arrive at violent intervals. The last time I woke up and saw the nurse leaning over me I started to cry.

There are six of us in the room, in our narrow iron beds, in two neat rows. When I wake in the morning I am so heavy I struggle to open my eyes. Every step is like walking uphill. My tongue is thick in my mouth and my brain is lead in my skull. Food has no taste to me but I shovel it into my mouth, obedient. My body in any case is a stranger, my stomach ridged with red welts as if I had been scratched by the claws of a wild cat, my breasts filled with small rocks. I am bleeding and do not know how long I will continue to bleed.

★

Today the fog rose to the level of the window and if the window would open I could reach out into it, I could tumble into that cotton-wool softness and rest.

Last night I dreamed of when I was a little girl. I woke up remembering how Bella and I used to make a little hideout by the river, of branches weighed down by large rocks. We pretended to be robbers and fairies and pirates and even bakers. Let's be mothers, Bella said one day. I was disgusted. Come on, she said. You can choose first, do you want to be the baby or the mother? I picked up a handful of mud and sticks and threw it in her face, then ran away. For days Bella did not talk to me. I saw her in the town, playing nursemaid with the other girls, holding a baby on her narrow hip. I decorated our hideout with feathers and speckled rocks. Four days later, I found her there. She had painted her face with mud and she brought cookies wrapped in a dishrag. Without a word, we returned to our old games.

I'm trying not to think of her playing house with my husband, like we used to play house when we were children. I'm trying not to think at all.

★

My favorite time of the day is craft hour. There is a light and spacious room full of tables and easels. Here and at mealtime we see the men. Otherwise we are kept separate.

One man is always in the art room when I arrive and there when I leave. He has a spot by the window, where the light is best. He is fair and tall and seems almost a guest and not a patient. Most of us use the art room as a chance to talk. The air is thick with gossip. I have never heard him say anything. He just paints, thin horizontal lines that blur into each other like a fading sunset.

I hear one of the nurses call him Oliver.

★

Today, when I went to the art room, I went straight for the windows, where Oliver was already standing. He was standing with his knee bent and his chest twisted towards the easel. His nose has a little bump at the bridge, and he has a dimple in his chin like someone pressed a narrow finger down and left a dent. He wears his hair longer than most men. His concentration was fascinating to me, and as I watched him paint there was a clearer relationship between the soft lines he paints and the lines of sea and sky out the window. On his palate were slate, white, cream, azure, Prussian, cornflower, indigo, violet—I read the names on the tubes of paint. He used a very thin brush, and dragged it down the canvas slowly, like he was stroking someone's bare back with his index finger. I picked up a piece of charcoal and I filled my own page in a crabby nest of blurred black lines. I left no white anywhere on the page, and when I looked up again he was gone and my hands were black with charcoal dust.

★

I feel so wrecked and sagging. My breasts are bound so they will not leak, my crotch is bandaged in cloth, my hair is full of knots, my mind...

★

The women in my room have names after all. Sarah, Hetta, Sylvia, Amy, Anne. Sarah is the youngest, fifteen. She looks like a skeleton, like the people in the pictures in the papers after liberation. Her elbows and knees stick out and only her face is as round as a moon rising over her body. Hetta is the opposite, she is very fat, dimpled and round like a baby before it has begun to walk. She gets rashes on her skin because flesh rubs flesh everywhere on her body. Today she talked a lot and was full of warmth. Some days she stays in her bed, and the nurses, who make few exceptions in their rules, allow her to remain there. Sylvia seems completely normal, I can't figure out why she's here. Her hair is tidy in pin curls, her clothes are always neat, her movements are crisp, she seems like one of the nurses and not like one of us. She reminds me of so many of the women in the neighbourhood—practical, uninterested in politics. She has five children, she told me today. She just needed a rest. The only strange thing about her, really, is that her family never visits. And also, that according to the other girls, she has been in for nearly a year, which is a long time for a rest. Even if you have five children. Amy is the only non-Jew. The Virgin talks to her and makes her pray five times a day, on her knees, makes her repeat the words again and again until they are perfectly spoken, makes her check the door at night to see if it is locked, makes her rub the corners of the bed before she can lie down in it. Today she told me I am going to Hell but she is there already.

Anne is probably a hundred years old, we don't think there's anything wrong with her either, though she has been there longer than any of us. They took her for treatment today and when she came back there was no one behind her eyes.

In the afternoon, I played Mahjong with Sarah, Hetta, and Sylvia. Sylvia knows the names of the flower tiles: plum, orchid, bamboo, chrysanthemum. She told us that in China, they are called the four noble ones, and represent the seasons, winter, spring, summer, fall. While we played Amy prayed loudly in order to disturb us.

In here, it is always warm and stuffy, often the shades are closed. Only the sky over the river through our window tells us it is Spring. The light wakes us up early these days, and the room is not dark until nearly ten.

The child I must remember to forget is nearly a month old.

★

Today, Sylvia took me aside. She told me that after her last baby was born, she was full of fear and rage. In her mind, like a film loop that kept repeating, she imagined him being dropped on the ground, or worse, thrown out the window, she saw it again and again so it seemed like a prophecy rather than a fear. She begged for them to not leave her alone with him. She told me this and her eyes were hard and shiny. There is more, she said, but then she stopped speaking, Sarah came back into the room from the toilet, where she goes after every meal. She was looking worse, and her breath smelled like death. Last night, I heard her shifting in her bed, her flesh has left her no pillowing and she is all angles and bruises.

★

Today I was late to the art room because I was helping Sarah in the bathroom. She started to retch bile, she said that she could taste almonds, I searched the hallways for a nurse and could not find one. It was a nightmare. Finally, I saw a doctor, I dragged him into the ladies' room where he said he must not go. She was almost unconscious on the tiled floor, her arms hugging the toilet bowl, her head resting on the rim. I nearly missed my art time, I ran down the corridor and saw the spot beside Oliver was still empty. This time when he looked up at me his eyes were the colour of the river on a stormy day.

Later, I learned that he would not let anyone else beside him. Oliver guarded my spot like a dog until I came. That day, his painting was all black, drawn in the same way, line by line. Sometimes the lines were feathery and allowed the white of the paper to show through, and sometimes they were solid as the bars of a cage. As I looked at it I could see the light in the blackness. The paint cracked, dripped, and pooled into shapes that looked like crows rising on the picture plane, monster faces lurking in the shadows, tree branches reflected in a black lake at night.

★

Today I wrote a time on the page and I drew a map—a dead end corridor I have passed which seems like a place that has been forgotten, it leads nowhere and holds nothing. I waited until I feel his eyes flicker in my direction, heard the slight intake of his breath. Then I turned the images into a spiderweb until they were no longer legible.

I cannot sit still and Sarah keeps asking what's wrong with me.

★

He came.

★

When I came back Amy was on her knees, praying and rocking, and she looked up at me with hate, but I am not afraid.

★

Abe stopped visiting, I don't mind. When Sylvia tried to console me, it took me a minute to remember who she was talking about. Hetta has lost some weight, she is actually quite pretty, her family visits frequently and we know she will soon be coming home. We are all worried about Sarah, who faints frequently and has developed a faraway stare and a fine coating of hair on her body. She cannot get warm, and Sylvia now sleeps with her at night to comfort her.

★

Today Amy's parents came to take her home. She cried when she left and hugged each of us in turn, which surprised all of us. Her bed is empty. I cannot believe I miss her, but I do.

★

Oliver is not mute, but has taken a vow of silence as protest, he says, "against the frivolousness of language and the stupidity of the world." He will break his silence to speak to me, but he prefers to speak little, and he will answer no questions about his family or his past. I do not tell him about my lost homeland, about my crazy dead mother, about my husband and my child, about the life I have left behind that waits for me. As a cat waits for a bird.

★

Last night, Oliver talked about his paintings, the lines as thin as threads that he traces day after day. He told me they do not represent something, not the muscular bands of the East river or the phantom landscapes of the sky. They are something. He said he draws each in a single exhale and then inhales and begins again. He tries to modulate the colours as closely as he can so they shimmer and blur into each other. They are the invisible made visible, the cords of a spiritual reality, and painting them is not a form of creation, it is a form of worship.

He talked very fast, and then stopped suddenly as if his tongue had tripped and fallen. Then he said, it's no use, they are nothing and mean nothing. Just a way to pass the time. He buried his head in my chest and told me I am the only real thing he knows, he gripped my hips so hard I think I will see red marks when I undress for the shower.

Now I feel furious. I think that after all he is more like Abe than I thought, clinging to me as if I was his mother and could save him. When he tells me that I am real it sounds like an insult, when he tells me that I ground him I think that he wants me to be the earth so he can be the sky. He now paints only in the colours of the sky, slate and silver and pale blue. What if I want to be the sky? I do not think he would be my ground.

★

Today I saw Oliver in the hallway with a tall pale woman and a tall pale child who has his eyes. He did not meet my gaze, but he also did not seem happy, shuffled beside them like a man under a spell. Beside them, he does look sick, as if he has been sapped of that purpose that keeps the spine straight, that keeps you walking in a line towards the horizon. It is just that everything is horizon for him now, and the lines have collapsed.

★

You are not sick, the doctor said today. Soon you will go home. Are you not happy that you are going home?

★

Oliver must convince the doctors he is well. We will move west, somewhere that no one knows our names or histories. He has told me about a beach in Oregon where the sand stretches for miles and the tides are mirrors for the sunset. He will paint and I will be whatever I am without a family. I imagine a spare, white-washed cottage, a bed, a table, and two chairs, a laundry line with clothes hanging like white flags of freedom or surrender.

★

Tonight he did not come.

★

Today his spot by the window was empty.

★

Tonight he did not come.

★

Tonight he did not come.

★

Tonight he did not come.

★

Why leave the bed? Why get up? Why anything?

★

I feel sick. I cannot eat or move or sleep. Hetta rubs my head and feet every day. Sarah moves into my bed and huddles against me, she is a stray cat that is all bones, trying to warm me up with her own cold body.

★

Today Sylvia told me that it is time for me to go home, there is nothing for me here. She started to tell me about her own children, in slow and careful detail, at each stage of their development, from the very beginning, when they are still moist and unformed, and there is a terrifying and miraculous flutter at the top of their skull where the bones have not yet fused, and their veins show through as if they were drawn on top of their skin in ink, and their fingernails are thin and soft as flesh, until later, when the haze of their irises settles into color, when they begin to focus on objects and reach for them, when they recognize their mother and cry for her and begin to compulsively smile, to charm the world, to pull it in, as they pull themselves to sit and then stand supported, their balance so tentative, their need to grow, to reach, to touch, to laugh, to learn, to feel, so full it is as if the world is created anew in their discovery of it, she cried as she spoke and then I understood.

This was her kaddish for her own children. She was so painfully raising them from the dead in order to tell me I must live.

★

Today when I got out of bed. I washed my face and in the place of Oliver, I put my own child into my heart. I told the doctor I am ready to go home. When Abe came to get me, he looked troubled. I have to tell you something, he began, and I said, I will not hear it. Bella has been in our house long enough, I say, it is time to her to find her own place now. I have been very ill but I am better now. I am better and I am ready to keep my own house.

★

I have not written in this diary for a long time.

This morning a letter arrived in the mail. There was a strange address on the envelope. I pulled out a photograph, and felt something else, something heavy on the bottom. An opal ring, that stone which signals black magic, curses, early death. I put the ring on my finger, and rested my hand on my stomach.

Yesterday the store clerk asked me if I was pregnant. I am in my fifth month and only now beginning to show. This has been an easier pregnancy. I am busy with Moshe, who will soon turn two, I look after my house and my husband. I put the ring and the picture in the back of the closet. I will disturb nothing.

END

The diary ended there, and I got up from my bed stiffly, surprised by the daylight, and by the world unchanged. I went to the kitchen to make a cup of coffee, and my mother was home, sitting at the table, leafing through an old photo album. She looked startled as I walked in and closed the album quickly, as if she were ashamed. I sat beside her and put my hand on her hand.

"I have something to tell you," I said, thinking of the ring that I had lost, of the diary I had just found.

"I have something to show you first," she said, and opened the album.

There was my father as a young man, in one picture pushing me on the swing, in another smoking his pipe, in another sitting in the lawn chair he liked best and wearing a straw hat I remembered. My mother pointed to the first photograph.

"He loved to push you on the swing" she said, "and you never wanted to stop. More, more, you'd cry, every time he slowed you down. You wanted to go faster and higher, he'd push you until his arms were sore. He was so proud of you, do you remember, when he had colleagues over he would show off the books you were reading, he would get you to spell difficult words out loud. You were only six. He used to swing you by the arms into the air, I was always afraid he'd dislocate a shoulder, you couldn't get enough of it. He would swim with you on his back, he called you a barnacle and tried to shake you off, but of course, the trick was to keep you on as long as possible, do you remember?"

I did not. I remembered very little from my early childhood, and later just a cold and distant man who left the house at dawn and came home after we were in bed. But as my mother spoke the memories from the picture seemed to emerge and lift, like paper lanterns that rise with fire and light the dark night.